You Should Pity Us Instead

YOU SHOULD PITY US INSTEAD

STORIES

AMY GUSTINE

SARABANDE BOOKS ⟨SB⟩ LOUISVILLE, KY

No part of this book may be reproduced without written permission of the publisher.

This is a work of fiction. Any resemblance to actual persons or events is entirely coincidental.

Library of Congress Cataloging-in-Publication Data
Gustine, Amy, 1970-
[Short stories. Selections]
You should pity us instead : stories / Amy Gustine. -- First edition.
pages cm
ISBN 978-1-941411-19-3 (paperback : acid-free paper) -- ISBN 978-1-941411-20-9 (ebook)
I. Title.
PS3607.U788A6 2016
813'.6--dc23
                    2015017017

Cover design and interior by Kristen Radtke.

Manufactured in Canada.
This book is printed on acid-free paper.

Sarabande Books is a nonprofit literary organization.

This project is supported in part by an award from the National Endowment for the Arts.

The Kentucky Arts Council, the state arts agency, supports Sarabande Books with state tax dollars and federal funding from the National Endowment for the Arts.

To Erma, Charlie, Leona, and Henry for playing conductor and chauffer, for picking out the grapes and being the Solid Gold dancers, for telling me to put my fingers on ASDFJKL;

CONTENTS

ALL THE SONS OF CAIN

After they find out where she lives, they start coming every week, sometimes every day. Wednesday morning they come especially early, waking her. R's mother stays in bed, yearning for coffee and the bathroom, but fearful of nearing the window. She knows what she'll see below: her son's scrawny face imprinted on cheap poster board, hoisted on stave and dowel by protesters who misspell his name. Sometimes they use him to protest another prisoner trade, sometimes to support it; sometimes to urge settlements, other times to condemn those already built; to push for a two-state solution or to warn against it. Once they were protesting a tax, another time something to do with toilets. R's mother doesn't want to know what they're using her son for today. Reconciliation and revenge. Hostages and prisoners. Murderers and soldiers. It all sounds the same from up here.

She turns to the wall and pulls the blanket over her shoulder. Retired from her job as a nurse, she has nothing to do but think of R. What she thinks is that he's already dead. If not today, then tomorrow, or next year. And if we're sure to die, then aren't we already gone? Only time intervenes, and what is time? If you were a rock, there would be no time. Rocks do not die. It occurs to her symbols don't die either. As a symbol— inert, permanent—her son still matters.

Sitting up, she looks toward the street-side window. She ought to love the protesters. Whatever they're protesting for, they're keeping her son in people's minds. But she can't love them. She doesn't give a damn about them.

R's mother lies back down. What is the math of a mother's love? *Infinity*, she thinks. She would let everyone in the world burn for him. Including, and especially, Gilad Shalit.

They took R after Shalit, Israel's common son, came home in exchange for 1,027 Palestinian prisoners. Terrorists, some say. Freedom fighters to others. Regardless, Hamas wanted more. It was six months ago that they grabbed R under cover of tear gas near the Gaza border. The pain of his capture has not attenuated. Instead, it is like a cancer swimming through her veins to plant pieces in every pocket of self: her eyes, her ears, her taste, her dreams.

R's mother is sliding against the wall, staying clear of the window on her way to the bathroom, when something smacks the outside of the building. Enraged, she rushes toward the window, about to yell "bomb" just to make them stop jousting with his face. That face, that name, belong to her. To hell with them. But before she can speak, a few words break free of the crowd. *Muslim. Tape. Proof.*

She slams the window and turns on the TV, channeling past women singing and a show about desert climates to a local news program. Hamas has released a videotape of R in which he claims to be converting to Islam. His mother barely registers these words. She is staring at the newspaper her son holds, a British paper dated just last week.

The possibility that an Israeli soldier is becoming a Muslim takes hold of the country. The protests become larger, the pundits more strident. One morning R's mother is watching a local channel broadcasting a protest outside her own window. A banner, painted in slurred red letters, reads: "A Jew is worth a thousand Muslims. A traitor is worth a thousand deaths."

She finds a pair of scissors and cuts the TV's power cord.

For a month she doesn't go out, doesn't answer the phone, doesn't read the newspaper or turn on the radio. A boy in the building goes to the market for her, a boy who can be counted on never to ask how she's feeling or what she thinks about the tape. Like a prisoner herself—a prisoner of uncertainty, of history, of other people's prejudice—she spends her time reading old novels, their familiar stories a great comfort. No more surprises.

Then one Friday afternoon she is forced to venture into the street because her cousin's daughter has had a baby and there is a party. No protesters are about, but she dons a disguise anyway—old glasses, a hat, her nurse's uniform—to walk the ten blocks to her cousin's house. When she arrives, an aunt on the baby's father's side, a woman she has never met before, shakes her head sympathetically and says she heard what they are saying about R. "Don't worry," the woman assures her. "We all know it isn't true. It is impossible for a Jew to become a Muslim. Muslims are dogs." She lights a cigarette and puffs. "Putting a collar on a human doesn't make him a mutt."

The other women in the room blanch, casting silent apologies to R's mother, who returns their pained expression with a neutral stare, as if she doesn't know what the problem is.

As a distraction, someone asks the new mother how her labor was. Long, she says, and lots of back pain. This sparks a round of birth stories. The new mother's trials are trumped first by a mother allergic to pain medication who delivered a ten-pound girl, then by one who gave birth in the hospital's waiting room. Finally, a tiny woman tells of delivering twins on a moving bus. She wins, yet the stories continue—strange places, strange pains, rude medical staff. R's mother remains silent. Her birth story can't be told.

On the way home, she passes a café she used to like and glances in the window, thinking of their pastries. There, on a TV monitor hanging from the wall, is her son, his features digitally removed from the structure of his face and superimposed on a missile embossed with the star and crescent. Grabbing the door from a young couple stepping out, she goes inside. One of the pundits, a chubby man with a bad comb-over, is saying it doesn't matter whether R has converted to Islam or not. "He was born a Jew, so he is a Jew. We must get him out."

R's mother thinks of the blood-lettered banner, the old woman at the party. What would they say if they knew the truth? It's only a matter of time before a journalist goes digging—before the truth creates lies, and lies become facts.

At home she packs quickly, a change of clothes, a few toiletries. Then she gathers pictures of R. Recent ones, in which he's recognizable—one on his fifteenth birthday with his favorite red shirt, one at the beach, one from high school graduation—but also older ones, to show him at his most vulnerable. On his seventh birthday with both front teeth missing. On the day he took his first step, his hands flung in the air, his expression shocked and joyful. Finally she takes the first picture of all in which he isn't even visible. Only she can be seen, standing outside an airplane bound for home, holding something wrapped in a yellow blanket.

She leaves behind the picture of R in his IDF uniform, his long-toothed smile hidden in an ambivalent twist of the lip, his eyes lost in the shadow of an Israeli flag unfurled at the edge of the frame.

As her plane descends into Cairo's International Airport, R's mother looks down on the glittering high-rises lining the Nile's shore, then inland, to the raw-concrete worker's homes, squatting in twilight. To the east is the City of the Dead, crumbling, necropolitan mustards, and to the west the dark, ancient deserts of Giza's tombs, so singular and grand they strike her not as burial plots, but as alien settlements. Everywhere there are minarets, looking from above like missiles. As they near the earth, a few small crosses appear, then smokestacks, antennas, and satellite dishes, then finally bags and bags of garbage held in check by brick walls.

Her plane lands, opening to air that smells like home, hot and dusty. She wears black to blend in with the married women. The customs official examines her blue passport closely, but it doesn't arouse suspicions. Her last name is common in Israel, one of the favorites for immigrants looking to shed their European identities.

R's mother spends the night in a hotel, and the next morning the young man at the front desk locates a driver to take her east. Two hundred and fifty miles on two-lane roads, her peripheral vision tainted by a head scarf. At one point the driver takes a dirt road that can't go anywhere good and R's mother thinks he's figured out who she is and plans to make short work of a troublesome Jewish mother, but it turns out to only be a clever shortcut. The driver returns to pavement and in another few miles looks over his shoulder. "You are Jew, no?" he asks in English.

She hesitates. "Yes."

He taps the dashboard. "I am Christian. The government, they kill my pigs, so I get this. They cannot kill a car, no?"

Many of the Christians in Egypt were pig farmers until the government slaughtered all the pigs to pacify Muslims worried about swine flu. R's mother understands the garbage now. The pigs used to eat it. She smiles sympathetically. "They can kill anything, but for now you have a very nice car."

Another few miles before the pig farmer asks why she is going to Rafah. "Not a good place for Jew."

R's mother considers whether to tell the truth. The Muslim government killed his Christian pigs. What are the chances she'll find a more trustworthy Egyptian?

When she admits where she really wants to go, he looks shocked, then nods and holds up her money. "You pay me twice this, I get you to somebody. Understand? I know nothing."

She affirms, "Nothing."

In Rafah the pig farmer deposits R's mother at one of the few open businesses, a market with red metal tables. The rest of the street is lined with chalky buildings leaning against one another. Most appear empty. The proprietor brings her a Sprite, staring at her a moment before going inside and shutting the door in a way that tells her she's not wanted. At the red table she sits bolt upright, half-expecting to be shot from a passing car. They pass only rarely. When they do, R's mother tightens the muscles around her spine. If she dies, she'd like to do it looking forward.

The pig farmer returns at dark and says he's found her a place to stay. "Tomorrow, the tunnels."

She offers an open hand of bills, and he selects five. "This is good."

They drive through streets edged in dirt mounds and concrete shards to a building with a green flag. A woman shows R's mother to a room with a white iron bed. That night she dreams of carrying R under a sky glittering with stars. When the earth opens up in a great zigzag crack, she drops him.

The next morning the woman brings her bread with a paste of mustard-flavored chicken and tells her a man is coming. R's mother nods. A man is always coming.

The pig farmer returns. "Why do you go to Gaza?"

"My son is in there."

The man asks who her son is.

She tells him.

There is a long pause. He repeats the name.

She nods.

He taps his temple. "You are not thinking."

"I know."

They sit awhile in silence until the man sighs. "Promise me you will not say his name. Tell them you have family, but make up a name. Do not tell them the real name."

She nods again, and he hands her a bag with a thobe, slacks, and a white hijab.

"They will want to check you, understand? For safety." He pats down his own chest and sides to demonstrate.

He returns after dark with a flour sack. "For your eyes." She slips the sack over her head and submits to loosely bound wrists. They drive in what feels like circles for an hour before he helps her out of the car and unties her hands. They are in a home with pink floor tiles, a young man at the kitchen table. R's mother hands over more money. The pig farmer and the man debate something in heated undertones until the pig farmer sighs and comes over. While he runs his fingers over her sides, her thighs, and then briefly, barely touching, over her breasts and buttocks, he keeps repeating, "I am sorry, I am sorry."

The pig farmer and the other man leave. A boy remains, stationed inside the kitchen doorway. He watches her with a look of amusement alternating with blankness, as if he's having brief seizures. Over the next hour two new men look in on her, each asking why she is here. She tells them her son is in Gaza and pulls out the older photographs. The men have all looked through her purse, but only for weapons. They showed no interest in the pictures.

At one point a woman comes in holding a newborn and looks to the boy. He gives no indication of approval or disapproval, so she sits down to nurse.

"Was it a difficult birth?" R's mother asks in her passable Arabic.

"Easy," she says. "It is my fourth."

"Any more?"

"If Allah desires." The woman's tone says Allah is a pesky boss. "My first was hard." She dips her head to indicate the boy. "Fifteen hours and he gets stuck."

The woman describes her other children's births and then the tales of nieces and nephews, neighbors and friends. Sick babies, big babies, small babies, babies who can't wait, and babies who must be coaxed free. Babies who die.

"If Allah wants so many babies," the woman asks, "why make them die?"

More men come, blindfold R's mother and put her in a car. In a new kitchen two of them get down on the floor, heads inside a cabinet whose pressboard doors have swollen from water damage and cracked along the edge. They work silently, then pull the cabinet free to reveal a hole in the floor lined by wooden braces that act as both wall and ladder. One of the men helps her get a footing. As she descends, surprised by the muscle required to lower oneself into the earth, the air grows cooler and begins to taste of sulfur and iron. Breathing becomes difficult and her fingers begin to spasm from gripping the wooden braces.

At the bottom a man hands her a blanket. "Cold."

The tunnel is twice the width of her shoulders, its height an inch above her own. Light bulbs dangle from exposed wires, and cigarette butts dot the dirt floor. Every six feet a wooden brace supports the roof. She fears losing her resolve, but the nonchalance of the men emboldens her, and she dares to ask why the tunnel smells of fish.

"You don't let them take to the water," her Egyptian guide explains, rubbing index to thumb in the universal symbol of cash, "so we bring them fish."

At the tunnel's end her guide fits a harness around her and uses a phone on the wall to give the order to lift. Three men pulley R's mother from the earth. Her first glimpse of Gaza is a girl's bedroom with blue birds flying in lonely, far-flung formation across a pink wall. In the corner four children sit on a dingy yellow bedspread playing a game with stones and broken crayons. One of the men unbuckles the harness and motions for her to follow him. They walk through a room which several families have divided with blankets and out the door to a dark street. The man is gone, the door shut, while R's mother is still thinking about who painted those lonely birds.

The first night she sleeps behind a dumpster, and the next morning her bones feel as if they've been hammered. Gaza looks like she'd expected: half-buildings, debris-littered streets, dusty clothes, graffiti. The few women outside are accompanied by a man. Her resolve wavers until she spots a pair of older women alone, but when she arrays the pictures, whispering, "I am his mother," they look frightened, shaking their heads, and quickly move on.

The next night she sleeps on the beach hidden behind a pile of cinder blocks, and in the morning her bones feel only gently pinged, like the keys of a piano too strenuously played. The men think they took all her money, but R's mother hid bills between the inner and outer sole of her shoe, so she buys a banana and eats it, watching a group of children yelling at a boy cowering against a wall. Every few seconds laughter bursts forth and the faces light up, including the boy against the wall. He switches places with one of the shouters and shows her how it's done, getting his face low, leaving her only a view of his dark, angry eyes. The other children clap at his performance. R's mother catches the words "soldier" and "tough." Instead of cops and robbers, the children here play IDF and Palestinian.

She shows them R's picture. "Do you know him?"

One little girl says he looks like her father. "But he's not."

A boy asks what his name is, then shrugs apologies and wanders off.

After that, R's mother talks only to children. Their skin feels dusty when she takes an arm, asks them to look. "He is here," she explains, "being kept somewhere. If you were kept, wouldn't you want your mother to be able to visit?"

The strip is twelve kilometers at its widest, forty-one long. For three days she lines up her steps with the sun's arc from land to sea. One time an older girl narrows her eyes. "My brother is in jail in Israel and my mother cannot visit." When the girl runs off, shouting something R's mother can't understand, she hurries away, hiding for an hour in an abandoned market.

Another time a different girl asks why she is stooped.

"I've been walking a lot and my back hurts."

"You should stop walking."

"I can't."

She traverses the sand and rubble fields between towns, and on the fourth day reaches Khan Yunis, a town whose busy streets add the smell of motorbike exhaust to the relentless odor of sea salt and fish. That night she hides in a yellow boat, a tangle of net for a pillow, for her blanket, a filthy tarp. The odors have become her. She will smell of dead things from now on.

Near dawn, her dreams are infused with a man's mourning call. R is dead. The man, whom she doesn't know, is rending garments, crying out during Kriah. *Blessed are You, Lord, our God, King of the universe, the True Judge.*

She starts awake, her heart beating fast. The smoky predawn sky swells with a quivering ululation. The voice rises, buzzing, hits a single bell-like note, drops again. Not mourning. Only morning. The muezzin's call to prayer.

R's mother drifts back to sleep and is wakened by a giggling group of boys calling her a fish, pointing at her feet, which have become entangled in a second net. One boy, around thirteen, with a face all teeth and eyes, helps free her. She shows him the pictures of R. In the most recent one R stands outside their apartment building on graduation day, squinting against the sun. The photo has absorbed water from the boat's bottom, and when the boy takes it, a gash opens across R's leg. The boy gazes at the photo several seconds before saying in slow, badly pronounced English, "I see him."

They make arrangements. She will wait for him to fish with his uncle and then he'll take her where she wants to go. R's mother, heart pounding, sits on a sewer pipe at the beach's edge. The day is overcast and boats can't go far without risk of being fired on by Israeli ships. Still, she keeps an eye on the boy's skiff, ignoring the women in the nearby camp who watch her while they hang laundry. They recognize an outsider, but hardly imagine a matronly Jew has smuggled herself in.

Two hours later the boy and his uncle drag the boat onto the sand, weight it against wind and tides with jagged cement blocks and carry their rods and buckets to a path that leads into the streets. R's mother follows at a good distance until they go into one of the cinder-block houses, then she crosses the street and waits inside the remains of a hotel, its first floor open to the sky. Creatures scratch in the rubble, so she climbs onto a section of fallen wall, using its exposed rebar as a ladder.

When the boy emerges, shuffle-running in front of a donkey hauling two men on a flat metal cart, R's mother scrambles down, and they walk several blocks to a house with a Palestinian flag painted next to the door, its colors turned cinereal over the concrete's porous face. The boy slips inside and returns shortly to ask for a hundred shekels, shrugging to indicate the greed is not his. They repeat this process at two more houses. In both, R's mother hears a baby crying and smaller children playing. At another market, she buys a loaf of bread and some nuts and they sit on the curb.

"Are we getting close?" she asks in Arabic.

The boy nods. "Yep," he says in English. "Okeydokey."

She's never heard the phrase before and asks what it means. He explains it is an American word, as if that is enough.

"How old are you?" she asks.

"How old are you?"

"Old enough for respect."

He smirks. "Yes, Grandma."

She fakes a glower. "What is your name?"

"Jamil."

She can tell he's lying. "Jamil, what is your favorite subject in school?"

"School is a waste of time."

"My son used to tell me that all the time. He liked to learn, but he didn't like to go to school."

The boy looks chagrined. "I know what I need to."

He takes her from place to place, asking for money sometimes, other times not. Once he disappears in a crowd and she doesn't expect him to reappear. This is all a ruse, of course. He can't help her. Then he's there, hand on her sleeve. They go down a street where most of the houses have been reduced to rubble. A group of boys is playing capture the flag. The boy is greeted warmly and huddles with the others, speaking in hushed tones. Light pours down on the dark, tousled heads. No trees or buildings to cast cooling shadows. Only broken trapezoids of gray scattered among the ruins. The boys are deciding how to fool her. She wants to suggest they write out directions on where to find her son and send her on her way. By the time she discovers their duplicity, they can be home, in bed.

The boys scatter among the ruins just as the ululating voice swells again for midday prayer. For the next several minutes R's mother stands frozen in the middle of the road, her own shadow creeping away, though her body knows not what to do. Which direction do you face? What name do you call out? How do you hold your hands in reverence? She is exposed, incapable of escape, a figure encased by a sniper's target circle. Then the boy emerges from a pile of concrete, motions for her to be quiet, grabs the pink rag and dances down the street, avoiding the telltale pebbles in favor of toe-sized patches of smooth concrete. The voice, still keening, camouflages the noise of her less adept escape.

At the base of a wall covered in blue Arabic letters R's mother can't read, the boy lays down the rag. On the other side of the wall is a field of tents. He signals for her to wait and disappears through a gap. He won't come back. There are probably a dozen entrances. She settles against the wall anyway. Occasionally men glance at her, but she is covered head to toe, and they must assume she is waiting on a husband. Motorbikes and the occasional mud-splattered car pass. R's mother grows sleepy, wonders what might happen if she lay down here and said *enough*.

At the backfire of a motorbike she opens her eyes. A trio of camels, tethered in line with a rope, gets away from an old man a block off. They lope past, followed at some distance by the man, limping and swearing. Just then the boy returns. Taking in the situation, he catches up to the camels and grabs at the swinging rope. R's mother shouts in Hebrew to be careful, he'll get trampled.

At the sound of the language, several men stop and stare at her. Four approach, one with yellow teeth like shellacked maple, another with sea-green eyes. The old man keeps running, hollering at the boy.

The stack of pictures, less the one the boy still has, sits like a brick in her purse. The man with green eyes snatches the bag, embroidered with reeds and a red-throated loon. Asking a question she can't understand, he holds up a picture. She opens her mouth, but her Arabic has fled. The picture is of R on his thirteenth birthday, his teeth at their largest, his hair its most wild. It is the day she told him the truth.

Hooves clattering in a great arrhythmic panic draw the men's attention. The camels are being driven back this way by a motorbike careening around potholes. R's mother presses herself against the tent-city's wall while the men scatter. The camels go by and the bike skids to a stop. She climbs on behind the boy, who just manages to restart before the men put it all together and chase them down the street, hollering in Arabic, "Stop, you Jew, stop!"

"We have to go back!" she shouts. "They have my pictures!"

The boy firmly shakes his head.

Khan Yunis goes by in gray, the occasional flash of red or purple through the open door or half-wall of a destroyed home. R's mother closes her eyes and releases her breath in short, shallow puffs, trying to fuse all two hundred and six bones into one solid structure. Pebbles kicked up by the bike's wheels sting her ankles.

Several minutes later, having lost their pursuers, they slow to a speed barely able to keep them upright, punctuated every few seconds by a sudden leap forward, as if the bike were being prodded by a whip. The boy stops in the rubble street where his friends were playing. "It's late," he says, "good luck," then begins running—not fast, like escape. More like exercise. But fast enough for her to know she can't keep up. Except he has her only picture. Without it, she can't find her son.

R's mother runs. A knife in her side, pounding heart, burning feet. It is only because the boy runs for fun, out of habit, that she is able to keep him in sight. All the streets look the same, and she knows if he makes even a single turn without her seeing, all will be lost.

She rounds a corner, eyes tracking every direction. In front of a building like all the rest, the boy is talking to a woman who, by her unabashed chastising, can only be his mother. She is pointing inside, then down the block. He should go, then come right back.

R's mother hangs back until the boy reaches the next block, then makes her way toward his mother. She is wringing out a towel, the water forming dark bubbles in the sandy street. As the woman turns to go inside, shoulders stiff and bent toward some urgent task, the ululating voice calls out. Over it a cry escapes the house, and she quickly shuts the door.

R's mother knows that cry.

Cautiously, she nudges open the door. In the back room of the two-room home a sheet hanging from nails in the ceiling partially conceals a woman in labor. When the boy's mother touches the rag to her forehead, she turns, and R's mother sees an elegant nose, high cheekbones, wet eyes. But she is not a woman; she is a girl.

"Can I help?" R's mother asks.

The story unspools quickly after the boy returns with the water. He thrusts R's photo at his mother, summarizes their afternoon of seek and flee, then explains the girl's plight. She is the daughter of his mother's childhood friend. Unmarried, she ran away from her home in a town north of here to hide from her brothers.

"If they find her," he says, "they will kill her."

The statement is equally true of R's mother. The boy's mother insists she leave. "You endanger us."

The girl's labor isn't progressing well, and when R's mother tells them she is a nurse and offers to check the baby's position, the boy's mother relents.

The baby is face up, with a shoulder lodged down. R's mother explains what needs doing. As she works, the girl whimpers and the woman hushes her, afraid the neighbors will hear.

Once the baby is righted, R's mother prepares to leave, but the girl grabs her arm. "Don't go."

Though the sun has set and the mourning voice must have called out, none of them hear it. They don't become aware of the call to prayer until the final voice of the day, by which time they've undressed the girl to a thin white shirt soaked with sweat. R's mother massages her feet while the boy and his mother kneel and rise, kneel and rise by the light of candles, their shadows pulsating on the wall like hearts imaged with sound waves. The world has been praying for thousands of years. When, R's mother wonders, does God plan to answer?

After prayer, the boy's mother goes to blow out the candles.

"I need to see," R's mother objects.

"They will be wondering," the woman says, "after Isha." This is the name for when all the light has left the sky. A house with precious candles lit so late will arouse suspicion.

R's mother considers how to hurry things along. "I need something to break her water."

It takes several minutes to put her meaning across, but finally the woman sends the boy into the front room, where under a floorboard he's hidden a bag of scrap metal.

"I sell it," he explains, laying out the bag's contents—copper wires, screws with damaged threads, shavings, one and two-inch pieces of pipe cutoffs. The copper could work. It's stiff enough to offer pressure, flexible enough to bend into a hook.

They sterilize the wire in boiling water, then R's mother ruptures the amniotic sac and the contractions intensify. The girl bites a rag while the woman describes her own labors. They all end happily, with shining baby and tired mother.

The girl looks to R's mother. "What about you?" she sputters around the rag. "You have a son. Was his birth easy?"

R's mother wipes her brow and smiles. "Happiness is sometimes the other side of another's misery." But she is speaking Hebrew, so the girl smiles back, assuming the best.

Another contraction begins. R's mother cups the girl's kneecaps in her palms. "I see a head," she says in Arabic. "Push, press down hard."

The girl lifts herself on her elbows, clenches her teeth, and lets out a tiny squeal. The baby's full head emerges. With a great huff, the girl lies back. "Tell us in Arabic," she says. "Your birth was safe?"

R's mother cradles the baby's forehead, waiting for the next contraction to release the shoulders. "My boy came from the earth," she says.

"Did you grow him on a vine?" the girl smirks.

From the other side of the curtain the boy says, "I bet he was a root vegetable, like a potato."

His mother leans around the sheet to give him a dirty look, but he and the girl continue to giggle until the next contraction takes them by surprise and the girl lets loose a soft scream.

"We're almost there," R's mother says.

The woman lifts the girl by her shoulders, and as she pushes, R's mother tells her story.

The year her son was born quakes shook old Byzantium, the earth mother's tectonic bones grinding against one another until a final shudder pushed him free, a dark-haired, olive-skinned infant set adrift in disaster's bulrush and washed up in the rubble of an Istanbul street. She was there as part of a medical emergency crew when he was brought in. No identification, no way to track down family. She cared for him for two months, waiting for someone to come looking, but no one did. No Kurd, Turk, Greek, Muslim, or Christian. So she took him home. "Why not?" she says. He was as likely to belong to a barren Israeli Jew as to anyone.

The day after the baby is born, R's mother announces she is going to resume her search. "I need the picture back."

The boy is drawing it from his pocket when his mother shakes her head and holds out a hand to stop him. "You will get yourself killed," she tells R's mother. "And us. Go back to Israel. There is nothing you can do."

"I just need my picture, and I will be gone." R's mother reaches for it, but the boy dashes from the house. He is a block away, running toward the beach, by the time she gets out the door. By the time her feet sink into sand, her breath is gone and a great pain has bloomed in her side. The boy is nowhere to be found.

Hours later he shows up with a falafel and offers her half.

R's mother is rocking the baby from a stationary chair, moving her torso forward and back in a steady rhythm to keep them both calm. "Where is my picture?" she asks, without breaking stride.

Laughing, the boy makes a wave with his slender brown hand. "The water took it."

For two weeks she wanders the streets, eavesdropping on conversations and occasionally describing R to a group of children. "Have any of you seen him?"

The boy's mother begs her to stop.

"If it were him," R's mother points to the door to indicate the boy, gone out combing the rubble for metal scraps and helping his uncle fish, "if it were him, would you stop?"

When she is not searching, R's mother holds the baby so the girl can sleep. The plan is to get her into Egypt, where the boy's mother has distant family, but she can't take the baby. "They won't help her if they know."

After the girl is gone, the boy's mother will claim to have found the infant abandoned in a dumpster.

One day a friend of the boy's is killed, backed over by a garbage truck during their foraging sessions at a nearby trash heap. After that, the boy stays home, stripping the insulation off copper wires with a rusty paring knife. His hands are crisscrossed with fine cuts where the knife slipped. He melts the lingering lamina over the gas stove, letting it drip onto a piece of cheap tin he's sacrificed for the purpose, the different colored plastics rehardened into an intricate, overlapping pattern like veins and arteries.

R's mother continues to go out, but increasingly finds her mind wandering when she should be examining faces, catching scraps of conversation. Everyone has begun to look familiar, harmless.

One afternoon she is in the market, standing half-concealed by a pillowcase hung to shade the orange vendor, a wizened old man who hums while rearranging his fruit. She's bought a bag of garbanzos, fish, and mustard greens, and is bagging her oranges when twenty men walking in pairs split the crowd, their presence moving ahead of them in a conspicuous quieting and turning away. Hamas. They wear black shirts and pants, green headbands with white writing in Arabic and white cloths over their faces. Only their eyes, two dark nostril holes and the inside-out flesh of lips remain visible. Even R could be hiding among them and his mother wouldn't know.

She dashes into the street and in a flash the men turn, point rifles, a few women let out screams, somewhere a box is knocked over and a hundred somethings click on the sidewalk. The oranges roll out of her bag and R's mother collapses, frantically gathering the fruit. She feels the men assessing her, deciding she is no threat. They realign and march on. The vendor resumes his hum, placing the good fruit in back, the bruised up front. R's mother looks up to see the last dark figure round the corner and pass out of sight.

Crying with humiliation and self-loathing, she doesn't notice the two men in jeans follow her away from the market. She is nearly back to the boy's house when the one wearing a blue oxford sneezes and she becomes aware of them. Something about the way they both look away when she turns alerts her, so she passes the boy's house, keeping her eyes straight ahead, walks three more blocks, then doubles back to the market. There, she dodges and sidesteps, getting lost amid the other women's thobes.

For hours she crisscrosses the city, looking for the blue shirt. By the time she feels it safe to go home, it is very late and she must make up a story about getting lost.

In the morning she takes the boy aside and tells him about the men. "Be careful."

The boy tells her not to worry, though of course she does. When he gets home hours later, she realizes she's been preparing all day to surrender in exchange for his long nose, his too-big teeth. The puff of hair on the back of his head that bounces when he runs.

"Did you see them?"

The boy nods at the curtain, behind which his mother mutters instructions to the girl about how to keep the baby awake until her second breast is empty.

"They're her brothers," he whispers.

*

R's mother has a little money left. She offers it to them. "The girl must go. I'll take her." R's mother will pretend to be an aunt.

The boy manages to get an Egyptian passport for a twenty-year-old male, so they weave a tale of marriage across borders to tell Egyptian customs officials, and cut the girl's hair short, find her a pair of brown pants and a dark shirt, boys' sandals.

But her hands are a problem. "Too smooth," the boy points out. "And too clean." He shows her how to dig through the bag of scrap metal. "Like you were looking for treasure."

When she is done, her nails, formerly half moons pumped red and shiny with a nursing mother's swollen veins, are torn, and her knuckles abraded. The boy rubs dirt from the floor on them. "Perfect."

The plan is to dress her as a girl leaving Gaza so she is less likely to be searched and found lactating, and where passports mean nothing anyway. In Egypt, where the passport becomes important, she will become a young man.

The morning they are supposed to leave, the boy goes out early to fish. Before he leaves, he sheepishly offers R's mother a wad of shekels, the money she gave him that first day to buy information. "You will need it to get out."

She takes a few bills, tallying how much it cost to get in, then presses the remainder on him.

R's mother and the girl are to meet a man who will take them in a taxi to Rafah, from which someone else will get them to a tunnel. R's mother keeps imagining the men between here and home to be the Christian pig farmer, his shiny pate and kind eyes, his gentle hands on her hips.

The girl insists on walking separately in case there is trouble. "You can get away."

R's mother agrees to go first, hoping she can recognize the brothers and distract them if need be.

A blue car with a white stripe is waiting for her as she reaches the corner. The man gives her the word—*tilapia*—they had agreed on, and she gets in, holding a finger up for him to wait. As the girl reaches them, a shifting lump under her thobe gives the baby away. R's mother pauses, then nearly shouts, her throat pulling closed, "Let's go. We're ready."

They drive out of the streets, anonymous in the early morning dark. As they reach the edge of town, the ululating voice swells and the taxi stops. The driver gets out first, then the girl. R's mother slides across the seat and stations herself between them. Clumsily, she mimics their movements, rising and kneeling, rising and kneeling.

As she gets back into the car, still shielding the girl from the driver's view, she glances down the street. Between two buildings the Mediterranean glimmers under an oblique sun. Dark heads dot the pale sand, their motion like birds alighting, then startling, then alighting again. She hopes her boy is among them, praying.

UNATTENDED

Joanne wakes with the worst earache she's had in years. Ryan is already gone and the baby is crying, of course. His diaper has come loose—she put it on in the dark, at three a.m.—and he sits in a yellow halo clutching his favorite toy, a stuffed elephant now marinated in piss. When she plucks the elephant from his grip, the scream intensifies.

"Jesus," she says, flicking the toy back at him. "Fine, take the fucking thing."

It hits him in the forehead and he stares a moment, startled, then grabs it like a life preserver as Joanne takes up the tears, kissing his head again and again. "I'm sorry. I'm sorry. I didn't mean to hit you with it. I'm sorry."

Dumbo sloshing in the Whirlpool, she gives the baby a quick bath, which only makes him scream louder. By the time she has a bottle ready he's too apoplectic to notice until she squirts a long line of milk straight down his throat.

Fine, take the fucking thing. While he drinks, Joanne repeats the words to herself as if they're a line she's trying to memorize instead of a confession she's trying to bear. She imagines cutting out her larynx, making all her mistakes in sign language. But then she'd have to cut off her hands.

Once the baby's done eating, she begins her penance, walking him in circles through the house until the ache in her back and arms is almost as bad as the one in her ear. When she was a kid the doctors wanted to do surgery, but her father dismissed it as profit-mongering. As an adult, Joanne had the surgery and for a time things seemed better. Now though, her Eustachian tube feels like someone used a tire pump on it. She'd like to turn off the air conditioning—cold makes it worse—but then the baby's thighs will sprout a rash and any chance of quiet will be destroyed. Not that there's much chance anyway. At eight months old, he hasn't had a single good day. The doctors claim he's perfectly healthy, that the crying is only a symptom of infancy, and Joanne knows they think she exaggerates, that he doesn't really wail twelve hours a day. Ryan probably thinks so too, but he can't prove it. Between starting a landscaping business and going to school, he's rarely home.

Minutes before the washer's spin rumbles to silence, the baby falls asleep. He'll definitely wake if she puts him down. Then again, he might also wake at the click of the dryer door closing. Regardless, she'll need that goddamn elephant, so Joanne takes her chances with the door.

A shudder, then the wail commences. She stabs the dryer's buttons and resumes walking.

The earaches began in early grade school and grew progressively worse until, one day in the summer of 1993, Joanne's eardrums burst. She remembers the summer well because that May, just before school let out, her father left her mother for a woman named Pamela and by June he was talking about moving to Florida. When Joanne's mother, Lou, wasn't railing about this—"He can't fucking commit to a state, let alone a marriage"—she worked at Redmond Financial during the day and went to school at night to become an accountant.

Joanne, twelve at the time, spent her days off school with her friend Tina, who lived down the block. Tina and her little sister Megan were alone all day too, their mother at her job as a checkout clerk, their father only a name they heard occasionally when their mother made a phone call late at night asking for money.

The girls' day began at ten o'clock, usually with spoonfuls of peanut butter and a bag of potato chips, then TV, lunch, and more TV. Sometimes Tina, who was long-legged and fidgety like an acrobat, convinced Joanne to play tennis in the street, but more often they spent the open hours after their soap opera ended sitting on the hill, waiting for Caid to appear. The hill was two streets over from their block, a small rise on an empty lot from which they could see Caid's driveway and the basketball hoop mounted above his garage door. Caid was older by three years and neither girl had a prayer of dating him. Knowing this, they were able to love him wholeheartedly, without a sense of competition. In fact, they each loved him more because they could share it.

But one day Joanne couldn't sleep until ten because of the pain in her ear. At seven a.m. it forced her out of bed and she snuck four aspirin from the medicine cabinet, grinding them with the end of her toothbrush before carrying the white powder into the kitchen and slipping it into her cereal bowl. Lou sat at the kitchen table drinking coffee and staring into space. If she found out about the earache, she'd accuse Joanne of kissing boys or not washing her hands often enough. Lou had a thing about germs.

That morning, when Joanne swallowed the first spoonful of cereal, a spike of pain surprised her and she coughed, spewing aspirin-speckled cocoa puffs across her T-shirt. Lou snapped from her reverie, her loud voice suddenly dulled and echoed, and shook her head. *Jesus, Joanne, you could fuck up a one-car funeral.*

Thinking of this, Joanne realizes she hasn't taken any medicine yet, so she fetches the elephant from the dryer, puts the baby in the swing and goes upstairs to get the ibuprofen off her nightstand. At the sight of her bed, she considers closing the door and putting a pillow over her ear, then pictures the swing, its shaky Chinese base, its white and red triangular sticker that reads, "Warning! Do Not Leave Child Unattended," and goes back downstairs.

The swing has found its soothing rhythm, though the baby's face is still red with rage and his cry has begun its raspy phase, which sometimes means he'll take a break, sometimes not.

Huddled beneath a blanket with her ear pressed against the sofa's blocky arm, Joanne feels the entire city reduced to the size of this room. She imagines the wail expressed in water, a tsunami of grief bearing down, down, down.

Twenty minutes and no break. Joanne transfers all hope to an egg, scrambled hurriedly. The baby throws it on the floor the same way he has orange sections, steamed carrots, and every other solid she's tried. Apparently chewing offends him. The pediatrician scolded her: "It's the mother's job to get children on table food."

"I'm trying," she argued, "but he hates everything. Everything."

Before the baby, Joanne worked in a lab, her beakers always clean, her experiments always consistent. In college, she made straight A's and never missed a class. In those days she believed that, unlike her parents, she'd look back on her choices and see a straight line rising steadily to the right at a forty-five-degree angle. As if life were like a smorgasbord: all you had to do was pick the vegetables.

Joanne takes the baby outside, to the relief of warm air, and holds him above her head, gently shaking—"What? What is so damned horrible?"—until the flap of a neighbor's upstairs blind sends her back into the air conditioning, where she roots through her CDs for a soothing voice, something like what she listened to that summer she was twelve, when she had Whitney Houston's "I Will Always Love You" on tape. She and Tina liked to sing along, using a banana or a hairbrush as a microphone and watching themselves in the big mirror that hung above the sofa in Joanne's living room. One time the windows were open and Caid rode by on his bike and the girls threw themselves to the floor, mortified and thrilled that they might have been seen, that he might have guessed they were singing about him.

The morning her eardrum burst, after Lou had left for work, Joanne put Whitney in their ancient walnut console with the lattice-covered speakers and turned the volume up to ten. Alone, she didn't sing, only listened, revolving slowly, arms spread wide, marveling at the absence of pain. As she turned, the music changed, swelling and receding. It never occurred to Joanne she'd gone temporarily deaf on the left, that the price to be paid for relief was silence.

Of course she doesn't have any Whitney, the tape long gone to who knows where. Maybe Norah Jones will do.

No to Norah. No to John Mellencamp, James Taylor, Bruce Springsteen, Janis Ian, Alison Krauss, Mickey Mouse, and Barney too. Joanne turns off the music and calls her doctor. With the baby on his activity mat, she listens to the recorded voice instruct her on the health benefits of daily exercise. Her son rolls over mid-scream, then rises on one fat knee. Joanne knows she ought to be delighted—it's the first time he's managed to get so far—but feels only impatience as she watches him inch forward, right knee leading. Unable to bring the left up, he collapses, head wedged in the crook where the gym's arch meets the mat. Reluctantly, she lays the phone down to free him, then rushes back, catching the nurse just before she hangs up.

"Please, I need to see someone today," Joanne begs when the icy voice says they have no appointments. "I'm desperate."

They'll squeeze her in at twelve fifteen. Joanne calls Ryan, but he won't come home. They're behind on a job.

"This is so typical of you."

"What?"

"Is a little help when I'm sick too much to ask?"

"I've been telling you to find a babysitter."

"Yeah, someone's gonna watch this baby. They'd kill him."

"Call your mother. She has nothing better to do."

"Yes, because Lou's the soul of patience."

"Well, Jo, you'll just have to take him with you, then. I don't see why it's such a big deal."

"Thanks a fucking lot," she says and slams down the phone.

After she changes out of her pajamas, Joanne installs the baby in the stroller, bribing him with a sugarcoated pacifier. Every three houses she swaps the one he's sucked clean for the one in the bag of sugar. At the end of the block a lawn mower rumbles to life, its motor ebbing, then ramping. Of course she's tried white noise—fans, the dryer, vacuum cleaners, burbling brooks. One time Ryan brought home fucking whale calls, like a saxophone in a child's hands.

As she nears the corner, Joanne sees it is a teenage girl pushing the mower. She has long legs like Tina and hair held back with a bandana the way Tina wore it that summer, the summer of the burst eardrums, of Caid and Pamela, of the fight on the hill. That summer mowing the grass was one of the last clues about Tina. The first clue was Megan, Tina's little sister. Four years younger, she had not been allowed to play with them since they'd started talking about boys and looking up dirty words in the dictionary. But sometime after school let out—who could say so many years later exactly when? Maybe in June, maybe the beginning of July—Megan began to follow Tina everywhere, and Tina refused to stop her. The morning Joanne's eardrum burst, the girls showed up and attacked Joanne's fridge as if they'd been on war rations. It wasn't the first time and Lou had noticed the amount of food disappearing. "Those girls better eat at their own damn house," she warned Joanne. "Your father's not paying child support for three."

That day Tina downed two bowls of Cap'n Crunch before fishing a folded yellow postcard out of her pocket.

"Somebody stuck this on our door." It was a notice from the health department about their grass. "Do you know how to start a mower?"

He's finally asleep. Joanne parks the stroller beneath the sycamore and gets the book out of her car. *Breaking the Cycle: A Guide for Mothers.*

Lou had a hollow plastic tube, maybe three feet long and half an inch in diameter. She called it "the whip," used it on Joanne's legs when Joanne lied about going somewhere after school, came home late, or left the kitchen a mess. The whip left red welts shaped like boomerangs. Where did it come from? And where was it now? It seems impossible to throw such a thing in the trash.

Joanne flips through the book from back to front, reading the headings, unwilling to begin at the beginning. When it's time to go to the doctor, she lifts the baby carefully, but he wakes while she's buckling him into the car seat and begins to cry. She backs out of the driveway, teeth clenched, checking her mirrors obsessively, as if the baby will appear in one by magic, directly in the path of her wheels.

Forty-five minutes of people staring in the waiting room—one old woman scowls when Joanne uses the sugar pacifier—then five minutes with the doctor.

"Probably a viral infection. Use a double dose of ibuprofen, call if it still hurts in three days."

"Three days?"

After a lecture about the overuse of antibiotics, the doctor escapes, allowing a sympathetic smile toward the crying baby.

Back home he refuses his bottle, spits out mashed banana, throws a popsicle at her white curtains. Trying to scrub out the stain, Joanne eyes the inflatable pool on the patio. The water will be warm by now, not like yesterday, when she spent an hour with the air pump and the hose only to snatch him out as soon as his toes touched the frigid surface, setting off another rage. He would like it now. He would float, right? And if he didn't float, he would be quiet.

Joanne calls her mother.

While she waits for Lou to arrive, she puts the baby back in the swing and goes outside to have a cigarette. Several times she's left him alone in the crib, which the pediatrician calls "the safe zone," and stuffed cotton in her ears, but today the cotton would be intolerable, so she dons the ridiculous pink fur-covered earmuffs her mother gave her for Christmas. What was she thinking? How can Lou help? Lou always makes every-thing worse.

Joanne realizes the old man behind her—out trimming his shrubs—is scowling over their shared fence. Assuming it's the earmuffs that have drawn his attention, she takes them off. The baby is howling as if he's just been sentenced to death. Joanne checks her watch. Lou lives ten minutes away. What the fuck is taking so long?

The old man goes in and Joanne tries to concentrate on pleasant things—sprinklers hiss-putting in circles, bees buzzing in the lavender, children called in to lunch. That day, at noon, when Joanne had tried to get Tina and Megan to go home for lunch, Megan began to cry and Joanne asked what was going on.

"Nothing."

"Then what's the big deal if you eat at your house?"

"No big deal. It's just." Tina paused. "My mom has a new boyfriend."

"Is he an asshole?"

"I don't know. We don't see him much."

"That's good, isn't it?"

Tina shrugged.

So Joanne made them all macaroni and cheese and they ate while playing Monopoly at the kitchen table, then they watched their soap opera. With only one eardrum, the dialogue came at Joanne as if from a cave, the pitch deeper and every vowel laden with echoes. Still, she remained unconcerned, attributing the strange effect to a problem with the TV station. Her other ear had begun to hurt by then, so she took more aspirin, crushing it this time in a cup of leftover frosting.

After the program, they fixed each other's hair. Joanne worked on Megan's, which was unusually dirty and knotted. She combed it smooth, then repositioned a homemade barrette of yarn and ribbon.

Megan kept warning, "Be careful. My mom and me made it."

Lou's voice, like a German shepherd's bark, pierces the patio door and Joanne immediately drops her cigarette, stepping on it as she swivels.

"What the hell are you doing? I was out there ringing the goddamn bell."

Inside the familiar carping begins. *Lay down? Aren't you going to shower? You stink. Well, what's wrong with him? Maybe he's got your problem with the ears. Have you had him checked, for Christ's sake? I'm turning off the air conditioning. The poor thing's probably cold. You keep it like a freezer in here.* Then to the baby. *Is that shit I smell? Did you shit your pants?*

Yes, Joanne thinks, climbing the stairs, let him take some of the heat. He brought it on himself.

Lou takes the baby outside. Moles have turned the yard into a treacherous expanse of lumps and divots. From the spare bedroom Joanne watches her mother plod, an anvil with legs, over the uneven grass. She bounces the crying baby roughly on one hip, her face turned away from his in a look of oblique disgust. By the garage she inspects the roses—in need of a trim—then marches over to the shade garden and scowls at the hosta riddled with slug holes. Coming back toward the patio, Lou steps on a mole tunnel, buckling her left knee. As the baby pitches backward, she brings the other arm around and before Joanne can even turn to run downstairs, she's anchored him on her hip and her face, stiffened with rage, pivots to the window. Quickly, Joanne steps out of sight.

After the fastest shower of her life, she goes down and pokes her head outside. "He okay?"

"Jesus, what the hell is wrong with your yard? I nearly broke my leg." Lou toes some limp annuals. "And these plants need water."

"That's Ryan's thing."

"Of course. God forbid you get off your ass."

"You can go," Joanne says, reaching for the baby.

"I've got him. Dry your hair, for God's sake. Go." Her mother pats the baby's back and he stops crying a moment, his loose eyes focused for a second on some bug or flower.

On her bed, Joanne curls into the fetal position, though the house is fast becoming too warm. Sweat runs between her breasts. She should change into something lighter, but doesn't move. A shout erupts, then another. Kids' shouts. Bicycle-speed, they pass the house.

Tina usually rode her bike everywhere, but Megan didn't have a bike and Joanne's bike had a flat tire, so after their soap opera ended, the girls walked to the corner of Caid's block and sat on the hill. While they waited, hoping he would come out and play basketball, they plucked tufts of grass and threw them into the street. In a while, a girl with bright red hair rode by on a yellow bike. Tina muttered something about Raggedy Ann. Joanne let it go by and circled back to the boyfriend. "You think he might move in?"

"I don't know!"

"Tina," Megan warned.

Tina flapped a hand at her. "Just shut up."

The red-haired girl rode by again, staring at them. Tina threw a clump of grass at her, its soil still clinging to the roots. "What are you looking at, you ugly little shit?"

"Whoa," Joanne said. "Don't let your mother hear you say that."

Lou comes back inside. The baby's cry has taken a sudden upswing, its pitch sharper, more like a bird's shriek. What is she doing? Joanne gets up and goes out in the hallway, leaning over the stair rail.

What's the matter? You don't like your swing? Your mother doesn't make you stay in it, does she? She's always hauling you around. There's the snap of the safety bar locking in place. *Just try it,* the voice directs, low and quiet, like a secret. The broken-sounding click-grind of the mechanism starts up. Joanne returns to bed and presses a pillow against her ear.

After Tina yelled at her, the girl on the yellow bike rode down the street and went into a dingy gray house five doors down from Caid's. There were big American cars parked half on the front lawn, their long rusty hoods and broken taillights suggesting shipwreck. She came back out with five older kids, three boys in dirty T-shirts and two girls in black tank tops. As they neared, Joanne could see a flamingo tattooed on one of the girl's arms. It had the name "Rick" in blue-black along its neck.

"You been throwing dirt at my sister?" the girl asked.

Tina tried to wiggle out of the accusation, but the older kids weren't fooled. One of the boys smirked. "Maybe we oughta teach these bitches a lesson."

The other girl said something Joanne couldn't catch and nodded toward Megan.

Tina said, "Megan could whip her ass."

Megan looked both doubtful and thrilled. "Sure," she said. "I'll fight her."

As Megan stepped into the street, Joanne noticed the same stain on the seat of her shorts from yesterday and the day before. She put it together then—Tina's letting Megan tag along, the tall grass, the girls' unreasonable hunger, Megan's unwashed hair. The boyfriend wasn't moving in. Their mother had moved out.

Joanne takes four Tylenol knowing they won't help, then strips down to her underwear. Crawling back in bed, she freezes at the sound of Lou's voice.

"Joanne!"

"What?"

"Where's his cups? These cupboards are a mess."

"Upper, right of the sink."

A few seconds pass. The baby continues to cry. Joanne puts the pillow back over her ear.

"Joanne!"

"What?"

"Get down here!"

In the kitchen Lou stands in front of the open fridge, the baby propped on her hip, howling, his back arched against her iron grip. She eyes Joanne in her bra and underwear as if they were in public. "What the hell do you feed this kid? Your fridge is empty."

"I tried to feed him earlier. He wasn't hungry."

"Well, he's hungry now."

"He can have baby food."

Lou bangs baby food jars on the counter. "All you've got is pudding. He can't live on pudding."

"He won't eat anything green."

"You've got to make him. You're his mother." Lou slams the cupboard doors one after another. "Jesus, Joanne, when was the last time you went shopping?"

"There's plenty to eat." Joanne opens the cupboard above the stove. A box of old saltines, some granola bars, Oreos, and a can of Cheez Whiz. She thrusts the crackers at her mother. "Here, he likes these," she lies. Let Lou try to teach this kid something.

"Do you have any real cheese at least?"

Joanne checks, finds a hunk of cheddar hiding in the crisper drawer.

"Here. Cut it small."

Back in bed Joanne hits upon a solution. Poke a hole in each eardrum. How has she not thought of this before? Instead of removing her larynx, she could remove all sound. And the pain right along with it.

Having decided this is what she'll do, she drifts between sleep and waking, remembering how the little girls fought—pulling rather than punching, each of them grasping for a hold on bare flesh, loose hair. Megan's barrette snapped free and fell into the storm drain. She took the redhead by the hair then, shook her like a doll. "Let go!" the girl shrieked. Megan did. Wound through her fingers was a large clump of bright orange. The girl was crying and one of the boys muttered what sounded to Joanne like "tons," but Tina told her later was "cunts," and started toward them.

Joanne sits up to Lou yelling. For a moment she curls her face into repulsion. What have I done now? Then the words begin to line up.

She tears downstairs and finds her mother hitting the baby on the back. His mouth hangs open, eyes wide, color gone. Joanne shoves Lou away and fumbles with the high chair's strap.

"God damn it! What did you do? What did you do to him?"

"Just a cracker. I gave him the cracker!"

Joanne pulls at the strap, screaming, "I can't get him, I can't get him!"

"Push!" Lou hollers. "Push the button, for Christ's sake!"

Joanne pushes and the straps pop free.

"On his back!" Lou keeps screaming. "Hit him on the back!"

Joanne hits him hard, slung over her left arm, praying for the first time in years—*please God, please*—but she can tell by the silence she hasn't dislodged the cracker.

She puts him back in his high chair and sticks her finger down his throat, probing, afraid she will lacerate his windpipe, the panic closing out all time, all sound, all smells. She feels it way down, almost out of reach, the mush of Nabisco that will kill her.

"It's okay, Mama's here, Mama's here. It's okay." Joanne circles through the living room, kitchen, and dining room, patting the sobbing boy while Lou follows.

"You told me he was used to it. Haven't you been giving him crackers?"

"Yes, mother," she lies again. "Did you break it up?"

"For Christ's sake, he's eight months old!"

Lou prepares to leave. Joanne tries to remember the last time she saw Tina and Megan. Someone took them away. A grandmother maybe. She is ashamed not to know, but that block of years is hazy, after her father moved to Florida and Lou failed her first two tries at the CPA exam.

Before her mother leaves, she puts a hand on the baby's head. "I'm sorry, little guy. You all right?"

Joanne sees it again—Lou coming down the block that day, her anvil step and cold eyes testifying that she'd already been in the house, where the frosting bowl, cereal boxes, a mac and cheese pan and several dirty plates lay on the table next to Pacific Avenue. Then her eyes shifted to the boys' dirty T-shirts and angry faces, and for a moment Joanne actually expected her to turn around, to deny them. Instead, Lou's anvil pace quickened, a hard, relentless click, and she shouted, "Joanne, you okay?"

As Joanne jogged up the sidewalk, turning her back on those other, motherless children, pain spiked again, this time in her right ear, and the world fell away. All except her mother's face, where she is sure she saw relief, which today, even more than then, saves her life.

GOLDENE MEDENE

D r. Spencer looked up from his misery to the long, winding lines—
dark eyes, brown clothes, the occasional red and yellow native
costume—and each day before this and after seemed a wretched same-
ness to him, as if Ellis Island were a prison rather than a reception point,
and he was the one locked inside. It made him wonder for the first time
if these people were worth all the trouble.

Dr. Hauss, down the line, was new, so his inspection—just clubfeet
and goiters—still took twice as long as it should. Waiting for him to
finish, Spencer slumped against the metal railing and pressed his palms
over his ears, gently rubbing his temples with his extended pinkie fingers, aware that he looked haggard, but not caring. These people's mur-
murings—a dozen disparate languages ricocheting like a symphony of
ignorance off the tile walls—made his head throb more than last night's
bottle of brandy. Who were they to judge him? Human flotsam. Desperate castoffs. They had no right. They did not know him.

The next person was a woman in her forties, then a man in his twen-
ties, followed by a family of four who all had conjunctivitis. He passed
them on, then stopped and glanced at their backs. Really? Had he run
his finger under every eyelid? Of course. It was so automatic he did it
without thinking.

Spencer reached for his face, then jerked his hand back. Damn her!

He'd almost touched his eye without disinfecting. Spencer dunked his hands up to the wrists, splashing solution onto his instrument stand. It took only a moment to risk his sight, his whole life.

Just like it took Laura only a moment to excise him from hers. Six words—*I don't want to marry you*—had reduced thirty years of confidence, work, friends, and good looks to the simple, ridiculous fear of not being good enough to love. It felt as though she'd stamped his forehead "undesirable" and he would walk around trying to hide under his hat the rest of his life, tripping over obstacles with his brim pulled down too far. Spencer wasn't sure whether or not to believe what she had said—that there was no one else—but what did it matter? Was it better or worse than what his sister had said—that Laura came from a different class of people. "I'm surprised she ever went out with you."

While Hauss muddled through the next large family, Spencer absently arranged the things on his stand—a row of blue chalk, a flat piece of metal like a buttonhook for inverting eyelids, a notebook for interesting observations and a gold-plated, new ballpoint-style pen Laura had given him. Spencer opened his notebook and looked at his name, written with the pen in the top left-hand corner of the inside cover. The crisp lines of his signature, the perfectly round dots between his M and his D, suddenly seemed a mockery. He decided to throw the pen out as soon as he could get a different one.

Spencer had gotten a job on Ellis Island right after he finished his training and last year he'd been promoted to the eye and brain man, responsible for diagnosing trachoma, a highly contagious infection that caused blindness, and mental deficiencies. Like all the physicians, he used blue chalk to mark his diagnosis on the person's shoulder, in his case CT for trachoma and a circled X for the deranged and retarded. Inspectors further down the line separated people based on their marks. People marked with CT were sent to the infirmary for a second check. If confirmed for trachoma, they joined those with a circled X back on the boat, bound for wherever they started. Which is why Spencer's position was left to the most experienced.

Finally Hauss sent up a group of eight and Spencer worked through, starting youngest to oldest—the best way since younger kids got scared off if they saw him use the buttonhook.

Done, he leaned on his podium, head in his hands. God, Hauss was so damn slow! Perhaps he could go to the administrator's office and tell them he was ill. Who would question a doctor's diagnosis of himself? But with Hauss's speed, if he went home sick, they might have to shut the whole line down for the day. People whose relatives were waiting for them to disembark would get stuck on the boats. Maybe he could at least get a damn chair to sit on. Wasn't he entitled to that much? A chair? He was a doctor after all.

Spencer pushed his glasses up on his tall nose and rubbed his eyes, then glanced quickly at his hands. What the hell was wrong with him? He never touched his eyes at work. Had he remembered to disinfect? Of course, he hadn't seen a case of trachoma all day. Still.

He dipped his hands in the bowl of disinfectant on the stand's lower shelf. Some of the doctors on the Island didn't bother with this precaution—as if they had no common sense at all. Sometimes, seeing this, Spencer wondered if he should feel proud of his job. Was it true what Laura had implied, that only the desperate take a job on the Island? Spencer's father owned a grocery. He had no medical connections. So what of it?

A man approached with red, watery eyes. Spencer swirled his instrument in the disinfectant, flipped up the man's eyelid and ran his finger along the underside. It took only a second to feel the white granules. The man forced his eye shut, face wrinkled in outrage, and muttered something in Yiddish. Trachoma and the Jews. They had it the worst, especially of late.

Spencer marked him on the shoulder with a CT, then smiled kindly, eager not to alarm him—he looked as though he could be trouble—and motioned for him to go on ahead.

Waiting for the next group, he scanned the lines, focusing on the women, wondering what they thought of him. Were they ashamed to have a strange man touch them? Or did they admire him, a doctor, an American? Did they resent him for judging them or seek his approval gladly, like a child seeks a parent's?

Spencer washed his hands again, straightened his tie, then glanced up. Laura stood in front of Hauss. Laura? The same crackly red hair, like fall leaves. The same white neck. The mole? Was it there? Hauss had his hand on the woman's neck, checking for goiters. She looked afraid and angry. Spencer's stomach felt bound like a tourniquet on a wound. He knew now: that's what Laura went to last night. Someone else's touch.

He passed the next two people without the mental exam—they seemed good enough, just go—and picked up a fresh piece of chalk, rolling it slowly between his hands, the dust leaving blue trails in his fingerprints.

Fredek held his book high so that he could appear to be reading while actually watching the pretty girl from their ship. Her name was Macia, but he thought of her as Goldene because she'd told him that's what the Jews called America, Goldene Medene.

She approached the first man along the pipe and he took her throat in his hands. He seemed to be massaging it, which Fredek thought a strange way to greet someone.

Fredek began to scratch his head, but the Old Loaf slapped his hand away before he could get any satisfaction. "How many times do I have to tell you? You want them to think you have lice? Hm?"

Fredek smiled and stuck his hand in his pocket. At least she was moving again. For weeks his grandmother had sat on her bunk aboard ship as if she were a baker's sample, long gone stale in the window. Fredek couldn't even remember seeing her get up to use the toilet. Now that they were on land, her body had begun to expand to its normal shape, which he thought of as a paczki, sweet and thick and soft.

If he had asked her, Wicktoria would have said she was more like a dinner roll—hard crust, good slash across the top for bursting. She'd have explained to him there was nothing to worry about, though. It was only natural after weeks of sitting in rail offices, waiting in ticket lines, riding on strange buggies, walking on unfamiliar roads and sleeping in common beds that she'd become flattened, like unleavened bread. Which was fine. Such bread lasted longer.

And last she would have to. The journey had taken an extra week due to rough waters, and then they'd been forced to sit on board, just off the coast, for three days waiting for the Island to clear. On day two the rumor started that they were not going to be let off at all, that the whole ship would be turned around and sent back. In the wavering darkness of steerage Wicktoria had listened to the mumblings in Magyar and Russian, Yiddish and German, and tried to remain flat. No hope. No fear. These were the opposite ends of useless.

She knew her grandson was only pretending to read. She followed his eyes to the redheaded Jewess in front of them in line. On the ship the girl had a berth just across from them and Wicktoria had warned Fredek to stay away from her. Everyone knew the Jews were infected with a disease of the eye which kept you from getting into America.

"She looks fine to me," Fredek had said a hundred times over the past few weeks, but Wicktoria wasn't taking any chances.

While the man examining the girl made notes, she dabbed at her eyes and Wicktoria nudged Fredek. "See, I told you."

"She's crying, Babcia, because of the bags." When they'd come in on the first floor the men in blue made them leave their suitcases in a pile before they were allowed in line. It kept the lines moving more smoothly, with less congestion. The Old Loaf had heard rumors of this policy on the boat and had taken the precaution of concealing their valuables—

cash money, her late-husband's pocket watch, some dried biscuits, her Bible and her mother's rosary—under her knitting in a small bag she could easily carry. While they waited in line, the knitting would also keep her occupied.

Goldene had argued with one of the men in blue and Fredek had tried to help, translating for her, until the Old Loaf had pulled him away. "You want us to go back on the ship? You want to go to prison for talking like your father?" It was the first time since they'd left home he had heard real fear in her voice.

Goldene dropped her handkerchief. Fredek grabbed it and handed it to her before the Old Loaf had time to interfere. "Cheer up," he told her. "It's just stuff."

She grinned and reached to pat his cheek. Wicktoria slapped away her hand. "No touching!" She'd already told the girl why they preferred not to associate.

"It's nice," Goldene whispered in Polish, "to have a young man think of me." She turned back to the man at the pipe, who pantomimed removing his shoes. She leaned down to unlace her own boots and Fredek enjoyed the view of her wide hips and her hair, like fired clay, falling across her face.

The Old Loaf whispered, "Mind your manners."

Embarrassed—did she miss nothing?—Fredek turned his attention to his book, a small volume covered in blue, wrinkled leather. Gilded letters rubbed brown read, "An Emigrant's Guide to the United States of America." He read the book slowly, puzzling out each word from context and the English his father had taught him. He marked the passages that seemed most important with a light pencil dot.

Here he can do everything which is right, and no man can with impunity do anything to him that is wrong. If he is not in debt, an event necessary only from sickness or decrepitude, he is absolutely his own master, and the master of all his possessions.

www.thomascranelibrary.
org

Title: The best place on
Earth : stories
Author: Tsabari, Ayelet,
1973-
Item ID: 31641009361381
Date due: 6/21/2016,23:59

Title: The bigness of the
world : stories
Author: Ostlund, Lori.
Item ID: 31641009351051
Date due: 6/21/2016,23:59

Title: White sands :
experiences from the
outside world
Author: Dyer, Geoff.
Item ID: 31641005378439
Date due: 7/5/2016,23:59

Title: Felicity
Author: Oliver, Mary, 1935-
Item ID: 31641005367820
Date due: 7/5/2016,23:59

Title: You should pity us
instead : stories
Author: Gustine, Amy,
1970-
Item ID: 31641009354956
Date due: 6/21/2016,23:59

Fredek didn't know what "impunity" or "decrepitude" meant, but he knew what "his own master" meant—he would be free, just as his father had promised.

It is only the sober, the honest, and the industrious who succeed. Fredek marked the word "industrious" to look up when he bought an English/Polish dictionary.

Despite her admonishment, Wicktoria did not judge the boy harshly for enjoying the pretty girl's backside. She was proud of him, in fact, that amid all the loss he'd suffered—both parents gone, his home, his friends, everything left behind—he could still find joy in what God had made. Nonetheless, there were matters of respect to consider.

The last night on the ship, Fredek asleep and the lights all extinguished, Wicktoria had decided to put on her good dress. She knew she'd get better treatment on the Island if she looked more presentable. It still plagued her, whether she'd made the right decision to save the money on second class and take steerage. After she'd bought the tickets she'd heard second-class passengers were given a more cursory inspection.

When Wicktoria slipped her dress over her head and turned her head to free her long hair, she saw him—the man across and one bunk down from her. She'd thought he was asleep, but no—that was clearly a glint off his wet eyeball, open, staring at her. She paused, holding her dress in front of her. What interest could he have in an old woman like her?

She looked at him questioningly, then slipped her top off, letting her pendulous breasts sway out nearly bare, covered only in the thin fabric of her undergarment. He smiled and nodded in appreciation. She'd proceeded to pull off her old stockings—thick, black wool with tiny, random moth holes—then slid her fresh stockings—white with red poppies embroidered along the outer calf—up her dimpled, fine-veined thighs, and fastened them to her garter.

The man smiled at her, then closed his eye, the glint gone.

Finally, on the third morning, the doors opened and the darkness began to move, the long, wide skirts, leather bags tied shut with rope, pillowcases full of nothing worth having, only worth not losing.

On the ferry Wicktoria sat at the window, cheek against the cold glass, eyes closed while Fredek strained over her, looking out. She tried to imagine a moment of complete rest, complete aloneness, a moment when she could let go all her bags, take off her coat and dress, shed the papers with her fake name and pretend husband, crumple the damn tag they'd pinned to her collar, and return to a world in which she could lay down without another pair of eyes to see her drift away.

Now Wicktoria watched the second man further down the line at the elbow in the pipe. He handled each person like a mother who'd had enough—grabbing their faces and peering in their eyes as if they were peepholes, asking questions, writing directly on their clothes. Would this be the end of it? She doubted that. At least it was warm in here.

Wicktoria breathed in a great quantity of air. Her whole chest rose, the papers with her false name, her pretend husband waiting in America, pressing against her breasts. She turned her face toward the high windows above and felt an intense desire to fly, to be able to rise up far away, just her, not even Fredek, into the enormous open space above her, the towering arch of the ceiling, where she could touch the cool tiles on the upper wall, curl up in the immense chandeliers under the gentle warmth of their electric light.

The man waved Goldene down to the next station at the elbow in the pipe and consulted his clipboard again. Fredek glanced at the Old Loaf to ask if he should go on up, but she was staring at the ceiling, her gray head twisting in circles. Fredek followed her eyes to the arched windows, where a faint snow fell against the gray light. He, too, thought of flying— out the windows, out into the new world of rules, laws, languages, and the only thing he feared was leaving behind the Old Loaf. His parents were dead, but she had saved him. He looked at her wrinkled, spotted hand. The knuckles were especially wide and flat, like a man's. She wore a gold band that had grown too tight some time ago and now sat in a permanent depression which made it seem that removing it would require amputation. Fredek took the hand in his and squeezed it.

Hauss, so miserably slow, seemed to have been manhandling the poor girl for hours. Finally he'd waved her down to Spencer.

"Your name?" Spencer asked, his voice almost a whisper. Her high-necked blouse made it impossible for him to see if she had a mole like Laura's, a soft-brown spot, perfectly round, just above the clavicle.

She didn't reply, so he asked loudly if she knew English.

"No," she shouted in Yiddish.

Another Jew. Spencer wondered if she was trying to escape the Pale of Settlement the Russians had set up.

He asked in his limited Yiddish where she was from. The girl looked at him with that expression, the way they all stared, defiant and vacant, resentful, assuming you had something against them, which you didn't.

"Oh, for God's sake, I don't have time for this." He snapped some papers out of her hands. Macia. He was fairly sure that was Miriam in English. "Miriam, where's your husband?" It wasn't his job to ask these questions, but really, what was a woman her age doing coming to America alone?

She said something he didn't understand, this time in Polish. Why was she switching to that awful language? Did she think he was a bohunk? That he might understand it any better than Yiddish?

The old woman behind Miriam took several steps forward, then stopped under his glare and spoke in Polish to the girl.

"I'm not ready for you yet," Spencer said sternly, hoping his tone, if not his words, would convey the message.

A boy took the old woman's hand and pulled her away, mumbling "sorry" in English. Spencer frowned a warning, and went back to Miriam.

He was going to just wave the girl through—she was clearly not insane—when he noticed her eyes. Red, puffy. He wiped his hands slowly, rubbing his chalk-laden fingers white again. Then he cupped her jaw. She looked frightened. "It's all right," he whispered. "I just have to check your eyes." Instead of using the buttonhook, he took her fragile, blue-veined lid between his thumb and forefinger. The girl muttered something in Yiddish. He caught the word "don't."

"It's okay," he muttered, but she pulled away from him, shaking her head and blinking.

"Healthy!" she said in English.

And so she was. No granules, no weeping. At most, she had viral conjunctivitis. More likely, she'd just been crying. "I thought you didn't speak English," Spencer said flatly.

"A little," the girl replied.

If he marked her with a CT and they held her over for examination, Spencer would have a chance to speak to her. He glanced behind him out the window—the gray swirling day, the Statue of Liberty in the distance. If it were sunny they could sit in the wooden folding chairs on the dock and watch ships come in. He would teach her English, then explain America, where to live, how to get a job, warn her against the charlatans on the trains and in the bus stations. She would grow to depend on him. At the board of inquiry he would defend her, explain that his diagnosis had been overly cautious. She'd be indebted.

Spencer waved the boy behind Miriam in line up to him. The old woman followed.

"Do you speak English?"

"Some words," the boy said.

"Your name?"

"Fredek."

Spencer nodded. "Frederick," he immediately amended the name by adding a syllable, "you tell her what I say, all right? You can do that?"

Frederick nodded.

"Ask her how old she is."

"Twenty-three," Frederick translated.

A year younger than Laura. Dr. Spencer smiled. "Ask her if she is alone."

"Yes," Frederick said.

"So she's not married?"

"No, sir."

"How is she going to make a living?"

Frederick shook his head.

"Money," Spencer said, "how will she make money, live, pay rent, buy food."

Frederick nodded and asked Miriam. She said she was a seamstress and she was meeting her brother, who'd come over last year.

Spencer reached out slowly and touched her hair, winding a lock around his finger. It was just like Laura's. Even dirty, it felt like hers, crackly autumn leaves in huge piles. Miriam pulled away, looking to Frederick for an explanation. Frederick shrugged. The old woman addressed the boy. He answered her in a word.

Spencer spoke sharply, "You are not up yet. Tell your mother to be quiet." Hauss had gone through two more people. They waited respectfully several feet away.

The boy said something to the old woman. She replied and Frederick began to translate, but Spencer waved him off, nodding toward Miriam. "Tell her to unbutton her blouse." He felt sure she had the mole, and he wanted to see it.

Frederick translated, but Miriam pulled her gray shawl more tightly around her shoulders and glanced at the old woman, who stepped forward and spoke. Frederick translated. "Sir, it is a problem, uh, young woman," he nodded at Miriam, "she is..." He stumbled. "Not want to open blouse, not with men."

"It's a medical exam. You have to submit," Spencer said. Frederick didn't translate. Spencer slapped him on the arm. "Boy, tell her what I said. People are waiting!"

Frederick told the two women something. Spencer was beginning to doubt he could speak English all that well.

"I need to check her out," he said. "I'll take her down to the nurses. Tell her to come with me."

Frederick explained this to Miriam, who took a step back, next to the old woman. The woman put her arm around the girl and told the boy something. Frederick hesitated, whispering to the old woman.

Spencer reached out for Miriam's arm. "Come with me."

She pulled away from him. "No," she said in English.

The boy said, "She is my sister. Where are you taking her? She is with us."

"You said she was alone. What do you mean she's your sister?"

"I..." Frederick stumbled again, then listened for a moment to the old woman. It was clear to Spencer there was something fishy going on.

"She is my sister," the boy repeated.

Spencer demanded their identification papers. "You don't have the same last name. Now leave us be, step aside." He shoved Frederick, who stumbled into the old woman. She spoke sharply to Spencer, clearly reprimanding him for pushing the boy.

Spencer tried to talk above her. "I need to get this girl to the infirmary. She needs to be examined." He grabbed Miriam's arm. She yanked it away. He grabbed again and tried to pull her down the line.

The girl's face had gone blotchy. The old woman and the boy rushed forward. Spencer tried to dodge, but she hit him with her canvas bag while the boy grabbed the girl's free arm and knitting needles clicked out onto the tile floor. The old woman was shouting. He thought it sounded like the universal language of profanities. Miriam's shawl fell on the floor. People were staring. The boy hollered, "You hurt her!"

Spencer realized he could feel Miriam's humerus. He let go. Hauss was staring. The bedraggled faces of those in line were staring. The damn old woman and her boy refused to look away.

Spencer walked back to his station and snatched a piece of chalk. He wrote CT on Miriam's pleated blouse, then motioned for the old woman to step forward. On her right shoulder he drew a large blue X with a circle around it.

An inspector had come up to see what the ruckus was. "Mental defective?" he asked, watching the old woman move down the line with Miriam and the boy.

"Yes," Spencer said. "I could see it in her eyes. She's not all there." He hadn't bothered with the boy. He would go back with her automatically, and later, Spencer would find Miriam in the infirmary and comfort her.

The inspector walked off. Spencer rearranged his chalk into neat, clean lines. Hauss had returned to work, but seemed distracted, checking and rechecking his damn clipboard. God, they'd be here all night! Spencer smoothed his shirt and tie. Everything was fine. The old woman and her boy would be gone soon. He motioned with his finger for the next person. A man stepped forward, Spencer looked him over quick—catch up now or never, he figured—and waved him through. Then a woman and her daughter, a young couple.

Spencer waved them through quickly, then scanned the line for Miriam. She, the boy, and the old woman were still several people short of the next station, where inspectors checked for chalk marks and put the ones for return in one wired area, the ones for treatment in another. The three of them were deep in conversation. Then Miriam smiled and turned away, stepping forward in line as he knew she would. She had nothing to do with that annoying kid and his mother. Spencer was about to look away when he saw Frederick motion to the old woman's shoulder. She slipped off her coat and looked at the mark, then said something to the boy.

"Put the damn coat on and get going," Spencer muttered. He glanced down the line. Hauss was still flustered. He could see it in his hands, the way they fluttered the pages on the clipboard.

He looked back. The old woman and the boy were hunched together, talking. Then she began to roll up her coat. She removed a pile of yarn from her little bag, stuffed the coat in the bottom, then replaced the yarn on top.

Spencer began to step out from the iron pipes, the words almost in the air—"What do you think you're doing?"—then stopped. The boy was tapping Miriam on the shoulder, saying something. After a moment, she rubbed at the mark on her blouse vigorously, then covered the smudged blue with her shawl.

In three years not one person had thought to do anything about the marks he chalked on them. Of all those he had diagnosed—which must add up to thousands—the old woman and her boy were the first to understand: it is not good when they mark you apart.

Spencer watched the three of them proceed past the wire compartments, down into the main inspection lines, where they would be asked for their papers, which he'd already seen were in good order. Afterward they'd retrieve whatever remained of their luggage, then step out into the cold and the strangeness of a land they had never seen, didn't know, couldn't speak to. For those who left here there was no language, only sound. There was no knowledge, only hope. Once you stepped off the Island the marks you carried could not be stuffed in a bag or washed off a garment. Spencer wanted to call after them, to tell them he was sorry. To holler out "Good luck!" but someone had walked up, another old woman, this one with two boys and an old man. Spencer laid down his chalk and slowly reached for their eyes.

YOU SHOULD PITY US INSTEAD

Whohen Simon and Molly moved from Berkeley back to her hometown in Ohio, Molly was surprised to discover how many people still believed in God. They'd bought in a neighborhood with an excellent public school, near the university where Simon had snagged Chair of Philosophy. There were conflicted Jews, closeted Muslims, casual Lutherans, and hennaed Hindus, but it soon became clear the diversity provided no cover. For most people Adonai, Muhammad, Christ, and Vishnu could be treated as vernaculars. Same thing, different name. The particular dogmas didn't have to be debated or justified. Everyone could just get along. Except atheists. They still offended people.

Last year the subject of religion came up at school. Molly's oldest daughter, Kate, was asked "what she was" and when she said she was nothing, the other kids insisted this was impossible. "You have to be something!" After that Molly started coaching the girls—Kate was in the fourth grade and Emma was in first—on the polite things you say when asked about religion. It was all working out fine until Simon's book came out.

Riding in on the same wave as Harris's, Hitchens's, and Dawkins's condemnations of religion, *The Great Cults: How Religion Warps Minds and Hearts* received both more attention from the lay public and less respect from academia than it otherwise would have. Several reviewers called it "derivative" and now Simon has to come up with something "ground-breaking" for the next book. Under this pressure, he's been in no mood to help Molly negotiate the social fallout from the front-page story their local paper ran quoting *The Great Cults'* most inflammatory passages. Because of the article, invites to card nights and progressive dinners have dried up and the girls have been skipped over for several birthday parties and sleepovers. At school, no one gives Molly more than a perfunctory nod during pickup and dropoff.

To smooth things over, she tried placing Simon's criticism in light of Catholicism's more spectacular failures. Surely some of the other mothers had been traumatized by a crucifixion movie? Questioned why billions of Chinese were eternally damned for not worshipping a God they never heard of? No dice. The word had gotten out: it wasn't the mistakes of a few or the odd papal ruling Simon questioned. It was the basic intelligence of those who had faith.

Last month Molly began trying out a new line. With a little wave and a grin, as if she were apologizing for an overgrown lawn or unpainted shutter, she'd say, *You should pity us who have no faith. We're lonely and anxious.* A few women took her seriously and suggested she try their church. The hippest ones forced a burst of air through their noses to indicate they weren't too old for irony. The rest gave a one-sided, closed-lip smile, as close to a sneer as forty-year-old mothers get. Molly knows it's time for a new line, but as yet nothing's come to her.

Tuesday morning she picks up her grandfather for the weekly grocery trip. His house, a box at the end of a row of other postwar boxes across from a cheese-processing plant, is nearly as small as her garage, but when she pulls onto the makeshift gravel curb, the crunch under her tires sends a primordial comfort through Molly's veins. After her parents divorced, she lived with her grandparents during the week. In the summer Grandma Alice played make-believe with Molly on the platform swing—train conductor, trapeze artist—and in the afternoon they watched soap operas. Now Grandma Alice is gone and Molly's mother lives in North Carolina with a man she met there named Dave something. This leaves Grandpa Hank to Molly and she doesn't mind at all. In fact, it's the most fulfilling time of her week. For the next few hours they will go shopping for bran cereal and talk of things that can be fixed. Leaky gutters. Drooping plants. Overdue library books. Her grandfather will thank her for her trouble and try to pay for her gas, which she will laugh at and refuse.

As Molly gets out of the car, her phone beeps to remind her of the school talent show later that afternoon. She plans to arrive late, sit in back, and slip out as soon as Kate is done with her dance. She'll wait for school dismissal in her car, avoiding the awkward silence and forced smiles she would endure if she waited in the hall with the other mothers.

At the back door Molly wiggles the key into the lock, pulls up on the knob, then turns. Inside, Grandpa Hank sits on the edge of the kitchen's vinyl booth tying the neck of a plastic bag around his ankle. A hernia of blood swells the bag's seamed corner.

"Oh my God." Molly trips up the two stairs into the kitchen. "What happened?"

Beneath his heel, a dark spot bigger than a dinner plate mars the carpet. "I broke a vein and I can't get the thing to stop bleeding."

"I'll call an ambulance."

"No, no. You can drive me. I tied things up real good. It won't make a mess in your car."

"I'm not worried about my car, Grandpa."

"Well, that's a nice vehicle you got and blood's hard to get out." He nods at the carpet stain.

On the way to the ER her grandfather asks how the kids and Simon are. He doesn't know about the book, doesn't read the *Times Book Review* or listen to NPR. He lives where Molly used to live.

"Everything's good," she tells him, watching the blood move higher in the bag. "I should have called 911."

"We're almost there." A block away the brick wall of the hospital rises, its narrow, uniform windows like gravestones and morgue slabs.

In the ER Molly flags down an attendant, then fumbles in her purse for her grandfather's Medicare card, thinking the mothers should see her now. Now there's no disputing how lonely and anxious an atheist can be.

At two o'clock she skulks into the elementary school talent show, sliding into the nearest free seat next to Mrs. Gupta, a bindi between her eyebrows. On the other side of Mrs. Gupta is Elizabeth Randolph. The Randolphs have six natural children plus a boy adopted recently from South America. Molly knows only the outline of his incredible story. A member of an isolated tribe, his people went uncontacted by modern civilization until a group of illegal loggers infected them with the common cold. Only nine children survived. A Christian organization arranged for their adoptions in the U.S. and Canada.

Elizabeth leans forward and waves at Molly. "You missed them!" Kate and Elizabeth's daughter Sarah are best friends, which Molly assumes is the only reason Elizabeth still speaks to her.

"My grandpa, hospital," Molly whispers. Elizabeth frowns and Molly mouths, "He's okay. It's all right."

If she'd known she was going to miss Kate's dance, she'd have skipped the whole damn show, two torturous hours of ten-year-old violinists and jugglers who can't catch a ball. Last year Simon told people, "If I'm wrong and there is a God, He's no doubt preparing a perpetual elementary school talent show for my personal hell." This year Simon is lucky enough to be out of town.

In the hall after the show, Kate throws her arms around Molly's waist. "Where were you? I looked and looked and you weren't anywhere. I thought you were dead!"

Several people glance at Molly in shock, as if Kate isn't supposed to know about death. Molly rubs Kate's back, the sequins of her dance costume like sharp fish scales. "You were great up there!"

"You saw me?"

"Of course I did! I was just a little late. You probably couldn't see me in the back."

Death became a problem last year, after Molly's grandmother passed away. The girls couldn't accept her disappearance. *Grandma Alice was gone? Gone where?* Without heaven as a destination, Molly struggled to explain. "It's kind of like sleeping forever."

"Where is she sleeping?"

"Underground."

"Can I see her?"

As Molly stumbled, they stared at her like a teacher waiting for a slow student to finish *Dick and Jane*. Finally she had to admit death wasn't quite like sleep. Since then her credibility has suffered, which is no doubt why Kate continues to question her about the talent show until she exposes Molly's lie. At dinner, she is still pouting and Emma needles her.

"Kate looks like a frog with her lip out that way."

"Sweetheart," Molly pleads, "it's not like I skipped on purpose."

"Kate has blood in her eyes," Emma observes. "Does that mean she's going to die?"

"It means she's a drama queen," Simon says, then asks how Molly's grandpa is.

"They used a special bandage, like stitches."

"Is Grandpa Hank gonna die?" Kate asks miserably, but with resignation, as if he were the family cat.

"Everybody's going to die," Simon says.

Molly glares at him.

"When?" Emma wants to know.

Simon lowers his voice. "We don't know, sweetie. He's very, very old."

The girls glance at one another.

"What's the matter?" Molly asks.

"Sarah told Kate she's going to hell," Emma announces.

Simon laughs. "How does she know that? She call God's 1-800 line?"

"There is no hell," Molly insists.

"Yes, there is. Daddy said so," Kate says.

"When did I say that?"

"You said your hell was going to be a talent show."

Simon looks chagrined. "I was joking. Hell is illogical. If God is good, why would He have a hell?"

Emma stabs a big piece of chicken with her fork. "Maybe," she says, "God isn't good."

At eleven o'clock Molly is pouring herself a glass of wine to toast the end of this day when Kate comes into the kitchen. "How old was Grandma Alice when she died?"

"Why?"

"Emma and I are trying to figure out how long we have to live." She holds up an Audubon calendar. "I counted three hundred and sixty-five days in one year. Now I need to count how many years."

Both girls have their father's Scandinavian coloring. At bedtime, the inside rims of their eyes grow as red as raw meat. "Go to sleep."

"I will. Tell me how old she was first."

"Eighty-eight," Simon says. He's cleaning the sink and counters. They have to be disinfected before he can fall asleep. "Now go to bed."

Kate goes back upstairs.

"Why did you tell her that?" Molly asks. "They'll be up for hours counting three hundred and sixty-five eighty-eight times."

"It's like counting sheep."

They hear her padding down again. "What's Emma's birthday?"

"Why?" Molly sighs.

"Because we have to take away how many days we've been alive from the total to get how many days we have left."

"You can't count how many days you're going to live."

"Why not?"

"Because it's late and you need some sleep and both of you could easily live longer than Grandma Alice. Look at Grandpa Hank. He's older than Grandma Alice was and he's healthy as a horse. Now go to bed. Dream about ice cream or something."

"So I don't have to die before Emma?"

"Not necessarily," Simon says. "Age is only one factor..."

Molly interrupts. "Go to bed. Go!"

Kate runs upstairs, hollering, "I don't have to die before you! I'm older, but Daddy says you could die first!"

On Friday Molly takes Kate to play softball. It's pure Americana—a miniature baseball diamond bordered by a ragged row of folding chairs and blankets. Toddlers play near the field, though in no peril as none of the fourth-grade girls can achieve better than a slow-roll grounder. At halftime Molly goes over to talk to Elizabeth Randolph, whose one-year-old sits in her lap eating cheese crackers and smearing the orange paste across Elizabeth's pants. Adoo, the boy from South America, leans against a nearby tree. The color of red mahogany, he has a flat nose with splayed nostrils and a sharply defined, narrow bridge. Dashed, black lines bisect both of his prominent cheekbones. Molly can't tell if the lines are tribal tattoos or the handiwork of a bored eight-year-old with access to eyeliner.

She kneels by their blanket. "Hi, how are you?"

"I'm good. And how are *you*?" Elizabeth says. The emphasis on "you" crept into her voice after the book came out. It makes Molly suspect she's warming up to proselytizing.

"Actually I'm wondering if you can do me a favor. Kate's been upset since my grandmother died and I guess she talked to Sarah about it."

"Oh, I'm sorry about your grandma."

"Thank you." Molly pauses to regroup. "The thing is, Kate is a little upset because..."—she flips her palms up to indicate she might have this wrong—"...Sarah said Kate is going to h-e-l-l."

"Oh no!" Elizabeth gasps.

"I was wondering if you could please ask her not to say that kind of thing to Kate. She's pretty freaked out."

"Of course." Elizabeth nods vigorously. "I will definitely talk to Sarah." She touches Molly's hand. "Also though, I would appreciate it if you ask Kate not to tell Sarah God doesn't exist."

The game has restarted and the first batter connects. Elizabeth claps. "Way to run, way to hit, Kate!"

Molly glances behind her. Kate's already made base. She looks back, aware she should simply say yes, of course, and let it go. Instead she says, "I can't stop Kate from telling people what she thinks. I'm not asking *you* to stop *Sarah* from saying she *believes* in God."

Elizabeth claps for a girl who's tagged out. "Does Kate really not believe in God?" Her voice is sympathetic. "Or is it your husband? He's told her not to believe?"

Molly shrugs. "And you tell your kids to believe. That's what parents do, they poison their children with their own convictions."

Elizabeth's face goes stony and Molly attempts to recover by explaining her brain/jail theory. "Our minds are like jails without a jailer. There's no one to let you out. Trying to believe something that strikes you as false is like asking the mouse nibbling on crumbs outside your cell to unlock the door."

Elizabeth scowls. "So I'm a mouse?"

"No, no. I mean you can't make your brain think differently just because you want it to."

Elizabeth continues to frown.

"It's like a cat," Molly tries again. "Like asking a cat to do something."

Elizabeth wipes the baby's mouth with the edge of her blankie and focuses her attention on the game. Molly looks over her shoulder. The teams are changing and on her way to the outfield Kate shouts, "Did you see my hit, Mom? Did you see it?"

"It was great!" Molly says. Elizabeth gives her a soft, knowing look, as if granting dispensation for the lie. This angers Molly more than anything else.

The next week when Molly arrives to take her grandfather to the grocery store she finds him on his knees in the basement. "I was changing the furnace filter, and I couldn't get back up."

Molly helps him to the sofa. "How long have you been stuck?"

"Only about four hours."

"Four hours! On your knees?" She tries to keep her voice light, like Mary Poppins in distress.

"I guess these old legs aren't what they used to be."

Molly brings up subscribing to an emergency service. Her grandfather scoffs, "It's silly to pay all that money every month, and I don't want to be calling strangers. They'd send those ambulance folks and have my whole door busted up just getting inside."

"Maybe you should consider moving in with us, then." Molly knows Simon won't like this.

"No, I'm fine just where I'm at. You don't need some old fart hanging around."

"I don't like the idea of you being hurt and no one there to help."

"People get old. You can't worry. You just got to accept it."

She buys him a cell phone, tells him to carry it in his pocket, but he has trouble with the buttons, and a week later Molly finds it on his dresser. "You're supposed to carry this all the time."

"Oh honey, that's too bulky."

That afternoon Molly picks Kate up at the Randolphs'. The girls are making habitat dioramas for an end-of-year project. While she waits for Kate to gather her work, Molly tells Elizabeth about her grandfather.

"You should try the thing I bought my mother after she broke her leg," Elizabeth says. "It's an automatic dialer your grandpa wears around his neck. If he pushes the button, the machine calls you with a recorded message to let you know he's in trouble. No monthly fee and no strangers."

Before they leave Kate and Molly go out to the rear deck to get a papier-mâché tiger Kate's left to dry in the sun. Adoo is standing at the bottom of the wooded ravine. The sun, which has emerged following hours of rain, strikes his face, making it glow. In the moment before he turns away, she sees the dashed lines again on his cheeks, but he's too far off to tell if they're the same as before.

Grandpa Hank agrees to the automatic dialer. Molly gets it wired up and helps him record a message. "Molly, it's Grandpa. I need help." The prefiguring of illness and injury unsettles her, but her grandfather pronounces the system "very practical," and hangs the button on a chain around his neck.

During summer vacation Sarah becomes a fixture in the house. Molly can't think of a reason to object. There's been no more talk of hell. The girls spend hours alone, Emma a tolerated arbiter, gofer, test subject, the third leg of their otherwise intense twosome, heads bent together over braids of thread or yarn, twenty fingers sorting plastic gems and letters. Molly never interrupts. Neither does the phone. No one calls to invite the girls swimming or ask Simon and her to a cookout.

While the sun rides its reliable path through the upper leaves of a neighbor's elm, Molly lies on a musty futon in the screened porch reading about the history of places that aren't usually thought of as having a history. Switzerland. Canada. Zimbabwe. Before Kate was born, she'd been working on a Ph.D. in history, but no matter what subject she tried, Molly couldn't find a beginning or an end. History just went on and on in infinite directions, a recursive, progressive web spun at a hundred trillion points of ricochet. There was no point from which to make a sensible judgment. When she got pregnant, Molly felt relieved to stop trying.

In the porch, she just reads the facts, makes no attempt to judge them. One day she looks up from her book and sees that the elm's ten thousand pods, which blanketed the gardens in late May, have sprouted. Somehow this mindless, unwanted propagation make being lonely okay. Even in the form of a plant, the world has violence and invasion at its core. Being lonely is the least you can expect. It's so light a disappointment, it almost counts as a blessing.

One Friday Simon invites two professors from his department over for dinner. Despite her supposed brilliance, Helen looks like a truck-stop waitress—bloodshot hyperthyroid eyes in a pale narrow face and a bony chest she advertises in midriff tank tops. Her husband, Dugan, twenty years older, wears his hair in big waves like a '70s porn star. Helen was Dugan's PhD student before they married. The rumor is he's number four.

"Maybe she doesn't believe in premarital sex," Simon joked.

Helen has two PhDs, in anthropology and English. She wrote her thesis on Gertrude Stein. "What I'd really like," she announced the first time Molly met her, "is to be a lesbian."

Molly laughed. "I don't think that's the kind of thing you choose."

Helen shrugged. "When I was twenty I moved to Israel. For two years I was a Jew."

Dugan is near retirement and Simon has caught wind of Helen scouting positions out East. Hence the dinner invite—as Chair it's his job to make sure she stays. Molly serves pasta and brie with cheap white wine. Outside, on the patio, overgrown bushes along the edge crowd the chairs, requiring her and Dugan to scoot off axis to avoid being scraped on the neck. Helen winds her pasta around her fork like paint on a brush and scans the yard. A sparse patch of sun-starved lawn has greened up in the temporary gap between winter's cold and summer's worst heat. Within a few weeks it will be brown again, except for places where crabgrass has taken over.

"I have to cut stuff back," Molly says.

"It's too late," Helen shrugs. "You've lost control."

Molly looks at the yard. "We haven't had time, with the girls."

"Emma's in first grade this year, right? You been working?"

Molly shrugs. Simon likes to keep alive the myth that she hasn't given up on a Ph.D.

"So how's it going with the crazy Christians?" Dugan asks.

Simon laughs. "The usual. Death threats mailed care of my publisher. Oh, the new thing is Kate's going to hell." He tells them about Sarah.

"That's why the East Coast is better for people like us," Helen says.

Dugan's face tightens, deepening the creases that divide his narrow cheeks into sections like a sliced loaf of bread. "Is it that bad, Molly?"

"Well, I wouldn't say we're terribly popular in the neighborhood. No one except Sarah's mother gives me more than a perfunctory hello."

"Which is ironic," Simon says, "since she's the craziest Christian of them all."

Molly scowls. "Be nice. The Randolphs are good people."

"Are you sure she knows about the book?" Helen asks.

"Everybody knows. This neighborhood has the Ford assembly line of rumor mills."

Helen looks at Dugan meaningfully. She's published several essays on atheism with a feminist twist. Simon smells a book in them, another reason to worry about her getting snatched away to the Ivies.

"Could be fun," Dugan raises his eyebrows. "You enjoy pissing people off."

The doorbell rings and Molly goes through the house to answer.

Elizabeth is there with Adoo to pick up Sarah. Molly invites her in, but Adoo remains on the porch.

"Now that it's warm, he likes to be outside," she explains, keeping an eye on him through the storm door. "When he first got here he was afraid of the cold."

"So he's adjusting?" Molly asks.

"He's doing great with English, and he's teaching me his language."

"Does he always put those lines on his face?"

"They're from his tribe. They burn the skin and use a plant sap to dye the scar tissue as it heals."

Molly blanches. "So it's permanent?" She puts a hand to her own cheek. "Have you talked to any of the plastic surgeons around? Maybe they could do laser removal."

"Oh no!" Elizabeth exclaims. "I wouldn't want to take that away from him. He had a whole life before us, and I want him to hold on to it." She pats Molly's shoulder. "It'll be okay. It's all in Jesus's hands."

As the girls come downstairs, Adoo opens the door and presents a garden snake to them with a big smile. Sarah screams and clutches at her mother.

"Sarah!" Elizabeth snaps. "That's enough." She unwinds Sarah's arms from her waist and gently pushes her backward, then takes the snake, muttering a foreign word to Adoo that sounds like "beda," and releases the animal into the bushes. "Please tell Adoo you're sorry."

Sarah wrinkles her nose. "Sorry."

"In his language, please."

"Minto," she mumbles.

Simon comes in from the kitchen. "What's the uproar?"

Elizabeth explains Adoo's fondness for snakes, smiling at him as if he's been discovered to like cubing three-digit numbers in his head.

"He's probably an animist," Simon says. "Snakes are often seen as role models. He may even worship them as gods."

Sarah scrunches her face into exaggerated disbelief. "The Bible says snakes are the devil."

"The serpent in the Bible is a *symbol* of evil," Elizabeth corrects. "He's a form the devil took. Regular snakes are just snakes, all God's creatures."

"How do you know the difference?" Emma has come into the hall, her lips rimmed in blue from an unapproved popsicle.

Everyone looks at Molly. Why is she supposed to have an answer? "Go wash your face," she orders. "And stay out of the popsicles."

That night when Simon goes to kiss the girls good night, he finds them on their knees, fingers laced together.

"Pascal's Wager," he explains to Molly. "Sarah told Kate she should pray to God because nothing bad will happen if she's wrong, but if she doesn't pray and God exists, she'll go to hell."

Kate looks sheepish. "I'm sorry, Daddy. Are you mad at me?"

"No, of course not. Why would I be mad?"

"Because you think praying is stupid."

"No, he doesn't!" Molly repeats her canned speech on different beliefs being okay.

"Do you believe in God, Mommy?"

"I'm still thinking about it," Molly says, "I do know this, though: I'm not going to hell and neither is Emma or your father. If there's a God, He's more interested in what we do than what we think."

"How do you know?"

Simon sits on the bed and puts his hand on Kate's knee. "Just think about it, honey. The idea of God is that he created all other beings, right?"

She nods.

"So if he created us, including our brains, then he must know how we think, sort of like the people who invented computers know how they work. It follows that if you pray without really believing in God, then God will know you don't believe, and it won't matter what you do."

"So I'm going to hell even if I pray?"

Molly shoves Simon out of Kate's room. Downstairs she tells him to lay off the logic. "You're scaring the pants off that poor kid."

At one a.m. Molly wakes to sounds in the hall. Kate lies outside their bedroom door clutching Grubby, the musical bunny she's had since infancy.

"What's the matter?"

"Nothing. I was just hot."

Molly takes her back to her own room and they lie together like gears in the twin bed. Kate tucks Grubby under her chin and rubs his foot against her lips. "Mom, can I go to church with Sarah and her family? She invited me."

"Sure, why not? It's fun to have new experiences."

"I love you, Mom."

"I love you too."

While Kate's breath slows and deepens, Molly does the math in her head. Twenty-nine thousand, seven hundred and sixty-four. The paltry number shocks her, so Molly does it again more carefully, but comes up with the same answer. If Kate lives to be ninety, that's how many days she has left.

The next morning, Molly feels as if she slept in the stockade. Simon cheerfully greets her at the breakfast table. "Where were you?"

"Crammed into Kate's bed. How about this for your next book? Parental fatigue is the source of religion. We don't need God to explain things to ourselves. We invented him to shut the children up."

Simon laughs until she tells him about Kate wanting to go to Sarah's church.

"Isn't it enough they're trying to convert that poor pagan kid, they want mine too?"

"You're trying to convert every Christian into an atheist," Molly accuses. "What's the difference?"

"Technically, I'm an agnostic."

"That's not what your book says."

Molly sits down and splays her hands on the table. "Has it ever occurred to you God is a comfort to kids? He answers a lot of tough questions."

"What we need is somewhere to take agnostic kids. I want to invite Elizabeth's brood to a big room where we all sit around singing songs about logic and reading the Bible for inconsistencies."

"You work there. It's called a university."

Simon waves this off. "I get them too late. The brainwashing has already taken hold."

"Yes, except Kate's being raised by us. For us God is like the Easter Bunny and Santa, maturity will take care of him."

"That's only because adults agree Santa doesn't exist. As long as there are people like the Randolphs, that's not going to happen with God. The girls are going to get confused."

Molly shrugs. "Life is confusing." She remembers Emma, age one, falling through a banister down a flight of stairs. That night in ICU Molly caught herself praying to Jesus as if he were an old friend who'd moved to Bangladesh—these days, he could be reached only in case of emergency.

"One visit," she assures Simon. "Kate will be bored to tears and never go back."

But church neither bores nor comforts Kate. Rather it seems to strike a flame of curiosity edged with suspicion. Molly finds her reading Simon's book.

"Why does Daddy get to write a book about God if he doesn't believe in him?"

"That's what the book's about. Why he doesn't believe."

"Does anybody besides you agree with Daddy?"

"Sure, lots of people do."

Kate looks unconvinced. Molly takes the book away. "This isn't really appropriate for you."

"Why? Does it have bad words?'

"No, it's just complicated."

"Yeah," Kate conceded. "There were a lot of words I didn't know. Some of them had fifteen letters!"

The following week she announces she's going to church with Sarah again.

"Why?" Molly asks.

"It was interesting." She tells Molly about Adoo. "Sometimes he stays outside during church and Mrs. Randolph stays with him, or sends one of the big kids. And he doesn't like music. He covers his ears when they play that gong piano thing."

"Organ," Molly interrupts.

"Yeah, organ. People started singing, and he crawled under the bench thing and wouldn't get out."

"What happened?"

"Mrs. Randolph laid down with him."

"In the middle of church? On the floor?"

Emma appears dressed in her only skirt, a black and white houndstooth wool. She's wearing a white blouse Molly doesn't recognize with an orange stain on the sleeve.

"I'm going too. Sarah said I could."

Simon gives Molly a told-you-so look. "Nobody's going," he says. "We don't go to church."

Both girls demand a better reason.

Molly takes Simon aside. "I told you encouraging them to think for themselves wasn't a good idea," she jokes.

"Yes, and now seems like a good time to stop that."

"Come on, they'll lose interest eventually."

"You said she wouldn't go more than once."

"Adoo makes it interesting."

"Sounds to me like they're torturing that poor kid."

The Randolphs arrive to pick up Kate, but there aren't enough seats for Emma. Molly is about to offer to drive her and Simon is suggesting neither girl go when Adoo comes out of the van and signs something to Elizabeth. They talk in gestures and a few broken words of English and his native tongue. Molly gathers he is offering his seat to Emma.

"Adoo can stay here." Simon shrugs, Mister Innocent.

Adoo seems to have understood and nods his head. "Stay, yes."

Elizabeth hesitates.

"It's fine," Simon says. "It'll be interesting."

Within half an hour Simon has exhausted what he can learn without a translator, so Adoo goes out to wander the yard and Simon goes inside to clean the fridge. From the porch, Molly watches Adoo examine plants and rocks, then climb up into the crotch of the willow tree and begin chewing on a leaf. When the Randolphs pull in the driveway, Molly goes outside to call him down. He hands her a long, shallow basket he's made from the willow switches and mimes for her to collect flowers or pick up sticks. After he leaves, Molly looks up willow trees and finds out the salicylic acid their leaves and bark contain is the precursor to aspirin. She wonders if Adoo is in pain.

The girls delight in the basket and next time Sarah comes to play Kate invites Adoo as well.

Elizabeth thanks Molly. "He doesn't have any friends yet. I really appreciate Kate being so nice." She pauses. "Not everyone feels comfortable with Adoo."

He shows the girls how to make the baskets. It's harder than it looks and the twigs leave narrow welts on their hands. To weave the bottom, crosspieces have to be inserted through slits in a thicker branch. Adoo demonstrates how to make the slit with your front teeth, holding the wood like corn on the cob, but the girls recoil from its taste, so he does it for them.

The following week Elizabeth calls to say they can't take Emma and Kate to church. "Adoo and Sarah don't want to go, and I think I might have better luck with them if it's just family."

"I hope the girls were behaving."

Elizabeth assures her they were, but Molly can tell there's something more to it. A week goes by and Sarah isn't free to play. Kate leaves four messages, none returned. After the fifth message, Elizabeth calls.

"I enrolled Adoo and Sarah in Bible camp, so they won't be around as much."

Molly stews for days, then calls back. "If you aren't going to let Sarah be friends with Kate, I would prefer you tell me that straight out. I don't want her to think Sarah is mad at her."

Elizabeth insists she adores Kate and that Sarah's just been busy.

Another week passes with no Sarah before Kate tells Molly she wants to attend Bible study too.

"You can't. You have to be a member of that church."

"I can go with Sarah. Please!"

Molly puts her off with excuses about Simon not liking it and Emma wanting to tag along, but Kate continues nagging until Molly snaps, "No, we aren't religious. We don't belong to that church and you can't go to Bible study. You can't go to yeshiva or join a sangha or hang around the mosque either. We stay home Sundays. We do yard work and go swimming."

"You just read," Kate says. "You don't even like to swim."

Kate mopes around for nearly two weeks before Molly calls the Randolphs. Simon is lecturing out of town, so she won't have to argue with him about it.

On the phone Elizabeth sounds different, her tone less cheerful, more intimate. "Sarah would love to play, I'm sure."

"Kate would like Adoo to come too, if it's okay. They have baskets to finish."

On Saturday Elizabeth drops them off. The kids, including Emma, go into the backyard.

"How's it going?" Molly asks.

"Well," Elizabeth shrugs. "It's harder than I thought."

"Harder?"

"Adoo. I knew he'd need a lot of love and patience and extra work to socialize..." She stumbles, correcting herself. "Acclimate himself."

"I admire you," Molly says. "What you're doing for him."

Elizabeth looks embarrassed. "I'm not so sure anymore I did the right thing. For him, I mean."

"Why? What's the matter?"

She glances at the van. The one-year-old is asleep in her car seat and the three-year-old is watching a movie on the van's video system. "I think we'll be moving to a new church."

"Why?"

"The pastor and I disagree about Adoo."

"How so?" Molly makes her voice gentle to invite confidence.

Elizabeth sighs. "He's not sure Adoo can be saved."

"Maybe he should move in with us. He'd fit right in."

Elizabeth smiles, scuffing her sandal on the pavement. "You'll be fine. God isn't interested in what you think. He's interested in what you do."

Emboldened, Molly asks, "How come you've been so nice to me? No one else is talking to me since Simon's book came out."

Elizabeth shrugs. "Being offended is a sin of pride."

Molly bristles. "So I'm your good deed for the day?"

"No, no. I admire you guys. Most people are afraid to be honest. What's the point in having a friend if they aren't who you think they are?"

Simon has made a similar point about God.

"I'm going to say goodbye to the kids." Elizabeth nods toward the backyard. "Give me a call when you want to get rid of them."

Molly follows her along the garage through a tangle of shady plants she doesn't know the names of. She's beginning to suspect they're mostly weeds.

Three baskets sit half-finished on the table. The women poke their heads into the house, but don't hear anything. Elizabeth goes around front while Molly does a quick check in the living room and calls up the stairs. Nothing. She goes back outside.

"They couldn't have gone anywhere. We were here the whole time."

"Maybe hide and seek," Elizabeth says.

They return to the yard and peer between the tangle of plants along the fence. In the back, where there's a huge lilac, Molly catches sight of a bare foot on the ground. For a crazy second she imagines Adoo has dragged the girls' bodies to a hiding place. Plunging into the bushes, Molly shrieks at the sight of Sarah, Kate, and Emma lying in a row, a garden snake slithering across their necks. In a flash the snake disappears into a pile of leaves and grass clippings.

"Mom!" Emma complains. "You ruined it!"

"What were you doing?"

"We were trying to see if there's a God," Sarah says, then sees her mother and goes pale. "I mean, I was proving it to Kate."

Emma brushes off the seat of her pink shorts and rolls her eyes. "Adoo says snakes are special and making friends with them gives you magical powers."

"No," Sarah objects, "I did it because Kate is afraid of snakes. I told her if God doesn't want you to die, nothing can kill you."

Elizabeth and Molly exchange a glance, then Elizabeth sits down and pulls Sarah into her lap. "That's not quite right. You still have to be careful. If you purposely do dangerous things, that's like testing God, okay? And we can't test God. That's wrong."

Kate looks at Molly, the need in her expression plain. Molly puts an arm around her shoulders. "Don't mess with snakes. Wild animals are unpredictable."

Though she knows it's only her grandfather's recorded voice—"Molly, it's Grandpa. I need help"—in the haze of four thirty a.m. the digitized sound summons the altered voice of kidnappers demanding ransom and stalkers knitting terror. In her panic, Molly makes it as far as the garage before remembering Simon is out of town, she'll have to bring the girls.

It's a ten-minute drive if you go like a bat out of hell, take the freeways and catch all the lights. Molly doesn't catch the lights, but she clocks ninety on the interstate and once, after slowing and looking, runs a red. She thinks mostly of what she'll find at the house. Did he fall down the stairs? Another broken vessel, this one's flow too generous for a bread bag to contain? If he had to use the emergency button that means he can't get to a phone. Molly doesn't know what to do about the girls. What if he's already blue? For several minutes before Molly's grandmother died, she would stop breathing, then her whole body would shudder and she'd grab a single, long breath as if trying to capture something going by. Molly cannot get that shudder and gasp out of her mind.

She skids onto the loose stones. "You girls stay in the car. I'm locking it."

"No!" Kate protests.

"It's too dark," Emma agrees.

The darkness isn't what bothers Molly. It's the pink-orange of the sodium lights across the street in the cheese plant's parking lot. They remind her of *The Twilight Zone*. Nothing is safe, nothing can be anticipated, even in the end everything remains a mystery.

"Okay, but you girls sit in the kitchen. Don't move. I have to help Grandpa Hank."

Key in the lock, Molly hears movement and the door is opened from inside. Her grandfather has on an undershirt and khakis. "Oh, shucks, I tried to call you. I'm just fine. Relax."

Molly looks him up and down. No blood, no palsy. He's had time to put on socks and shoes. "I must have rolled over on the button while sleeping. I tried to call you, but the phone was busy."

Molly guesses she left it off the hook.

"Hi, Grandpa," Emma says.

"Hi there, little one. Your mother got you out of bed this time in the morning?"

"We had to come. Daddy's out of town."

There's already water boiling for tea. "You want some eggs and toast?"

"No thanks, tea's good."

"I think what I'll do," he says as he gets out a bag of the girls' favorite cookies, "I'll take that thing off at night. Then it won't be causing all this trouble."

Molly reminds him he could fall out of bed or forget to put it back on the next morning.

"I won't forget," he says. "The old noggin still works pretty good."

The girls want more cookies. Molly nods, too tired, yet buzzed on adrenaline, to deal with complaints. She stares outside. The pink-orange sodium lights cast an alien glow over her car. *Assimilation is the mortar and pestle of humanity.* That's what Simon said when she told him Elizabeth was having second thoughts about bringing Adoo to America. Suddenly, Molly feels sure he won't make it. The modern world will swallow him. Maybe not at fourteen, or eighteen or twenty. But it will. Does that mean they should have left him in the jungles of Peru? It seems to her if you don't belong where you're born, you'll never belong anywhere.

Grandpa Hank sits down with his eggs and toast, asks again doesn't she want anything. Molly shakes her head. "I'm just glad you're okay."

"Well, sure I am. Next time don't be rushing out so quick. I don't want you getting hurt hightailing it over here."

Of course, one of these times he won't be okay. But most likely she won't get a call. At the morning or night check, his answering machine will pick up. Molly will wait ten minutes, then call back in case he's in the bathroom. After the second call, then one from her cell on the way over, her car will crunch onto the familiar stones, but she won't feel the familiar relief. She'll put her key, hand unsteady, into the lock, and lift the warped door, her grandfather's name already vibrating on the air. "Grandpa Hank? It's me, Molly." She'll step up to the vinyl booth, proceed through the narrow kitchen and into the future without expecting an answer. One thing she has learned—death is like God: it answers every question with silence, but that doesn't mean it's not waiting for you.

AN UNCONTAMINATED SOUL

It is a hot day in June when Lavinia returns from the market, the scent of burned diesel in the air, sun shining on her house with a glaring light that does it no favors. She rolls her groceries—canned fruit, bread, peanut butter, milk, coffee, spaghetti, tomato sauce, forty cans of wet and three bags of dry cat food—behind her on a rickety dolly. Every few steps she stops to be sure the bungee cords are still secure.

For thirty years Lavinia and her husband Carl lived in apartments, moving whenever the appliances broke and the landlord wouldn't fix them. Then, five years ago, long after their son Christopher had moved on, Lavinia inherited her mother's house at the corner of Newton and Wade, just across the street from where three tracks converge at the Amtrak station. Brown and gold asbestos shingles cover the outside, as if someone used roof tiles for siding. The front steps are crumbling, pried away from the sill by fifty years of freeze-thaw cycles. A plastic pot of geraniums, gone to twigs three seasons ago, slumps from a rusty bracket.

Lavinia turns up the gravel path between her house and old man Pultwock's—no garages in this neighborhood—and trudges to the back door, coming to a breathless stop on the five-foot-square patio Carl laid. Propping the screen door open with a bag of cat food, she unlocks the main door. Taped above its lock is half a used envelope: *At the heart of all beauty lies something inhuman.*

With the door barely ajar, Lavinia reaches in to dispel the cats and grab the baby gate. "Shoo, get, go. Back, you beasts, back." She's locking the gate into the opening, hissing at Casey, Wallace, Rodeo Roy, and several others trying to escape when Jason, a sneak with a white-masked face like the killer in the *Friday the 13th* movie, leaps, passing through her reaching fingers silky, muscular, untouchable, already gone.

A nail protruding from the metal weather stripping gouges Lavinia's finger. "Dammit, Jason!" She gets the storm door shut, then trips down the stairs, sucking salty, warm blood from her hand.

Jason has stopped, a bit dumbstruck, in the middle of the yellow yard. A rotting privacy fence barricades his route to Newton Street and a thick stand of yews in front of a chain-link obstructs the alley behind, so Lavinia positions herself between her house and old man Pultwock's, barely six feet apart. "Here kitty kitty, here." She crouches seductively. "Come on, Jase. I got food in the house." He plops on his side, turning his black body in the warm grass as she stoop-walks toward him, cooing, "Here kitty kitty, come to Mama."

Just when she gets close enough to touch him, reaching out with a tentative, inveigling rub of her forefinger and thumb, old man Pultwock's screen door whacks shut. Jason darts toward the back fence and disappears inside the yews.

Pultwock slaps down his steps in scuff slippers, waving his finger. "Mary, you let that damn cat go! That's what we need, a mass exodus, a diaspora!"

Lavinia is the name of Emily Dickinson's sister who liked cats. Mary started to think of herself as Lavinia after Carl killed himself.

She scowls at old man Pultwock. It's a bad omen, this old man knowing the word "diaspora," her just learning it last week. She read it in a book she bought at a garage sale about a Jewish woman forced to put her cat to sleep when Hitler forbade Jews to own pets. It struck Lavinia as the most horrible thing she'd ever heard about Nazis. It was one thing to want someone dead, but the capricious, petty denial of even this love? That seems altogether a different class of cruelty.

"I know what you got in there," Pultwock says.

"Sh!" Lavinia flashes over her shoulder, finger to her lips.

"Let him go. Probably be happier free." As he leans to peer into the yews, a gap opens in Pultwock's robe, revealing the inside of drooping, white thighs, like raw chicken on a hook.

"Walter, he's not going to come out with you there."

Old man Pultwock straightens up. "Be for the better. What would your mother say to this? You think she'd approve?" He flicks a cigarette nub into the gravel between their houses, where at least fifty others lay scattered like toy infantry after a fire bombing. When Lavinia's son Christopher was a child he made up whole army divisions from their ashtrays. Carl's butts were the brown army, Lavinia's the white. When she wore lipstick, the opposing army became communists.

Lavinia parts the yews, calling "Here kitty kitty kitty, here," then holds her finger to her lips again and listens, hoping to locate Jason by a telltale rustle, but a train becomes audible just then. The ground vibrates and Lavinia raises her voice, going further along the fence line, toward Pultwock's yard.

He follows, complaining. "I saw you take my paper on your way to work last night."

Lavinia clerks nights at a convenient store ten blocks down on St. Claire. "Yep," she says. "You know I need those."

Pultwock always puts the papers on the top of his garbage cans, then hauls the cans to the curb, pretending to know nothing about what Lavinia needs.

"I see you got boxes this morning. What's them for?"

Lavinia has a new plan for the basement, so she brought home several empty cardboard boxes from the store. She's not surprised Pultwock saw her. He has always made a point of knowing her routine.

To get rid of him, she lies. "I'm using them to pack some things up, you know, clean house."

"You? Clean?" Pultwock's saliva trembles on his thin, red lip, one bubble balanced on the tip of a chin whisker. The bubble's utter unlikeliness, its dogged persistence, galls Lavinia. She imagines grabbing Jason out of the bushes and tossing him—claws fully extended—at that chin.

"Would you please go inside, Walter? Jason's never going to come out with you here."

"Shit, I don't see as he's going to come out with or without me here. What do you think? He appreciates you? Cats are stupid animals. Now dogs, they'd know what they got. A dog would come back."

Lavinia returns to her own yard, still stoop-walking to peer into the yews. Pultwock follows. "That dog your mother had, he was something. He could shake hands and if you held up a hot dog he'd dance like a goddamn ballerina."

Lavinia is annoyed by the mention of her mother's dog. She took him to the pound after her mother died, mainly because Carl had just gotten her Fritz and they were not getting along.

Lavinia continues to croon for Jason, on her hands and knees now.

Pultwock laughs. "Jesus, Mary, look at you? You think that cat would care if you lived or died?"

Lavinia stands up and brushes off her jeans, belatedly aware of how her rump must have looked from Pultwock's view. "Shut up, Walter. Just shut up."

"So you going to tell me why you really got them boxes?"

"I'm sending some things to my son and his wife, okay? The family china."

"China, uh!" Pultwock guffaws. "You and that girl are on the outs, right? I sure don't see her come round here after that fight a while back."

"They're busy," Lavinia says. "They've got little kids." Patti was pregnant last time Lavinia saw her. She would have had the baby by now.

Suddenly Pultwock shouts, "You're moving, aren't you? That's what they're for. You're moving out!" He says it with shock and anger, as if they were lovers.

Lavinia trudges up the back stairs. "You caught me, Walt. I'm leaving you."

Just as the door shuts she hears him mutter, "Crazy bitch."

The corner of Newton and Wade is an island of five houses cut off from the adjacent neighborhoods by the interstate, the Amtrak station, an empty warehouse, a bar called The Rusty Tavern, a boarded-up building still advertising on a wooden sign "Bait and Grocer" in cracked red paint, and a few oddly contemporary businesses—ZZ Graphics, a brand-new post office. On the far side of the warehouse the High Level Bridge rises across the Maumee. Its blue-gray steel is lit all year round with white lights.

Of the five houses on Lavinia's street, she and old man Pultwock are the only permanent residents. The house on the opposite side of Pultwock is boarded up and the two on the far side of that are rentals, their occupants changing each year, sometimes in the course of a few months.

Lavinia's mother bought the corner house with life-insurance money from J&M Stamping, where Lavinia's father worked as a machine operator for better than thirty years. Her parents, Catholics, had ten children, and could never afford to own until her father died. By then all but one of Lavinia's siblings had moved out. Her brother Luke went all the way to Texas. He made money in the concrete business and built a huge stucco house that reminds Lavinia of a cult compound, with its two wings and guest house clutching a courtyard where he and his wife installed a Jesus fountain. In the pictures they sent, Jesus stands on the middle of an enormous concrete lily pad, hands outstretched, geysers of frothy water shooting from his palms.

Later Angela, the youngest, went to Idaho on a college scholarship and lost touch. Lavinia's brother Todd moved to Detroit and died of pneumonia in the mid-'80s. As for the rest, Lavinia has argued with all of them over the years, and now that their mother is no longer a common thread, no one bothers making it up.

Inside the tiny kitchen white oil paint, long yellowed, flakes from the walls. Exposed wooden shelves hold Corelle plates. In the middle of the room, a Bakelite dinette set with green vinyl seats scored by claws into patterns like the veins on a leaf. Lavinia shuffles around forking canned Friskies onto two dozen plates.

The gluttonous—Adrienne, Plato, Camus, Ginger, Peter, Wally, Fyodor—dominate the plates while she stands at the sink waiting for Pultwock to go inside, but he seems to have settled in for the duration on his back steps.

When Lavinia's mother died it was Luke who called. Apparently his phone number was the first on the yellow scrap of paper her mother kept affixed to the fridge with a plastic Virgin Mary magnet. He said a neighbor found her. Lavinia had never thought to ask how the neighbor got in, or who it was, but it flashes to her—Pultwock, of course, even though before today he's never said a word about Lavinia's mother. Until this moment Lavinia would have said they hardly knew each other, though that would be nearly impossible with the houses so close, their backyards the only grass for blocks around.

Emily, an all-white stray who regularly disappears for days in the basement rafters, jumps up and butts Lavinia's elbow. She pets her in a circular motion between the ears, a light touch the skittish cat prefers. "Be patient, Camus is almost done. Can't you see his little belly swelling?"

On top of the fridge Fritz wails. Lavinia drums the counter. "Come on down, Fritzie. Come on. They'll be done. You and Em can eat soon." Fritz meows with increased pitch, a formal complaint against her coldness. "No, you don't need help. You got yourself up there, now get yourself down." Nonetheless Lavinia shuffles amid the swirling bodies and offers her arms. Fritz hesitates, then leaps, his claws piercing her shirt and the tender skin of her breasts. She grips him to her.

Several of the cats have clogged tear ducts, so every day she wipes the corners of their iridian eyes free of a brick-colored ooze which, left untended, would stain their delicate faces. She scissors out matted clumps of fur or dried feces caught in errant, long-haired tails. When brawls occur, she applies first aid with a lightning swipe of a damp paper towel and a glob of Neosporin. After Rodeo Roy, a clumsy gray tabby, broke his leg falling between the back of the couch and the wall, Lavinia made a splint out of popsicle sticks and caged him to heal in a kennel fashioned from a cardboard box. For circulation, she cut out the words "Get Well" on one side and "Be Careful" on the other.

Lavinia shoos Peter and Virginia away from one of the plates and installs Fritz, then shuffles through the living room to peer out the front window. The cats, fifteen or twenty at the moment, dominate the furniture like a collection of stuffed toys in a store window. The answering machine is supposed to be on top of the TV, but today it's wedged behind, knocked off by Lucifer, who crouches on the warm set, which Lavinia rarely shuts off.

She rights the machine. Its light isn't on, but Lavinia pushes the "play" button anyway, holding the little box as if to coax something from it. What if the light has burned out? No. It's the same message, unerased by future calls for over a year. "Hi, Mary, look, after what happened today I just don't think it's a good idea for the kids to see you for a while. It's..." Christopher says something in the background, then a child laughs, and Patti resumes, speaking more quickly, her voice lowered. "It's better if we just don't come down for a while. Better for Hannah, you know, and maybe, you could just be *reasonable*, and get rid of some of them. Just some. Not all. Anyway, I have to go. I really do."

Lavinia lets the tape run out, then rewind itself. Has it really been a year since she's gotten a message? Working nights, she's mostly home during the day for solicitors and an ancient aunt who lives in Michigan. Lavinia lays the machine back on top of the TV, next to an old car-wash coupon taped face down. The back reads, *If it were sufficient to love, things would be too easy. The more one loves, the stronger the absurd grows.*

Lavinia returns to the kitchen and looks out the window. Pultwock remains. She watches him as she cracks open another eight Friskies cans. "Do you think he's ever going in?" she asks the cats. "What's he waiting for? Rotten old man."

The last time her daughter-in-law Patti came over, Lavinia put most of the cats in the basement, but while she had her back turned making peanut butter sandwiches, her granddaughter opened the door. About twenty of them flooded up and Hannah leapt into her mother's lap, clawing her throat.

Lavinia had stood on the porch hollering as Patti fumbled to buckle the girl in the car. "The struggle itself toward the heights is enough to fill a man's heart! Camus said that! Not your crazy mother-in-law. I didn't say that! Camus did!" Of course, Patti hadn't read *The Myth of Sisyphus*, which Lavinia found at a garage sale six months after Carl's death. She could not possibly have appreciated the significance of the simple truth Lavinia was trying to impart. The cats are alive. What else can she do but feed them?

As Patti drove away, Lavinia spotted old man Pultwock peeping out his front door. "Oh, you've never even heard of Camus!" she'd hollered. "What would you know?"

After breakfast the cats settle down to nap.

Poppy, Frank, and Clover curl up on the back of the sofa. Venus, Emily, Moss, and Trevor take over the cushions. Norma Jean's tail peeks out from beneath.

Rose, Stanley, Pinky, Lucy, and Mabel balance on the window sills, tucked behind the drawn curtains.

Lily, Daisy, Roger, Oscar, Opal, Ruby, Eliot, and Lion sprawl on the floor in the narrow lines of sunshine that break through, turning the brown carpet tan.

Everyone else is either in the kitchen, the basement, one of the two bedrooms off the living room, or the bathroom, a jigsaw of chipped porcelain with a pocket door—no room for swinging.

Lavinia settles into Carl's recliner, where she can see Pultwock from the side window and keep an eye out for Jason coming around front as well.

If you have four, or ten, or maybe even twenty cats, the sound of their sleeping is silence. If you have fifty or sixty, their breath can be heard, a collective purr rising in the air. Lavinia closes her eyes and listens to the hum, the cats' breath the song of life, reminding her what it's like.

She rocks back and forth in the old La-Z-Boy, a blue tweed recliner Carl bought with money he won in the Ohio Lottery. Six hundred and forty-seven dollars. His only winnings in twenty-five years. A dollar ticket every week for twenty-five years comes to one thousand three hundred dollars. Lavinia can't remember if the lottery always cost a dollar. She is sure that Carl sometimes bet two or three, so either way the money he spent was far more than he got back.

Carl knew that. Of course he did.

Maryann and Ginger jump up and arrange themselves, spooning, one brown-haired, the other red. Lavinia found the girls on her way home from work a month after she found Carl in the basement. Two kittens huddled under a car parked illegally on St. Claire. Nearby, bloody and still, an adult cat. Lavinia wrapped the kittens in her scarf, tucked them inside her quilted black coat with the nacreous buttons, and took them home. They slept on her chest all night and she lay awake listening to the flutter of their infinitesimal hearts, picturing the organ's incredible precision, its vulnerable red slickness, its mindless, perfect pumping.

Soon, other cats began to arrive. Fritz objected, peeing in her bedroom, first in the corner, then on the bed, finally on Carl's pillow. But eventually he became accustomed to the influx of strangers, or simply lost track, as Lavinia imagines God does of all of us. "The anonymity of abundance," she mutters, rubbing the girls' backs, going against the lay of their fur so that she can feel the prickly spot where each hair joins the skin.

The house is closed up, curtains drawn against the heat and Pultwock's prying eyes. Lavinia parts them and checks. Still there. He has been since the day she moved in, his house crowding toward Lavinia's like a petulant child who keeps scooting his desk over until it touches his neighbor's. The house itself has always menaced Lavinia, its peeling paint around narrow windows, its shingles the color of baby poop, some of them hanging loose to reveal a darker, rotting sheathing underneath. One day when she was raking leaves, she looked up at her own house and for a moment mistook it for Pultwock's. Shabby and menacing in the same way. She felt overburdened, she and Pultwock, the only owners left, expected to hold off the highway bearing down, the crumbling streets with patches of original brick showing through, the charging trains cutting through pebbled parking lots. They called it a railroad yard, but there wasn't one speck of grass as far as Lavinia's eye could see.

Lavinia learned that if she kept the drapes closed in the winter, she could go months without seeing Pultwock, but in the summer, he becomes unavoidable, sitting on his porch, blowing smoke through the screen of the window just opposite the one Lavinia wants to open. Her mother told her their houses have identical floor plans, hence his bedroom right across from her living room. A few times she has caught him looking at her at night from this window.

.

Lavinia succumbs to sleep and dreams old man Pultwock is in her bathtub singing "Amazing Grace." The girls wake her, stretching across her lap, then jump down, square on the carpet stain—a blue-gray shape like a mollusk.

Lavinia gets up and looks out all the windows. No Jason. Pultwock still sits on his stairs. "Bastard," she mutters. She'd go out to tell him off, except it would only make him more apt to sit on his stoop, spying on her, so she decides to clean the basement instead. As long as he's there, she doubts Jason will leave the yard.

With some old tennis shoes on and her pant legs rolled up, Lavinia gathers the boxes to carry down. At the top of the stairs, above the light switch, the back of a receipt says, *Suicide is prepared within the silence of the heart, as is a great work of art. The man himself is ignorant of it.*

The day after Carl was laid off the last time, he woke up earlier than usual and sat for two hours at the kitchen table looking through the newspaper. He read each employment ad twice, then neatly folded up the paper and said to Lavinia, "Well, you can't waste a day of freedom. How about a drive?"

Their '74 Olds Cutlass sat on blocks again—no money for repairs—so they borrowed a friend's car and drove twenty miles down toward Bowling Green to a farmer's stand.

What they had they spent on blueberries.

Lavinia made a pie while Carl tinkered with the Cutlass.

Then, after dinner, Carl dropped the pie.

He dropped it, the whole thing, flipping it upside down, right in front of his recliner. He'd been on his way to the front porch to watch the lights of the High Level Bridge emerge from the dusk. "Come sit with me, Mary," he'd said. "At least we still got the bridge, right?"

Then he tripped. Over what Lavinia has wondered many times.

When he started screaming, "God damn it! I loved that pie. I loved that pie!" and fell to his knees, Lavinia thought he was joking. He had that way, a spontaneous burst of brilliant humor in the face of minor tragedies. Then she saw the tears, the snot, his face blurred by anguish, and all sound stopped. Without sound he appeared ridiculous, as if he were acting out a mime's routine: grown man kneeling on a dirty carpet plucking furiously at a cat's endless fur, his whole life dependent on one ruined blueberry pie.

"Oh, for God's sake," Lavinia said, "get a grip on yourself."

A week later Carl hanged himself from a rafter in the basement. A while after that the city towed away the Cutlass.

Lavinia shovels soggy newspaper and feces into several garbage bags which she steals from work. She is careful about it, taking only individual bags, never whole boxes. She feels no pang of guilt because she would gladly buy them if she could, if she weren't already barely paying the heat and the food bill. Suicide nullified Carl's life insurance.

As she works, she half-reads the quotes written in black marker here and there on the concrete block.

Next to the bare hookup for the washer and dryer: *Is one going to die or take up the heart-rending and marvelous wager of the absurd?*

Near the water heater: *A whole being exerted toward accomplishing nothing is the price that must be paid for the passions of this earth.*

Above the laundry sink, where Lavinia turns on the water for the hose: *I have a liking for lost causes: they require an uncontaminated soul, equal to its defeat as to its temporary victories.*

The ten or so cats who had shown interest in her shoveling flee upstairs at the sound of the water. Lavinia squirts diluted Mr. Clean as she goes, trying not to get the furnace wet. It's shorted out once already from the cats urinating on it and she is still paying for the repair.

Done mopping, she washes the mop and reads the quote above the sink again, wondering what souls become contaminated with.

As the floor dries, Lavinia breaks the boxes down flat, then spreads them out to cover the concrete. Their purpose is to reduce sweeping and mopping. At the next cleanup, Lavinia hopes to just pick up the boxes and chuck them in the garbage.

Some of the cats prefer the carpet to the newspaper, so Lavinia has cut several pieces out of the back bedroom and brought them down here. She scrubs each of them with a wire brush, then drapes them over the pipes to dry.

Standing on an old chair to reach a pipe, she reads the rafter Carl used to hang himself: *Revolt gives life its value.*

After climbing down, she begins to shred the newspaper.

An hour later she emerges from the basement. Pultwock is finally gone. Of course, Lavinia thinks, that asshole. Now Jason may have slipped away. She grabs a can of tuna-flavored food, the most pungent of the varieties, and goes as quickly and quietly as she can out the back door, wondering as she sneaks around her own yard just how old Pultwock really is, how much longer she'll have to put up with him.

She calls Jason's name, crooning "kitty kitty kitty," and waves the can of food back and forth at the height of a cat's pining nose. Nothing. She walks out front, still crooning, and glances up and down the street, first toward the High Level, then the Amtrak station, and finally past Pultwock's, to the end of the street, where cars race overhead on the interstate's enormous concrete arches. Even the train tracks must look like ants in marching formation from up there.

Lavinia turns left, away from the interstate toward Newton, where twenty-year-old cars list at the curb around the corner from The Rusty Tavern. On hands and knees she peers under each one, regretting she owns no flashlight, yet believing Pultwock is wrong, that Jason will recognize she is his savior and come out of his own accord.

Because Lavinia has always understood that cats strike out from the familiar in a circle, next she scouts the alley behind her house, where there are never any newspapers in the The Rusty Tavern's dumpsters, then trudges downhill toward the Amtrak station.

In the train yard, no attempt is made to shield the tracks. Lavinia walks right past where the chainlink fence simply ends—no gate, no purpose—and begins to call for Jason, a crack in her tired voice. Kneeling in the stone-pocked dirt to peer under cars, she begins to cry, thinking that Camus is full of shit. He claimed, *There is no fate that cannot be surmounted by scorn.* Sure.

Lavinia searches for over half an hour, going east from the station, trudging along the tracks, panning for the slightest movement in the bushes on the far side. Then she returns to the station and heads west. A dirt parking lot with several cars sits in the V formed where the tracks cross. Lavinia is getting back on her knees to look under these cars when she hears a faint meow. For a fleeting moment she thinks it's him, then realizes the meows are too high, too strained.

The kittens are in an ancient Bonneville. Lavinia presses her face against the hot glass, hands cupped on either side of her eyes. It must be over a hundred in the car. A mother cat lies in the back seat. Lavinia tries both door handles, but the car is locked.

She could go home and look through Carl's tools. He might have something she could smash the window with, but the kittens would likely get injured and she might be arrested. Lavinia croons to the three tiny, blind balls of fur, "It's okay, I'll get you out of there. Just hold on. Hold on." The kittens crawl back and forth over their mother, pulling at her dry teats, kneading her belly.

Lavinia begins to cry again as she runs toward Pultwock's. Shortly after they moved in, Carl locked his keys in the Cutlass and old man Pultwock used a slim jim to get them out.

Before Lavinia gets a fist up to knock, he opens the door.

"I need to borrow your slim jim." She's stopped crying, but her eyes tingle and she can feel the stretch of her swollen face.

"Why?"

"I need to open a locked car."

"You don't have a car."

"I know, Walter. Can I borrow it?"

"You don't have the touch," he says and disappears into the house.

"Walter!" Lavinia is about to go inside when through the haze of the screen door she spots a picture on Pultwock's end table of a woman who looks very much like her mother holding a dog.

Pultwock emerges from the kitchen, slim jim in hand, and slams the front door. Silently they go down to the station. Lavinia convinces herself the picture is of someone else.

At the car Pultwock grumbles. "Figured it had something to do with the damn cats." He opens the door and Lavinia scoops up the kittens.

"Check the mother," Lavinia says. "Is she alive?"

Pultwock prods her roughly with a single finger. "Nope."

Lavinia doesn't believe him. She climbs into the car, laying the kittens on the driver's seat, then reaches into the back, burning her bare arm against the vinyl seats. But as soon as she touches the mother, she knows he's right. Lavinia retrieves the newborns, eyes only half-open, all three small enough to fit in her cupped palms, and starts back home.

Behind her she hears Pultwock lock and slam the car. He grunts with satisfaction. "Somebody'll be wondering how the hell them cats got out."

He catches up to Lavinia without seeming to try. "Thought I was lying, huh?"

"You ran Jason off, why wouldn't you lie about that?"

"Who's Jason?" Pultwock says.

"My cat," Lavinia says.

"Oh shit, he ran himself off."

At home Lavinia checks the kittens' rectal temperatures first, glad to see they are within the acceptable range. Then she pinches their flesh and rubs her finger along their gums. Each is a bit sticky, so she sets up the humidifier in her bedroom, shooing out all the other cats, and installs the kittens in a box lined with sheepskin car-seat covers from the towed Olds.

In the kitchen Lavinia warms milk, corn oil, salt, and egg yolks on the stove, then feeds each kitten with a doll's bottle. Afterward, she massages their genitals with a warm, moist cotton ball and they relieve themselves in her palm. She prefers to do it that way at first, so she can be sure who did what and how much.

Fritz wails in the hall and Lavinia goes out to him, careful to shut the bedroom door where the helpless newborns sleep.

After she washes up, Lavinia goes through the newspapers stacked in the spare room. She's looking for blank sheets, the ones they sometimes wrap the ad sections in. On each one she writes with a black marker, "Cat Lost. Very Precious. Black with white mask. Reward."

She posts her signs, stapling them to every light post within a ten-block radius, then returns home and feeds the kittens again before lying down to take a nap. Sliding her alarm to on, she reads a piece of paper taped to the top of the clock: *I know men by the consequences caused in life by their presence.*

She tries to fall asleep, but Fritz wails relentlessly at the door. Lavinia fights the urge to let him in. What if he attacked the kittens?

A car pulls up. Lavinia thinks nothing of it. Her bedroom is on the front corner of the house. People come and go all day and half the night from The Rusty Tavern.

A few moments later there is a knock. Lavinia sits up and parts the curtains above her bed. No one has knocked on her door in months. Solicitors don't come to this neighborhood. Rarely do Jehovah's Witnesses. The last knock was the postman. He needed to verify that a package addressed to her house, but with a different name, was not hers.

A fat woman in a purple pantsuit and a tall man wearing a blue wind-breaker stand on her porch. The man faces sideways and on his back, in fancy, yellow letters, it says "The Toledo Humane Society." The woman sees the curtains move and waves her hand, catching Lavinia's eye. "Mrs. Simms, we're from the Humane Society and we'd like to talk to you a moment."

Too late to hide. Lavinia gets out of bed and stands for a moment to think. The doorbell rings—bleat, bleat, bleat.

Coming out of the bedroom, she stomps her feet like a schoolgirl—left, right, left—and waves her hands, scattering the cats to the back bed-room, the basement, and bathroom, closing each door, then counting the bold stragglers: Maryann and Ginger, Rodeo Roy, Lucy, Genie, Buck, and Fritz. Seven. That's not crazy, is it? They won't freak out over seven.

Lavinia opens the door as far as the chain will allow. "Yes?"

"Hello, Mrs. Simms," the woman says. "We've had a report about your home. Some animals that live here."

"Really? From who?" Lavinia tries to keep her voice pleasant and sur-prised.

"We'd just like to come in and assure ourselves the animals are well cared for."

Lavinia tells them to wait a second, closes the door, and turns up the TV, hoping to drown out the inevitable whining and scratching from the bedrooms and basement. A soap opera is on. Lavinia turns the dial two clicks. The woman outside hollers "Mrs. Simms?" so Lavinia settles on a game show, with its bells and frequent clapping. Then she unchains the door and invites the two Humane workers in.

The lady has a face that ought to be pleasant—soft cheeks, bright blue eyes, yellow eyebrows—but strikes Lavinia as arrogant and un-knowing. The man shakes Lavinia's hand and introduces himself as Tom Mitchell. "This is Dawn Kester," he says. Tom is very tall and thin, his narrow, too-small face split by a thick, straight mustache which obscures his upper lip. Dawn looks around appraisingly. Tom raises his eyebrows and nods at nothing in particular.

"Well, you can see I have a few cats." Lavinia waves her hand around the room. Lucifer jumps onto the recliner and stretches his paws against Tom's leg.

Eight is okay, Lavinia thinks.

"Hey, buddy." Tom reaches out to pet him, but Lucifer swats his hand away and a thin line of blood appears on Tom's finger. He glances at it with lifted brows, pursing his lips.

"Sorry," Lavinia grabs the cat. "He's like that." She puts Lucifer in the kitchen, and turns to find Dawn on her heels. Behind Dawn the small living room looks suddenly foreign. A bookshelf blocking half the front window and piled haphazardly with yellowed, dog-eared paperbacks. A threadbare autumn-gold loveseat with avocado stripes obscured by cat hair. A brown, sculpted shag carpet spotted with stains—cat puke, the occasional potty accident and, of course, the blueberry mollusk. A blue La-Z-Boy with a seat cushion pilled to gray by zealous paws. Above the La-Z-Boy the back of a culled calendar page is taped at its torn frill. In black marker, printed neatly in block letters, the page reads, *What is called a reason for living is also an excellent reason for dying.*

"Mrs. Simms, do you think you could turn the TV down?" Tom says.

With one long step, Dawn reduces the contestant's joy to a pathetic, distant screech. Lavinia wants to slap her hand. She can hear Plato crying, his squeaky meow like an unoiled bike chain.

"I'm sorry," she says loudly, tapping her right ear, "you'll have to forgive me. A bit hard of hearing. So what can I do for you?"

Dawn scratches her nose with her thumbnail and clears her throat. "Mrs. Simms, we need to take a look around. To inspect the premises. We've had reports you have a number of cats living in unsanitary conditions."

Was cat hair considered unsanitary? How about a few spots on the rug? She tried to get the blueberry stain out, but the rug is old, none of that stain protector they advertise these days.

"Well, as you can see, I'm a widow, don't have much money. My cats are healthy, though, and well fed. I take very good care of them."

"The report suggested you had more than a few cats. More than these," Tom says. "And to be honest, ma'am, the house doesn't smell very good."

"May I?" Dawn says, motioning toward the kitchen.

Lavinia steps aside. Tom and Jerry, a pair of littermates Lavinia picked up at a garage sale, stand on the counter peering through a smear of white bird poop on the dusty glass.

"Exactly how many cats did you say you have?" Dawn, looking at the plates and the scattered crunchers on the floor, shrivels her small, round nose.

Lavinia recognizes repulsion. It is the expression most often seen on a person before he hangs himself.

She checks out the window. Of course old man Pultwock is standing in the narrow strip of gravel between their houses. Lavinia sees the interest in his eager face, the bright, alert way he watches the van parked out front. He drags on his cigarette, then flicks the filter toward Lavinia and pulls out his pack to take another.

"Mrs. Simms? How many cats do you have?"

"What difference does it make?"

Tom calls in from the other room, "Dawn, come take a look."

He's standing in the doorway to the back bedroom. Lavinia hollers, "Who do you think you are? This is my home!"

Dawn continues toward the room as if deaf while Tom cocks his head to the side and sighs. "I better call my wife. She'll freak if I'm late for dinner."

They call the police, who must subdue Lavinia before the cats can be removed. It turns out the kittens are dead. Somebody broke their necks while Lavinia was talking to Tom and Dawn.

When they run out of cages, Dawn stays behind to write up reports while Tom drives the first load back to the Humane Society and returns with more cages and another woman, who helps him round up the remaining cats and load them in the car.

After everyone is gone, Lavinia sits at her Bakelite table, tilting to the left where the foot of one leg came off years ago. Her head aches from crying and her hip hurts where she fell, slipping on a pool of Friskies vomit by the basement door when she tried to bar Tom's way down. The plastic plates lie around her, scattered into the middle of the room, several upended.

This can't be right, she thinks. She must have some recourse.

She considers calling Christopher, but can't bear the thought of his perfunctory pity.

A knife lying on the counter catches Lavinia's eye and she imagines herself knocking on Pultwock's door and, when he opens it—all bathrobe and day-old cigarettes—stabbing him. She imagines the look of surprise cross his greasy features.

Lavinia gets the knife. She stabs at the air first with an overhand grip, then underhand. This would be better, she thinks, for getting him before he can see what is coming, a blow beneath the ribs, right where his flimsy robe ties around his disgusting potbelly, like a sack of skinned rabbits shuddering beneath the terry cloth.

Lavinia goes to the back door. On this side of the lock the other half of the envelope outside reads, *Rarely is suicide committed through reflection. If a friend addressed him indifferently that day, he is the guilty one.*

Lavinia opens the door quietly and looks across to Pultwock's porch, at his dark windows, giving nothing away. She goes out, holding the screen door until it latches, then crosses the gravel path, stepping on a pile of cigarette butts in the dark, fallen heroes under her slippered feet. Around back she tries to spot him through the kitchen window. The house sits on a high foundation, though, and even on her tiptoes, ingrown nails piercing painfully, Lavinia can't see in. She moves to the living room, where the windows are set lower, cups her hands beside her eyes, the knife held precariously between her thumb and the edge of her palm.

In the contrast between dark and light, Lavinia can now see the picture clearly. Her mother is hugging the dog Lavinia sent to the pound with one arm and clutching the throat of her bathrobe closed with the other, as if someone has caught her unprepared. But she smiles. The surprise is not wholly unwelcome.

Lavinia adjusts her hands and sees Pultwock at the kitchen table, just as she was a moment ago. He has a plate of eggs and a piece of toast, but instead of eating, he's smoking a cigarette.

He looks behind him, sees Lavinia staring and waves. He doesn't even seem surprised. Did he see her come outside? Perhaps tracked her progress around the house? She wonders if he sees the knife.

The back door opens and Lavinia hears his voice. "Fifty-five with the new ones!" he shouts.

"What?" Lavinia grips her knife in the underhand position.

"Fifty-five fucking cats I counted," Pultwock says.

Lavinia tromps to the back door and stands in the dark. "You were the one who called, weren't you?"

Standing on the lowest step, Pultwock cinches his robe. "I didn't call nobody. Fifty-four fucking cats is pretty hard to hide."

"I kept them in the house."

Pultwock shrugs. Lavinia steps toward him and jabs at the air with her knife. "I ought to gut you like a fish. Nobody would care, you know. Nobody would give a damn."

"You're right about that," Pultwock says. "But I want to know first—where's number fifty-six?"

"What?" Lavinia steps forward, having convinced herself she's going to do it. She's going to jam this knife into his belly because she doesn't believe him. He's a liar. He is the cause of her tremendous loss.

"You had fifty-four, but that Jason, he gone off today, and you got the kittens. I seen fifty-five leave. Should have been fifty-six, and I want to know, where you stash her?"

"What the hell are you talking about?" The numbers mean nothing to Lavinia. She's never actually counted the cats.

Pultwock takes a piece of paper out of his robe pocket, the back of a long grocery receipt, and lets its wrinkled length drop to his knee. "Gray one with white spots, black nose. Black one. Long white hair with gray face. Black and white (big). Black and white (small). Orange with black swirls. Gray with black stripes. White with orange circles..."

He reads for several seconds, describing by color and unique markings each one of Lavinia's fifty-four cats, kittens not included. "So what happened to the all-white one? The one you call Emily?"

She's in the rafters of course. Lavinia stands on the concrete floor, kicking aside newspaper, calling up, "Here, kitty kitty kitty. Here, Emmy Emmy Emmy. They're all gone. It's just us." She instructed Pultwock to stay upstairs so he won't scare her. "We're all alone here. Here, Emmy Emmy Emmy. Come to mama. Kitty kitty kitty."

The cat's eyes, glowing blue, appear out of the darkness. She meows and rubs against the fragile knob and tube wiring. Her face is dusty.

"Do you see her?" Pultwock hollers.

"Sh!" Lavinia hisses. "She won't come down if she knows you're here."

Pultwock walks gingerly down the stairs. He's staring at the floor, covered with the flattened boxes Lavinia brought home that morning. "You're not moving," he says, surprised.

"I told you," Lavinia says.

Pultwock holds out a can. "Here. They like this, don't they?" It's a can of real tuna. The scent cuts through the stench of ammonia.

Lavinia takes the can and holds it high above her head, waving toward the empty spot where Emily's face used to be. "Emily, look what I have. Look."

PRISONERS DO

B efore going into Shayla's house, Mike fired up the laptop to check on his wife. Via the home-monitoring website he could see her on the couch wearing sweats and his old Bulls T-shirt. She wore little else these days, needing comfort more than style.

A can of Pepsi and a plate sat on the stool beside her. For years that stool, pink with blue butterflies, had boosted their girls to the sink for tooth-brushing and hand-washing, but it looked ludicrous next to the Italian leather sofa.

Mike zoomed in on Fawn's face. She looked relaxed. No pursed lips, no wrinkles, except for the usual ones. He shifted the camera down and left to get a better look at the stool. There, on one of the old melamine plates with the kids' handprints, her yogurt with its foil top and a pile of cheese and crackers appeared untouched, and he wondered if she'd lost track of them, if he should call to remind her. That morning he'd told her he had a lunch meeting and it might seem odd if he called now, when he should already be in the meeting, but what did she know of odd anymore?

Mike had begun to dial before he caught sight of Shayla in the window. She held up a Mountain Dew, his drink of choice, as if toasting him. He signaled with a raised finger that he needed a second, slid the laptop under the seat, checked the volume on his cell, then put it back in his pocket, where he'd be sure to hear if Fawn called.

Shayla and Mike had sex, then over a quick sandwich talked about work. She was a breast surgeon; Mike a radiologist. He'd diagnosed Shayla's mother with lung cancer a few years ago and after that, when they saw each other in the hospital break room or cafeteria, he always asked about Norma. By the time they slept together, Shayla understood his situation, didn't expect anything more than what he could give.

At least she'd thought so, but that afternoon while discussing a medical conference in San Francisco, she started to say, "It's a combination clinical and imaging seminar. We could go...," then stopped. Laughing lightly, Shayla fluttered her fingers to indicate momentary confusion, harmless forgetting. "Right, sorry, never mind."

Later, as Mike got ready to leave, he took her in his arms and kissed her hard, as hard as he usually did when first arriving. "Thanks. I really appreciate it."

She smirked. "I'm so glad."

"I'll see you back at the hospital. I have a mammogram we should go over."

Shayla stood at the dining room window watching Mike start the car, then fiddle with something in the passenger seat. A laptop came into view, propped on the steering wheel, and she stepped back into the shadows, but as a radiologist Mike had been trained to identify things in patterns of dark and light that other people thought meant nothing. Glancing up from the computer, he hesitated, then gave an exaggerated wave. Embarrassed, Shayla waved back.

A mile away Mike pulled into a McDonald's and signed on to the monitoring site again, having decided against doing it in Shayla's driveway with her at the window, watching him. While he waited for the image of his living room to appear, Mike let himself play back what it felt like to slide that red sweater over her head, her breasts rebounding against his chest, her thick hair, streaked like tiger maple, tickling his face.

Fawn, slumped on the couch, popped into view. She looked exactly as she had before. So did the crackers and cheese. He dialed and watched her feel around for the phone. "It's on the floor," he said. "The floor."

Letting it ring and ring seemed like a kind of torture, but the new phone announced the caller audibly, so Fawn knew it was him and that he'd let it ring as long as necessary.

"It's on the floor, by your foot," he said again.

As if she could hear him, Fawn leaned over and saw the phone.

"Hey, how's it going?" he asked.

"Good. I'm fine."

"It's one o'clock."

"I know."

"The girls will be home in two hours."

"I know, Michael. I can tell time."

"Did you eat lunch?"

"I'm not hungry."

"You should eat anyway."

"Goodbye, Michael. Goodbye."

"Okay. I'll see you later."

The afternoon bolted past in a continuous stream of CTs, MRIs, a lumbar puncture, two complaint calls from the ER, and countless plain films. At three thirty his watch beeped and he called his oldest daughter's cell.

"How's Mom?"

"She's fine. We're just having a snack."

"What's the homework situation? Does Middie have math?" His middle daughter, Miranda, was struggling with pre-algebra and his oldest would try to help if she had time, if she didn't get distracted by Facebook, or Instagram, or some other thing Mike felt the danger of but didn't know how to control. Fawn used to handle things like that.

"Put Mom on."

He heard mumbling, then Rebecca. "She doesn't want to talk to you."

"Why not?"

"I don't know."

Mike became aware of a shadow in the hallway. He stepped to the back of the room and lowered his voice. "Give her the phone."

There was another pause.

"She won't take it."

"You sure she's okay?"

"I guess. I mean, she seems okay."

Mike could hear Fawn talking in the background. If he went home now, he'd have to read the rest of this stuff tonight, after she fell asleep, which was fine, he could do the MRIs and CTs. He didn't have the right monitor for plain films, though. His partners had been covering for him, but that couldn't go on forever. He'd have to buy a high-resolution screen, never mind the money.

Mike told Rebecca he would try to leave early. "Call me if she starts acting weird, okay?"

The shadow hadn't moved off. Mike stuck his head into the hall. Shayla stood there.

"Sorry. I just stopped by about that mammogram?"

Mike tore through the rest of the films and snuck out the back at four forty-five. On the way home, he thought of Shayla. Later he'd berate himself for getting distracted. For now, and despite the danger he'd sensed at her house this afternoon, Mike thought of her sweater, her hair, and imagined the two of them in San Francisco eating Mexican or sushi, then a walk back to the hotel and slow, quiet sex the way he liked it, with whispers. Afterward he would be allowed to fall asleep.

At home, Fawn lay in her spot on the left side of the couch staring at one of those cop shows, the ones that always began with some poor dead girl.

"Hey, honey, how are you?"

She turned and opened her mouth but nothing came out. Then a little grunt escaped and she frowned.

"Did you take your medicine?"

She just looked at him. In the kitchen he checked her pillboxes: purple for morning, yellow for afternoon, red for evening. Behind them a whiteboard with the day of the week and beside it a computer Mike had programmed to beep and play "It's time to take your medication." Still, she'd forgotten her noon meds, which is why she couldn't speak. Normally, he made sure she took them when he came home for lunch.

Mike went to the bottom of the stairs, ready to shout at Rebecca. Hadn't she noticed her mother's words beginning to slur? How long had she been upstairs?

Pounding rap music and a black man's voice filtered down. *Gonna ride you like a freaky train / Bitch all up inside my brain / I'm thinkin' what I lost and gained / feelin' if it worth the pain.*

Cupping his hands around his mouth, Mike took a deep breath and smelled Shayla. On his hands. Though he'd washed at least four, five times.

In the kitchen he washed again, this time with stinging hot water and dish soap, a strongly scented citrus type that cut grease "magically." Then he poured a glass of water and went back in the living room, Fawn's pills like little pink bullets in his palm.

Shayla's ex had wanted the divorce. The request stunned her as much for its delivery as its content, so matter-of-fact, as if divorce were a reasonable improvement whose time had come. After he moved out, friends and family kept asking how she felt. For a while she gave the right answers, until the day she realized she'd been lying. She'd confused expecting to be devastated with actually being devastated. One day Shayla decided not to be devastated, and discovered it was easy. Like taking off one outfit and putting on another.

She supposed now she wore the outfit of a mistress, except she didn't feel like one. Fawn had had a stroke three years ago, a freak kind of thing that left her permanently disabled. Mike didn't speak of it in those terms, though. He hardly spoke of it at all. After they started sleeping together, the subject of Fawn was off limits. Shayla tried hard to resist the urge to probe for more information from his partners or the radiology techs, but it was like a scab she couldn't stop picking at. Not because she wanted Mike to leave Fawn. Truth be told, Mike annoyed her at times. He talked too much, and insisted on things that seemed to defy certainty, like whether God exists, or whether there's intelligent life somewhere besides Earth. Still, something about Mike and Fawn fascinated her.

That evening Shayla stared out her kitchen window, mulling this while a filet of grouper browned and a cold wind plucked the leaves from her silver maple. She'd already changed into pajamas and planned to watch the news over dinner, so when the phone rang she let the machine pick up. With the exhaust fan running, she could hear her mother's voice, but couldn't make out her words. Shayla decided to listen to the message after dinner. If it wasn't important, she'd call back tomorrow.

Except later, on the couch, the message light blinking in her peripheral vision, she kept wondering what her mother wanted. It couldn't be urgent. If it were, wouldn't Norma have called her cell? Norma had no one else nearby to call. Shayla's brother lived two hours away, in a big house on a man-made lake with his Canadian wife and four French-speaking kids. She counted back. Could it be last Christmas that she saw them? It bothered her enough to lay down her fork and think. Yes. Almost eleven months. They'd met at Norma's the first week of December so Rick could spend the real Christmas in Quebec with his in-laws.

Shayla wondered if she'd see Rick for the holidays once their mother died. What else would change? Nothing came to her. That seemed wrong, so Shayla kept thinking, but there was nothing. Norma would be gone. That was it.

Once Fawn recovered her words, Mike asked if she was hungry.

"I am always hungry. Where is dinner?"

It hit him then that he'd forgotten to pick it up. "I thought we might order pizza."

"It's Monday, Mike. We get Olive Garden on Monday."

For a moment he was happy. She knew it was Monday! Then he realized that from where he'd left her, sitting at the kitchen table with a fresh Pepsi, she could probably read the white board. She'd remembered Olive Garden, though. That counted for something.

"I know, I just felt like pizza."

"Well, I don't. I don't like pizza. You know I don't like pizza."

"Okay, that's fine. What do you want?"

"Ravioli. I always get ravioli from Olive Garden. Don't change the schedule. I don't like it when you change the schedule."

Mike stuck his head in the dining room, where Middie and the youngest, Abby, sat doing homework. "I'll be right back. You want the usual?"

They nodded without looking up.

"Your mother's in the kitchen. If she wants to go back to the living room, can you help her?" Fawn got around pretty well with the walker, but it never hurt to have someone spotting her, especially this late in the day. His fuck-ups—the pills missed, dinner forgotten—meant it was already six thirty, only an hour before meltdown.

As he stepped into the garage, Fawn yelled, "And do not forget the breadsticks!"

After he fed her—Fawn could use a fork, but sometimes her hand veered off course, and he didn't need her poking out the one good eye—

Mike gave her a second breadstick. While she worked at it, holding it in her fist like a two-year-old, he loaded the dishwasher, wiped down the counters and put away the leftovers. Fawn had drunk the last Pepsi for dinner. If he hurried, he could start a load of laundry, put her to bed, run out to the store, and still catch the Bears' kickoff.

Mike's cell rang. He picked it up without looking at the screen and Shayla's voice startled him. He glanced at Fawn. There was never any telling when she'd come in or out. For now, at least, she appeared absorbed in her breadstick.

He stepped into the foyer, making for his study, where he could shut the door.

"I'm sorry to bug you at home," Shayla began.

"I'm busy."

The girls had gone upstairs and Mike glanced toward the heat register, whose duct fed his study and, above that, Rebecca's bedroom. He could go outside, except that would look suspicious.

"It's about my mother."

Relieved, Mike almost laughed.

"I just got off the phone with her and her speech is slurred. I asked if she's okay, and she's telling me she's had headaches for a couple weeks. Can I get her in tonight for a head CT? I mean, I know normally you'd do it in the morning, and I'm sorry, but I'm kind of worried."

Shayla's mother was only sixty-two, a reformed smoker, otherwise healthy, so they'd treated her cancer aggressively, taking out half the affected lung and blasting the rest with radiation and chemo. The symptoms Shayla described could be nothing. Or they could be a minor stroke. Or they could mean the radiation and chemo hadn't gotten all the cancer and it had metastasized to her brain.

Mike said sure, she could take her mother in. "I'll let the techs know she's coming."

"Can you read it?"

Mike hesitated. He'd have to tell the techs to send it to his computer instead of the radiologist on call, and they might wonder why.

"Mike? You there?"

"Sure, yeah."

"You'll call me?"

"Yeah."

"Thank you. Everything okay at home? Fawn okay?"

Taken aback, Mike said, "I'll call you as soon as I read it," and hung up.

Shayla drove Norma to the hospital, the silence between them both familiar and unsettling. There should be something to say to the woman who birthed and raised her and was now, possibly, dying.

"How're you doing?"

Norma shrugged. "I'm all right."

Shayla sat in the waiting room's blue vinyl chairs while they did the CT. On the way home she forced herself to ask if Norma had eaten dinner, and felt relieved she had. Shayla could take her home.

"I'll call you after I hear from…" She almost said *Mike*, but didn't want her mother to know he existed. Which was insane. Shayla knew several dozen doctors in town well enough to request a favor.

Norma pushed herself out of the car using the doorframe. Only when she was pulling herself up the porch steps by the rail did it occur to Shayla she should have helped her. Shayla rolled down the window. "You okay, Mom?"

Her mother lived on a busy street and couldn't hear over the traffic noise. She'd made the porch landing and was fumbling for her keys. Shayla watched, feeling the moment stretch to breaking. Get out now? Offer to help now? It's too late. But she's still fumbling. Shayla had just cracked the door, the dome light blinding her a moment, when Norma found her key. By the time Shayla reached the sidewalk, her mother had disappeared inside.

Norma had metastases. They showed up as the classic black hand in her cerebellum. Mike left the images on his screen and went back in to finish getting Fawn ready for bed. He'd left her on the toilet, so he tapped at the closed door. "You okay? Need any help?" He could hear the clink of the toilet paper dispenser followed by a flush.

"Fawn, I'm coming in, okay?"

Still sitting, she looked up at him, the unpatched, good eye stretching to a perfect circle, eyebrow raised.

Oh no, he thought, not this again.

"Who are you?"

"Fawn, it's me, Mike, your husband. You know that."

"What are you doing here?"

"I live here, silly."

"Right," she scoffs.

"It's time for you to go to bed."

"How do you know?" Pulling away from his reach, she banged her elbow against the wall. "Ouch! You made me hurt myself."

"I know, I know. I'm sorry. Here, let me see it." He inspected the elbow, just to be sure, pressing on the bone. "Does that hurt?"

"Of course that hurts. You are pushing on it, Mike."

Good. She knew who he was again.

He got her to a stand, underwear up, and into bed, first removing her eye patch and then fitting the latest gadget in her mouth, a guard that kept her tongue flat and her teeth aligned, supposedly to prevent sleep apnea, which he'd read could be the cause of severe fatigue. Since the stroke he'd been chasing his own tail, going at each symptom—crossed vision, nausea, headaches, confusion, fatigue, ataxia, forgetfulness—only to discover none of the devices or exercises made any difference. What helped was treating Fawn like a child. She had to be fed, exercised, bathed, and napped on a tight schedule. Early on, he'd hired caregivers, but Fawn didn't like them, and after the third one she refused any more. By then she could get herself to the kitchen and the bathroom, so he had the cameras installed and kept the feed up on his laptop almost all the time.

Mike had left his cell in his study. It rang while he was arguing with Fawn about her pillow. The sleep doctor had recommended a foam one to keep her head at the right angle, but Fawn preferred her old feather pillow.

"Dad?" Rebecca knocked lightly, then pushed open their bedroom door. "It's some doctor. Dr. Clayton?"

"I'll call her back," Mike snapped and Rebecca withdrew, looking hurt. He heard her mumbling shyly to Shayla and a bolt of rage went through him.

Fawn began to cry. His tone must have upset her. "Who was that? Who was calling?"

"Just another doctor. Her mom had a brain CT."

"Is it okay?"

"Mets," Mike said, not thinking.

"Oh, that's terrible." Fawn began to cry harder, her breath coming shallow and catching in her throat. It was odd, the things she seemed to understand and the things that seemed to have escaped her permanently. "Mets" still meant something, yet she wouldn't know if she herself had it. Mike could keep it from her, ignore symptoms. If he wanted to.

"It's all right. She's very old."

"Oh, oh." Fawn grabbed hold of this. "We all get old. We have to die when we are old. What can you do? You have to die."

"That's right, honey. And she's very old." Mike wiped the tears from Fawn's face with a tissue and helped her slide down in bed.

"Thank you," she said. "I love you, Mike."

"I love you, too."

As he started to close the door she said, "I'm thirsty."

He didn't like to give her something this late. She'd have to get up in the night and he'd have to get up with her. Hampered by fatigue and the dark, or the shock of a light turned on, she was too unsteady to go it alone.

"How about a sip of water?"

"No, I want Pepsi. Pepsi with a straw. I like the straws."

"I know you do, honey." He closed the door, thinking he'd give her a few minutes. Maybe she'd forget and fall asleep.

While Shayla waited for Mike to call back, her skin began to itch. It was a psychological reaction to being embarrassed. She'd always had it, assumed everyone did until it came up during her psychiatry rotation in med school. To calm herself, she poured a glass of wine and flipped through a clothing catalogue. What was he doing? How long did it take to read a CT? She had another glass, then called her ex-husband.

"My mom might have brain cancer."

"Oh shit, I'm sorry. That's terrible."

Her ex hadn't wanted kids, and Shayla was busy enough with work that this struck her as a reasonable life choice. He'd remarried quickly, though, and now had a one-year-old. Did that mean he'd changed? Been pressured? Or realized it was only Shayla he didn't want? She wished she could ask, and was glad not to know. And she was embarrassed to have called him. Her mind, soft with wine, didn't know this. Her skin did, though. She had a wicked itch on her upper arms.

"I just thought I should tell people," she said, "so it's not such a shock if it turns out it's bad. I mean, I didn't want you to open the paper some day and see her obit."

Shayla cringed, hearing too late, even with an ear callused by daily contact with breast cancer patients, how cold she sounded.

"You okay? You want me to come over?"

"No, I'm all right. I just took Mom home and I'm making some calls, and I knew you'd want to know."

"Of course I do. Sure. Norma's a great lady. Do you need something? Anything I can do?"

Shayla could hear a TV and a baby in the background. It was after eight, so it might be his baby, or a TV baby.

"No. No, I have some more calls to make. Maybe I'll send around an email or something. Keep everybody updated."

But Shayla couldn't think who everybody was. Her brother, of course, whom she would call once she knew something definite. And Norma's sister, Aunt Polly. Shayla's father had died of a heart attack five years ago and her grandparents were long gone. Cousins? On her father's side they didn't keep up, and Aunt Polly would take care of the others. Norma had friends, but Shayla wouldn't presume to tell them, and come to think of it, didn't know their last names, couldn't have contacted them anyway. If Shayla called her own friends, it would only be for pity, not because they had to know.

Still, there must be someone. Shayla poured a third glass of wine. When she finished it, she'd concluded no, there really wasn't.

Suddenly she felt very tired. Wanted to go to bed, to wait until tomorrow to know, but that was unacceptable. She'd just have to stay up until Mike called. His daughter had sounded very sweet, and that simple exchange they had—"Is your Dad home?" "Sure, may I tell him who's calling?"—had brought her heart into her throat and Shayla didn't know why. She really, truly had been fine with no kids. Was still, when she thought about it, fine. That wasn't the problem. The problem was something else.

Mike put in a load of laundry, then sat at his desk looking at the black hand, a dark gray mass with fingers separated by white matter. Shayla's mother was dead. Four, five months maybe. They'd radiate to reduce brain swelling, which would buy her lucidity and mitigate the headaches.

He stepped quietly through the foyer and down the hall to the master bedroom, listening at the door. Silence. Back in his study, he picked up the phone. He'd given patients bad news many times, their families even more often. This time, though, he felt strangely angry at Shayla, as if the situation were her fault.

"Hi, it's Mike, calling back about your mother."

He would have said the same thing to any colleague, except that usually he added his last name and he couldn't shake the fear that Rebecca could hear him, would notice his omission even with the 4/4 drum beat of her music vibrating the heat duct.

On the other end of the phone Shayla waited silently. "It's not good," Mike said.

She knew what that meant. There was little more to say. A few questions about location and size, then she said, "Thanks. I appreciate it," in the same tone she would have used if this were a patient, and he replied with similar dispassion, "Sure, of course. Anytime," and they hung up.

Anytime? How many mothers with brain cancer was she going to have?

Shayla thought about this for several seconds until she realized she should be thinking about Norma. Who was going to die. Who would be gone this time next year. Everything from here on out would be their last. Last Thanksgiving, last Christmas, last birthday. Just the thought of all those lasts exhausted Shayla. That's when it dawned on her that a good daughter would have had Norma come home with her tonight.

She called Mike back.

"Didn't you say you had a friend at Anderson?"

Mike's roommate from medical school was an oncologist at MD Anderson Cancer Center. "Honestly, I don't think he could add much."

"It never hurts to ask, right?" Beneath her jeans, Shayla's calves prickled. She rubbed one against the other, waiting for Mike to respond. At the end of a long pause a girl's voice, higher than the girl she'd talked to on the phone earlier, shouted, "Dad, I'm lost! Algebra makes no sense."

Middie. The one with the math problems. Mike had mentioned it before they started sleeping together. Shayla realized now that afterward he'd stopped mentioning the girls as well as Fawn. But it was too late. Shayla already knew from the pictures in Mike's office what Middie looked like. The willowy, heavily-freckled middle daughter, her nickname a play on that position and not, as everyone assumed, an echo of her given name, Miranda. Shayla imagined her coming downstairs, plopping on the bottom step, the book's tattered pages splayed across her knees. The scene played out in Shayla's own childhood house, not Mike's, because she had no idea what Mike's house looked like. A decent mistress would have driven by, caught a glimpse of the foyer or kitchen through glowing windows.

"I'll call you tomorrow," Mike said.

"I can have her there tomorrow. I could book a flight tonight."

A blurring of the background noise alerted Shayla to Mike's hand over the phone's mouthpiece. He said something to Middie and Shayla raised her voice, interrupting, "Why don't you give me the name of your friend at Anderson and I'll try to reach him? I don't want to wait. The gears grind slowly enough as it is...Mike? You there? Mike?"

Even with the phone several inches from his ear, Shayla's voice jumped from its holes, beseeching. Pressing the earpiece against his chest, Mike motioned for Middie to go away. She was scowling as if she'd recognized something in Shayla's tone.

"I said go in the kitchen and I'll be there to help you in a minute."

Ignoring him, Middie threw herself on the stairs, limbs splayed like one of the victims in Fawn's shows. "Ugh! I hate math so, so much!"

"Mike? Mike?"

He put the phone back to his ear. "We should go over the films and

I'll show you what I'm looking at."

"I can come over now."

"No!"

Startled, Middie sat up and cocked her head. He made a motion with his hand to indicate everything was all right.

"Mike, this is my mother," Shayla said. "My mother."

"Come by the office first thing."

"Maybe the guys at Anderson have some new therapies. We could buy some time."

"There's no point." Shocked by his own insensitivity, Mike considered apologizing, but it would be impossible to find the right tone with Middie planted on the stairs, listening to every word until he hung up and helped her figure out the value of *x*.

"Okay, then," he said, breaking into a silence he could no longer interpret. "I'll talk to you tomorrow."

Mike knew the answer but Middie wouldn't listen.

"That's not how Mrs. Reid does it."

He wanted to ask, who gives a fuck how you do it, as long as you get the right answer? He didn't, though. Parenting rule #382: don't undermine the teacher. Fawn had taught him that.

Abby came into the kitchen.

"What are you still doing up?"

"I'm thirsty."

Mike eyed her tangled hair. The girls used to bathe every other night, which proved impossible for him to keep track of after Fawn's stroke, so he'd established a Monday, Wednesday, Friday routine. Mike opened his mouth to tell Abby to get in the shower, but like Fawn without her meds, nothing came out. His youngest had blue eyes. Pale-eyed children were more sensitive to light and chemicals. She claimed that just plain water, even lukewarm, burned. Every shower turned into a battle of wills.

Mike turned back to Middie. "I have to go to the store. We're out of Pepsi."

He got his keys and wallet. "Tell Rebecca to turn that damn music off and listen for Mom in case she gets up."

Mike never swore at the kids, but Middie didn't seem to notice.

"I'll listen," she said, grimacing at her algebra book. It broke Mike's heart how readily she agreed to help him.

Shayla found Mike's house easily. Why this should surprise her, she didn't know.

She parked in the street and walked quickly to the front door. *Ding dong.* A deep chime, like a church organ, seemed to shake the house, and only then did she remember how late it was. Shayla's whole body itched—especially her neck, which, though bare, felt as if she were wearing a turtleneck made of steel wool.

Middie opened the door. "Hello?"

More poised than Shayla expected for thirteen, but freckled and long-limbed like the picture.

"Is your dad home?" Nervous, she continued in her Midwestern uptalk. "I'm Dr. Clayton, from the hospital? He was looking at my mother's brain scan and I said I wanted to come take a peek?"

"He went to the store. You want to come in?"

This was as far as Middie's manners had been trained. Once they were in the foyer she didn't seem to know what to do.

"How about I just wait for him in there?" Shayla pointed into the adjacent room. Through an open door she could see a bookcase full of radiology journals, an enormous computer monitor, and a view box for hanging film, which he probably never used now that everything had gone digital.

Middie drifted off and Shayla sat on the edge of Mike's desk chair, looking at the family pictures scattered on the bookcase. The most recent one, judging from the kids' ages and taken before Fawn's stroke, showed the five of them in front of the Eiffel Tower. Freckled Middie seemed to come from somewhere else. Rebecca favored olive-complexioned Mike and... Oh God, she'd forgotten the youngest one's name. Emma? Emily? She favored Fawn.

Shayla studied the shape of her lips and teeth, just like her mother's. Abby. That was it. The youngest's name was Abby.

Relieved, she decided to wait five minutes, then make an excuse and get the hell out, but the minutes ticked too slowly. After three, she ventured back into the foyer. The living room was empty. Just leave? That would be too weird. She followed her instincts to the kitchen. No one. Coming back she heard crying and a mumbled voice. Shayla froze. Suddenly it felt as if she'd broken into the house. Switching to tiptoe, she was making her way through the hall toward the front door when Fawn turned out of a room and stopped. She wore a long Chicago Bulls T-shirt and slipper socks. Tears streaming down her face, she looked beseechingly at Shayla. "Do you know where Mike is?"

"He went to the store."

"Oh. Oh." She seemed to gather herself.

"I'm one of his colleagues, from the hospital. He said I could stop by and look at a brain scan. Your daughter let me in."

"You are a doctor?"

"Yes. Dr. Clayton."

"Did Mike send you to sit with me?" She spoke in staccato, each word with its own fervent stress.

"Yes," Shayla said. "He told me to keep you company."

"Good." Fawn seemed to be waiting for her to say something else.

"Where do you want to sit?"

"The living room. I like the couch in the living room."

With a walker, Fawn made her way across the carpet slowly. Shayla moved the coffee table out of her way.

"You can sit next to me," Fawn said. "I don't bite." She patted the sofa's cushion.

Shayla sat down.

"What is your name? I forgot your name."

"Shayla Clayton."

"Oh, oh." Fawn seemed to remember something. "You are the doctor whose mom is going to die."

Startled, Shayla nodded.

"Mike said she is old."

"She's not that old."

"Mike said she is old," Fawn insisted.

"She's sixty-two. I don't consider that old enough to die." Shayla had to get out of here. She was arguing with a stroke patient.

"I'm..." Fawn paused. "Do you know how old I am?"

Shayla didn't know exactly, but she was about to take a guess just to keep the conversation going when she felt someone behind her.

"Hello?"

She jumped up and held out a hand to Rebecca. "I'm Dr. Clayton. Your dad said I could come over and look at my mother's brain scan."

Rebecca looked at her suspiciously.

"Middie let me in. I guess your dad went to the store." A mistake. How did she know Middie's name?

"Rebecca, I want a Pepsi," Fawn said. "Your father was supposed to bring me a Pepsi."

"I'll get it."

Rebecca came back with a root beer. "I couldn't find any Pepsi. Is this okay?"

Fawn frowned. "I do not want ice. I want it in the can. I like the can."

Rebecca was already heading back to the kitchen. Shayla heard the fridge open and close, then Rebecca returned holding the root beer can, the soda apparently poured back in. One bead trickled down the side.

"I couldn't find any Pepsi."

"You didn't look hard enough. You never look hard enough."

"I looked, Mom."

"Did you move things? I bet you didn't move anything."

"I'll look again."

Shayla and her mother used to have spats like this. Norma called her snobby when she was shy. She called her lazy when she was tired. Norma also cooked Shayla's favorite dinner every Thursday, came to all her volleyball games and helped her pick out her first bra, turning away so Shayla wouldn't be embarrassed.

While Rebecca clinked around in the kitchen, Shayla plied Fawn with simple questions. How old were the girls? What school did they go to? What were their favorite subjects? Fawn answered slowly and earnestly, as if after careful reflection.

Rebecca returned without a Pepsi and Shayla tried to calm Fawn down. "Maybe Mike is getting it. Middie said he went to the store."

Rebecca leveled a cold look at her. "We know. You said that already."

For a disturbingly long moment the sight of Shayla's car outside his house sent a bolt of pleasure through Mike. For a disturbingly long moment he forgot she shouldn't be here and didn't even consider why, most likely, she'd come.

Inside, Shayla sat on the couch beside Fawn, who slept peacefully with her head lolling against the sofa's back, a glisten of drool like a tear on her chin. Shayla held up a palm in greeting, the unmistakable look of regret on her face, then rose by inches, watching Fawn to be sure she didn't wake.

Mike followed through the foyer, out the door into utter darkness.

"She wanted Pepsi."

"I got some."

The wind flattened their coats, too light for the weather, against their bones. At the curb next to Shayla's car, Mike looked up at the bedroom windows on the second floor. The blinds were all pulled. No faces, no shadows.

He took her hand. "I'm sorry about your mother."

"I told your girls I came to see her scan."

Mike nodded. "Good."

Shayla took her hand back. "Fawn told me you love her too much." She had dissolved into tears when a Pepsi couldn't be produced, and that had led to the confession that Fawn wanted to die. "She said you won't let her."

Mike cupped Shayla's elbow. "I'll bring us Indian next week. You like that place by the mall, with the spicy chicken."

"You hate Indian."

"I'll have rice, and that flat bread."

"You can't live on bread, Mike."

He grinned. "Sure I can. Prisoners do."

Shayla wanted to lean against him one last time, tell him the failure was hers. Someone else could string a life together from moments like this.

A car turned the corner, catching them in its headlights. Mike dropped Shayla's elbow and looked over his shoulder. Quickly, she slipped in the car. Tomorrow, or maybe that weekend, she would move in with her mother. Take charge of medication schedules and doctors' appointments. Do the shopping and cleaning. Smooth the edges of Norma's last few months. It was a job Shayla could do well, she knew, only because its time was short.

COYOTE

S he sees him first at the back of the lot, belly-deep in snow by the wild grape. Alec sits at the table, eating the new organic eggs. It's Valentine's Day.

Cory calls her husband Scott. "What do coyotes look like?"

"Uh, like a dog, I guess. Long snout maybe."

"I think I saw one in the backyard. He went into the woods." A tunnel in the snow testifies to the animal's route, but the pack is too soft and deep to retain clear tracks.

"I've never heard of coyotes in the middle of a city."

"Last March, Manhattan."

"Was he living in a homeless shelter?"

"Ha, ha," Cory deadpans. When Alec was a baby and refused to breastfeed, Scott just shrugged. "Maybe he's gay—doesn't like a nice pair of tits."

Cory calls the municipal office. The city manager sounds tired. "Yes, we've had a few other unconfirmed reports. Nobody's sure yet. There's no real danger. As long as nobody feeds them."

But how do you know if anyone is feeding them?

When she asks Scott this over dinner, he scowls. "What kind of idiot would do that?"

That night Cory watches a special about kids with brain cancer. It's terrible, but compared to the other threats against her son's life, it also has a kind of innocence, almost a reprieve.

There's the yellow card from the doctor—measles, mumps, rubella—without a single mention of how they can be so damn sure vaccines don't cause autism.

There's the faceless manufacturers with their recall alerts. Apparently, the strap on her ninety-five-dollar car seat can melt in a high-speed crash.

The blank-faced sickos in her email alerts. *Sexually Oriented Offender, victim: Child Female. File last modified 2006-09-19. Unlawful sexual Contact w/a minor.* What is unlawful sexual contact? How minor?

The little girl Alec goes to preschool with. Once, in Cory's dream, green-eyed Lily handed him a syringe. After that Cory studied the other toddlers, trying to guess who will convince him to take a hit, pass along AIDS, make a bet about how much he can drink or how fast he can drive on a rain-slick road. Who will bring a gun to school?

Cancer may strike without warning, but at least it arrives without recrimination. Blame lies with God.

Cory tried to take precautions. Their upscale neighborhood has its own police and fire departments. Their house and the enormous pines on either side completely conceal the backyard from any passing sickos. The low-lying area at the back of their lot—thick with woody shrubs and large trees for a mile—discourages visitors with twig-sharp snow in the winter, boot-sucking mud in the spring, and poison ivy mosquito flats come summer. To be sure there are no tells, Cory refused to buy a swing set. When Scott mocked her, she snapped, "Why don't we just put an advertisement in *Pedophilia Monthly*." He doesn't hold the patent on sarcasm.

Then, less than a month after they moved in, Cory heard a piece on NPR about the West Nile virus. Suddenly that swampy area didn't seem like such a benign shield. It took some doing, but she convinced Scott to add the screened porch and buy carbon-dioxide traps. She knew enough not to mention West Nile by then. Instead she talked about bug-free outdoor meals, the way a porch balanced the architecture of the house, the possibility of making love on a hammock during hot July nights.

For a while Cory believed this would be enough. She hadn't taken into account predators with fur. They were not scouting from the street and the boot-sucking mud and dense underbrush would do nothing to dissuade them.

In April Cory sees two coyotes just inside where the trees begin at the back of the lot. She's at the kitchen table typing another letter to the utility people. Since they bought the house she's been filing complaints about the sagging utility lines entangled in wild grape that run along their property's west side. Alec's three now. How long before he can reach them and electrocute himself?

Scott rolled his eyes. "He can't get electrocuted. That's phone and cable."

It's a flash of something tall and long-legged that draws her attention away from the letter. Then, behind the adults, two smaller creatures—rust-red fur, long snouts, and low-slung tails between. The adults are in pursuit of something. Cory tries to see what, but the woods are too thick and all she can catch is the black puff of their tails moving quickly away.

She does some research. Coyotes aren't native to Ohio, but have spread across the state and favor woodlots in urban areas. According to one map, Cory and Scott live in a "light-density" area, but there is a "heavy-density" area immediately to their south. One source claims that coyote sightings during the day indicate they've lost a fear of humans. She finds a documented killing of a three-year-old in California.

To deter coyotes, experts recommend cleaning up around your grill and making sure there's no pet food left outside. Coyotes feed on any-thing they can—even fruits and grasses if small mammals aren't available.

In the winter they eat deer excrement. Cory has seen the black pellet-like droppings under the pines, near the deer-ravaged hostas.

She gives away their grill and calls the administrator of their village. Yes, he admits, the stray cat problem seems to have gone away. "I don't know what we can do, though. Coyotes are hard to trap, and we can't have people running around shooting at them."

Soon the local paper runs an article. Cory's name in it annoys Scott.

"You're going to incite panic. *A dingo ate my baby*." He mimics an Australian accent.

"Sure, it's all a big joke to you, the guy who nearly killed my son."

Scott has no smart-aleck reply to that. A year ago Cory went for a bike ride. On the way home, along a busy street, she came over the bridge and there he was, her two-year-old. For several seconds it hadn't registered. She attributes the delay to a horrified disbelief. Her brain calculated Scott must be beside him—he simply had to be.

But he wasn't. Alec stood at the corner, hundreds of feet away from her, looking at the traffic whizzing by. Cory sped up and literally threw the bike out from under herself, lunging in front of her son just as he stepped off the curb. She'd have surely been crushed except that the car coming up was stopping anyway. What she didn't know was that Alec had pushed the button to turn the light red. He must have seen her and Scott do it.

Turned out Scott was home watching baseball, sure Alec was in the kitchen eating a snack. She hasn't left him alone with the baby since.

At the Memorial Day block party Cory finds out a neighbor's Pekinese was killed. "I heard a yelp, so I went looking and she was behind the garage. I saw the thing running off, going down your way."

Cory has a fence put up. She didn't get a permit because it's ten feet, four over the limit, and she was afraid they'd turn her down. Scott isn't happy. "Seven thousand dollars! Do you know how much the average coyote weighs? For Christ's sake, Cory, he's not a mountain lion."

"Thirty-five pounds. And they can jump a six-foot fence."

Someone in the neighborhood complains about the fence. This woman doesn't have any children and her dog, who lives outside, is at least seventy-five pounds. Cory leaves her a phone message. "I'm trying to protect my child's life. What's your excuse for that outsize mutt who never shuts up?"

The village council make her take the fence down to six feet, so she finds a rolling bar sold out of New Mexico that mounts to the top and keeps animals from scaling it. Another two thousand. She puts it on the backup credit card, which Scott doesn't check. When he notices the bar, she lies. "That came with the fence. They just got around to putting it on."

For Alec's fourth birthday Scott brings home a Big Wheel. Outside for the inaugural ride, Cory catches Scott standing at the top of the driveway instead of the bottom, where he could block the street.

"What are you doing!" She runs out, startling Alec, who thinks it's him who's made a mistake. He turns the bike, riding across the grass and into the neighbor's driveway. The neighbor, Mr. Prout, is backing out of his garage. He stops, smiling amiably. *No big deal, your son's life,* his grin implies.

By dinnertime Scott is red with anger.

"Stop it!" he yells at Cory, throwing down his fork. "He was only smiling! Of course he thinks it's a big deal if he runs over our kid. You're the one who scared Alec into going off the driveway."

Cory can barely keep from slapping her husband. "You almost hit Alec with that fork, you fuckhead!"

Alec begins to cry and Cory immediately repents. "I'm sorry, oh honey, I'm sorry. Mama's not mad. Mama's just pretending. Smile for Mama." She kisses his hair, his cheeks, each soft eyebrow, glancing sheepishly at Scott.

"Sorry," he says, kissing her on the head, then his son. She's right. The fork did bounce close to Alec's face.

Midsummer the Prouts retire to Arizona, replaced by a middle-aged couple prone to parties, usually cookouts. The guests who arrive look just like them—thick black hair, dark eyes, olive skin. Some of them look young enough to be the couple's children. Maybe they're all family, but Cory can't tell because they speak a foreign language. On Saturdays she sits in the screened porch or takes Alec outside to play, finds reasons to linger at the fence line listening to their musical chatter. Googling their last name, she discovers it's Persian, another word for Iranian, almost certainly Shiite Muslims. Muslims usually blow themselves up in busy places. They don't kill single little boys, right? And Alec's not going to be taking the bus to school. But what about in school? The neighbors have no small children. She'd feel better if they did. They wouldn't blow themselves up in their own kids' school, would they? Of course, they seem very nice. They always smile and wave. Cory knows she's being ridiculous.

One day, she pulls in the driveway and catches sight of somebody in the backyard, crouching behind the fence. Startled, she runs the car into the side of the garage. Then she sees—it's a squirrel. He jumps on top of a fence post and stares at her, oddly unperturbed by the crunch of metal against the garage wall. Cory leans over the seat to examine Alec for injuries. He is buckled in tight—new car seat of course, this one researched through *Consumer Reports*. Whiplash? Concussion? He seems fine, but you can never be sure.

When Scott gets home, he's angry. "You made me leave work for this? How fast could you have been going? He's fine. The car's what I'm worried about."

•

Late July a coyote digs his way under the fence. "You don't know that," Scott says. "It could have been anything. A raccoon."

"Which carry rabies," Cory says.

Scott ignores her. It doesn't matter. She knows a coyote made that hole. It's too big for a raccoon. And a raccoon would have climbed the fence anyway. The roll bar wasn't designed to stop them.

She examines the spot he chose, at the end where only pachysandra thrives under a sycamore's dense shade. Within a week she has the tree cut down, replaced by a row of hawthorn that will reach thirty feet. In front of that she plants two rows of rugosa roses, a barbarously thorned shrub the man at the nursery claimed is "almost impenetrable." That is the word that makes her buy it—impenetrable. It sounds military.

She tells Scott the village took the tree down and paid for the new bushes. "Some contagious disease I guess." They'd had the ash borer, so he buys it.

A week later she finds another hole. Thorny twigs broken off the nearby bushes lie about, thin and brittle as uncooked spaghetti.

That night Cory pretends to go to sleep with Scott, then gets up when he begins to snore and takes up watch at the kitchen window. It's dark, though, and the yard is deep and large. At its furthest point shadows move without divulging their identity. Cory turns on the patio lights, then gets a baseball bat from the garage and stations herself next to the willow, where she'll be hidden by the weeping branches. They make her think of lynchings and hangings. She imagines waking up to find her son dangling midway up, just another limb vulnerable to the wind.

Cory leans against the trunk, ready, then eventually sits, kept awake on the bony roots. Around her, dozens of broken boughs lie on the ground like snakes in the grass. *We're insulated*, she thinks, *but falsely*. A little drywall, a metal cylinder in a doorframe stands between us and it. We can't hear it. But it's always there, the rustling in the woods, the crunch of twigs and old leaves underfoot, the new neighbors whispering below their densely-planted pergola.

Cory creeps over and peers between the branches of an old lilac. The moon illuminates two people, men she's fairly sure, leaning forward with elbows on their knees, glowing embers in their hands. Cory inhales, trying to identify the scent. Cigarettes? Pipes? Cigars? Pot? Some Iranian thing she's never heard of? They talk, their heads bent close together, and she strains to catch something comprehensible. Why don't they speak English? What do they have to hide?

She thinks about the door she has left unlocked, retrieves the extra key from the false sprinkler head and secures the house, then returns the key to its hiding place. If someone kills her out here, she doesn't want the key on her person.

Summer is her best chance. Knowing that neither Alec nor Scott are prone to wake in the small hours of the night, she spends this time outside, waiting. The sounds, shapes and movements of darkness grow familiar. In a stiff wind, the pine's branches wave like enormous fans cooling the undergrowth. In the moonlight the neighbors' forbidden trailer—hidden behind their garage and stacked with boards and lengths of gutter covered by a tarp—looks like a skiff, the tarp its sail, the hitch an emergency oar neglected and soon to slip overboard.

The first time Cory hears rustling in the woods, she readies the bat. The fiftieth time she can tell the difference between the crackles of a methodical, light-footed raccoon and the more infrequent rustles of an owl in flight. When they settle, they hoot, long and low, reassuring her. Every night the murmuring in the Persians' yard reaches her, humming speech that mingles with the owl's hoot and the raccoon's scurrying. It is definitely two men—she's gotten a moonlit look to confirm. If one is the homeowner, who is the other? No one would visit so late every night, which means he must live with the couple. A boarder? An out-of-work brother? An older son?

Of course Cory gets tired. Five nights outside, seven, eight. Once she falls asleep and wakes near dawn with a pattern like a healed burn impressed on her cheek by the willow's bark. Sneaking into the house, she stations herself on the couch with a book across her chest, where Scott finds her only half an hour later.

"Couldn't sleep," Cory lies. "So I came down to read."

Alec seems to be crying more often. Is he sick? Another ear infection? The doctor says no. Cory tries to comfort her son, playing his favorite shows and taking him to the park, where he falls and hurts his arm. At the ER they look at her like she might be to blame.

"How did you say he fell?"

She doesn't plan to tell Scott, but as soon as he walks in the door, Alec tugs his sleeve and says, "Mommy didn't catch me so I fall and the doctor say I lucky!"

"How much is that stunt going to cost us?" Scott asks, and Cory shrugs, not sure if the stunt is Alec's fall, her letting him on the park's climbing wall, or her taking him to the ER. If Scott knew about her backyard vigils he'd blame her outright. If she weren't so tired she'd have caught Alec like she promised.

At playgroup one of the women mentions that two neighborhood cats have gone missing and Cory brings up the coyotes. Everyone shrugs—"Well, that's what happens when you let your pets roam." No one seems concerned, even when Cory points out that the coyotes have been seen in the middle of the day.

"That means they've lost their fear of us."

The women all look at her as if to ask, "What is there to fear?"

In the second week of her vigil, a new scrabbling sound and there he is, coming snout-first under the fence. Cory doesn't move, letting him come fully under the fence and muscle his way through the rugosas. Pieces of the shrub are caught in his fur. He shakes the thorns free, then raises his head and sniffs. His erect ears quiver. What can he detect? Can he smell her boy's peanut-butter breath? Hear the murmur of his toddler dreams? Cory's hand is on the rough tape above the bat's knob. She closes her fingers around it, feeling the gritty texture.

The coyote moves toward the house slowly, with a self-consciousness that makes her sure he knows something is different about the yard tonight. How often has he been here? Does he know the lay of the land as well as she does? Better? Cory eases to a stand and the coyote turns to her. Even in such dark, between the hundreds of switches dense with leaves, he seems to catch her eye. Evidence of nocturnal talents denied her and more proof, she thinks, that we aren't God's favorite.

Cory comes from beneath the willow's protection, the bat held ready to strike, her feet swift on the familiar lumps of grass. The animal runs, and Cory's nerve, about to falter, strengthens. Her shoulders are stiff and her hips click at full extension as they haven't since she was ten, playing tag. "Stay away from my boy," she huffs, out of shape, her breath held low in her stomach. "Stay the fuck away from him," she snarls, as the coyote reaches the rugosas. She's behind him and then he's gone and she's tangled, tripping, falling on the useless roses.

The next morning Scott notices scratches on her face: long, narrow red welts, the dermatographia of pursuit. Or escape.

"I was in the woods yesterday, dumping out those old flowerpots. I think I'm having a reaction."

He looks at her quizzically. "I didn't notice that last night."

She shrugs. "Delayed, I guess."

•

For their wedding anniversary Scott asks his mother to babysit and makes reservations at Cory's favorite restaurant. During dinner she resists the urge to call home, but she does keep the phone on the table, where she'll be sure to hear it ring. Over dessert, Scott brings up having another baby. "It'd be good for Alec to share you." In the last year he's become concerned that Alec is too attached to Cory, unaccustomed to being without her for even an hour.

Cory reminds him—falsely—that she's been off the pill for months.

"We haven't really been trying, though." He wiggles his eyebrows like Groucho Marx.

She laughs. "Let's get to it then," she says, knowing her son is safe. Her attention cannot be divided.

Alec's moods don't improve. One night he wakes crying and Scott discovers she's not in the house. Cory doesn't hear the crying—windows closed, air-conditioning on—but she sees the light go on in Alec's room. Before she can get to the house, the slider opens and Scott's there. "What are you doing?"

She's holding the bat. "I thought I heard someone out here."

"So you came out by yourself with a kid's baseball bat?"

Cory hadn't realized until then the bat was small and remarkably light. She swings at him in mock menace. "I could do you some damage."

Alec begins to complain of stomach pains and when Cory takes him to the doctor and insists they scan him, they find a tumor. More tests are ordered. For a week she cannot eat. She exists on the brink of tears, her throat tight and chest weighted, as if someone is sitting on it. She sleeps next to Alec's bed on the floor, attuned to sounds of choking or a change in his breathing. She imagines the tumor expanding like a balloon. Can it creep into his throat overnight, like the coyote into their yard? How foolish of her to think cancer would let her off the hook.

When Alec plays outside, she sits in the patio chairs with the base-ball bat by her side, rehearsing what she'll do, how she'll spot the coyote coming up behind the pine, in the cover of the forsythias. How she'll rush him, yelling for Alec to run inside. *Run, run as fast as you can!*

Then on Thursday at ten a.m. the doctor calls: the new tests confirm it's not a tumor, but a harmless malformation.

She gets a second opinion, then a third and fourth. At that point she's run out of doctors in her insurance network and Scott insists she stop. "You're driving everyone crazy, especially poor Alec."

Cory buys a gun, locks the bullets in one box and the gun in another, carries the keys in her pocket. At target practice, the recoil hurts her arm, but the ache reassures. She's taking action.

Scott thinks she's at yoga. He's happy to be trusted again. "I won't let him out of my sight."

At night she takes the baby monitor outside with her. Alone, waiting for that scrabbling noise or a change in her son's breathing, she would find the predictable company of the neighbors, the faint, faint odor of their smoke, a comfort—if only she knew what the hell they were saying.

On the first chilly night in September he emerges from between the thorny roses. Cory's attention has been on the neighbors, certain words they use over and over that she is trying to memorize so she can look them up later. When the coyote finally catches in her peripheral vision, she freezes, then, regaining her focus, slides the magazine in as quietly as possible. She's placed some dog food and meat scraps in a bowl behind the pine. He finds them and begins to eat. Cory parts the willow's whip-like branches and creeps across the grass, moving closer than necessary for a foolproof shot. She cannot miss, cannot inflict merely leg wounds.

His shoulders are low, his tail down, his face intent on its find. Un-der the pine the ground changes to a million brittle needles. *Crunch* and his head turns. She raises the gun, thinks *aim, steady, squeeze*. It's only a few seconds before she realizes she's waiting for him to lunge. *Come get me you motherfucker.* She can't shoot him otherwise. This shocks her. Wasn't that the plan? Preemptive strike.

She moves closer. The animal takes a step back, easily clearing the lowest branch, and that's when Cory realizes it's a pup. The males strike out on their own in fall.

"Come on," she begs. "Come get me."

The pup sniffs the air, his tail still low, then takes off at a speed she didn't think they had and in a second is gone to the darkness, the trees, the future.

In the house Scott sits slumped forward on the couch. Out the window, the pine where Cory failed to protect their son is in full view.

She tries to hide the gun in the folds of her wide-legged pajama pants. "Sorry. Did I wake you up? I thought I heard something."

Scott doesn't even look up. He's staring at his hands, folded tight between his knees. "I thought you were having an affair."

"What?"

"I heard you creeping around. At first I figured bathroom, a drink. Then I caught you outside, with the bat, and I thought, oh, she's being paranoid, but one night I cracked the window and heard a man's voice."

It takes a moment before Cory realizes what he must have heard. "The new neighbor. Two men. They're out there all hours."

Scott nods. "Yeah, I know. I figured that out." He looks up at her. "Did you unload it?"

Cory hesitates, then drops the bullets in her hand and hands Scott the gun.

"So why didn't you shoot him?"

"It was a pup."

"He'll grow up."

"I know."

"Will you shoot him then?"

Cory shakes her head and begins to cry. "I can't."

Scott walks over to the window and stares at the backyard, streaked in light from the neighbor's porch fixtures and the moon, half hidden behind a bank of thunder clouds.

"What do you think they're talking about over there?"

AKA JUAN

Lawan would have been on time to pick up Gloria if he hadn't circled back for Tricia, thinking it will make breaking the news easier, though he knows the second he drives off—that's stupid. Tricia will make it worse. Because it's weird to introduce a new girlfriend in a situation like this, and she knows it too, but can't resist. She's wanted to meet his family ever since she found out they are white.

On the way to the hospital Lawan lets Tricia choose the music while he watches the clock. Time seems to be moving faster than usual. Yesterday, Karen told him to be at the hospital by ten thirty. "They should have Mom discharged by then. You can bring her home in the van and I'll meet you at the house."

Lawan drives disabled kids for the county. They're all in wheelchairs, skulls cradled by headrests and chins fixed by straps, like victims of mad scientists in the old black-and-white movies. The van he uses has a power ramp and bars to secure the chairs, and Lawan knows his boss won't care if he drives Gloria home in it, but the way Karen assigned the task, as if he were some Negro houseboy in the prewar South, pissed him off, so he let an uncomfortable few seconds go by before saying, "I'm not supposed to use the van for personal stuff."

Karen gave him that look. She cannot believe he works such a menial job. "This is for our mother, and it will take twenty minutes."

Lawan relented because he'd have to go regardless. Gloria might be able to get from her chair into a car, but just barely, and only with someone strong to lean on. Six months pregnant, Karen could hardly be used as muscle, Kevin has a bad back from the bike accident a few years ago, and Dennis is built like you'd expect of someone who sits in a chair all day. If Gloria started to go down, he'd only serve as something soft to fall on.

By the time Lawan pulls into the hospital's drive, it's eleven fifteen. He tells Tricia to stay put. "I'll go see what's what."

The automatic doors part, sending a burst of hospital-scented air at his face. In the far corner, Gloria sits reading. That morning, when she called to verify what time he'd be there, she said what she always says: "It's Gloria, your mom." He doesn't think she ever identifies herself like this with the others.

Before she even looks up, Lawan offers his alibi. "Long morning."

The kids release him from the weight of time. If he's late, teachers and therapists assume one of them was sick or had a meltdown. Which is sometimes true. Every week or two he has to pull over and get in the back, hold somebody's hand or stroke their hair. Once in a while, he sings. You can do stuff like that and nobody's embarrassed, or tells on you afterward. They all just smile. The ones that can anyway.

Still, he feels a shit for blaming the kids. What the fuck, though. They don't know.

Gloria tucks her book, something about Chinese farmers judging from the cover, into her bag. "No worries, honey, no worries. I was perfectly content."

"I'll get the bags and come back for you."

Lawan turns and there's Tricia, looking especially hot in a tight pair of red jeans. She introduces herself as Lawan's friend and gets behind Gloria's chair, popping its wheels free and maneuvering around the lobby furniture. Her son, Tyler, who has cerebral palsy, is on Lawan's route.

Once they're underway, Gloria in back secured to the bars, Tricia and she shout out get-to-know-you questions over the engine noise until it becomes too awkward and they fall silent. Lawan tunes to public radio because he's used to classical music. It soothes the kids better than the stuff with words.

At the house, they're all standing on the front porch—Dennis in his lawyer suit, Karen with her white doctor's coat peeking out below her jacket, and Kevin wearing his standard khakis and spike-soled bicycling shoes, their gleaming white and green plastic surface freshly buffed. Lawan figures they're out there just to make a point about how late he is. Otherwise, why not go in the house and sit down? It's only fifty degrees, a damp May day that can't make up its mind, and they have keys, of course. They all used to live here.

They appear to be arguing, but that doesn't worry him. They argue a lot because Frank and Gloria always promoted opinions as if they mattered.

Getting out, Lawan hitches up his jeans, rebuckling to the next belt hole, and tries to look a little harried, remind them all that he might be late, but he's the one who brought her. He pushes Gloria's chair with Tricia trailing and as they reach the porch, everyone looks at her a second too long before saying hello.

"Tricia," Lawan points. "Kevin, Dennis, Karen." He thumbs toward the house. "So what's the plan? How are we getting her inside?"

Everybody glances at each other and Lawan can tell they hadn't thought about that. "Never going to be able to do these stairs."

The house, a brick colonial with rotting porch columns, has five steps up to the front door. Lawan watches Karen squirm. She's the doctor. Should have seen this problem coming. Finally he says, "I think I can get her around back and take her in through the patio door."

The house sits on a hill, so the basement is a walkout, but it's been a few years since Gloria was strong enough to garden and maneuvering her chair down the weed-choked incline proves difficult. Lawan manages, though, and keeps her pitched back on rear wheels across the choppy patio, its bricks sunken and heaved because Frank didn't dig the base deep enough. He's dead now, and the next owner will have to deal with it.

Inside, they all realize Lawan has only changed the problem. This is the basement, with a pool table from the 1970s, an old couch on which he lost his virginity to a homely girl named Reisha and, in the other room, the furnace, water heater, and laundry. Between the rooms a narrow, steep staircase leads to the main floor.

"Well, how the hell are we going to get her upstairs?" Dennis says.

"Can you sit on the stairs," Tricia asks, "and scoot up backward?"

Karen looks at her with a suspicious, even hostile, glance, but Gloria deems it an excellent idea.

"I'll go up on my ass just like I came down."

She makes a move to stand and Lawan hustles forward, offering his arm. When she leans on it, he realizes she's lost weight, and she didn't have much to spare. Gloria has always been tall and bony, like one of those funny birds that can't fly.

"I'll just carry you."

Before she can object, he's swung her up and she's easier to lift than most of the kids, who flop or freeze or otherwise work against the whole process. At the top of the stairs, Gloria pumps her fist in the air. "Ha, ha! I'm not dead yet."

Lawan began life an only child. When he was eight, his sisters were born, Lawkaya and Lawnita. Soon after, a social worker took the three of them from their mother, Lawsandra, and sent them to live with a Mexican woman and her half-black, half-white husband, last name Miller. The Millers wanted to adopt the twins and one day a very tall, skinny white woman with red hair came to explain to Lawan that his sisters were "easy" because they were babies, but they wouldn't be easy forever, and didn't he want them to go to a good home? The Millers moved away and Lawan was forwarded to the home of Gloria and Frank Schmidt. Gloria was also a very tall, skinny white woman, and for some reason Lawan assumed she was the other white woman's sister, until one day he asked and she laughed. "No, we're not related at all."

He stayed in his old school for the rest of that year, then Gloria and Frank sat him down and asked if he wanted to be adopted. Lawan nodded. He knew he wasn't easy anymore.

Gloria switched him to the Catholic school Kevin, Dennis, and Karen attended. It was all white, if you counted the Hispanics as white, which he did. By then he'd figured out "Lawan" was what they called "a black name," so he introduced himself as Wan, the name that Kevin and Dennis used, hoping this was whiter because it had been bestowed by white kids. With the Hispanics around everyone assumed his name was "Juan," so he started spelling it that way on his papers, and for a while got away with it, until his birthday, when the vice principal came on the announcements.

"We'd like to wish a happy birthday to Lawan Schmidt. Have a great day, Lawan!"

The other boys slapped him on the back the rest of the day, exaggerating his name in two drawn-out syllables, "Laaaa-waaan."

He stopped cutting his hair that year. By the middle of the next teachers began asking when he might be "trimming" it. Kids wanted to know if he could hide stuff in there, like candy or the answers to the history test. Dennis suggested he join the Village People, and Kevin said he looked like he'd touched a power line. His hair became so tall they didn't know what to do with him for the spring concert. His face should be in row four, but his hair would be best in row eight. The music teacher solved the problem by putting him on the end of row four, with no one behind him. In the yearbook he protruded like an inked thumbprint at the edge of the page.

While Tricia helps Dennis carry the wheelchair up, Karen yells from the kitchen, "It smells in here! I told you to clean out the fridge, Kevin!"

"I did!"

They walk around looking for the source, find nothing.

"Maybe the place just needs a good airing." Dennis opens windows to the thick, wet air of spring.

Tricia and Karen run out to the grocery store and by the time they come back they're talking like old friends. Karen has given Tricia a bunch of medical advice on Tyler. Lawan isn't proud of it, but it occurs to him this could be good. If they all think he's busy with a girlfriend and her disabled son, maybe they won't be so quick to think he can take care of Gloria. Won't be so mad when they find out he's already halfway gone.

For lunch they've bought a bunch of Arab stuff. A paste the color of a drop cloth and two salads, one made of cucumbers, tomatoes, and a crunchy bread, the other dwarf lettuce wilted in sour dressing.

"Could I have the tabouli?" Tricia asks, winking at him to indicate what? She already seems to know his family better than he does.

"So do you have your stuff here?" Kevin asks.

The time has come. For a second Lawan pretends not to be aware that Kevin is talking to him, then he widens his eyes. "What stuff?"

"Your stuff. To move back in?"

"Your brother doesn't have to move in," Gloria says. "I'm fine alone."

"That's how we got into this mess," Karen says.

"We?" Gloria says. "I think I'm the one with the pins in my ankle."

She fell down the basement stairs, shattering her leg, because Gloria has multiple sclerosis. Living in a two-story house with all the bedrooms and the only shower upstairs makes no sense, but if anyone suggests moving, she gets angry.

"I could have done those stairs on my ass. Lawan didn't have to carry me."

"Somebody's going to have to get your wheelchair up, unless you're going to strap it to your head," Dennis says.

"I can use my walker up there."

A five-minute debate about whether or not Gloria is strong enough for the walker ensues. What if she has an attack? That's what they call the sudden spike in MS symptoms that come unpredictably, sometimes not for years at a time, sometimes only months apart.

"You could have died falling down those stairs," Kevin says. "It was pure luck Wan was here." Kevin is six inches shorter than Lawan. He has to reach up to knuckle his hair, still two inches thick.

Lawan heard the thumping sound of Gloria's head hitting the wall and the cracking as her legs caught between balusters because it was his laundry she'd been carrying downstairs. He'd stopped by to do it and while he was rummaging through the freezer, she snatched it up. Lawan was pretty sure Gloria hadn't told anyone this part of the story.

That day he'd waited for the ambulance outside, feeling safer in the fresh air. When they pulled in he said right away, "My mother fell," to be sure they knew he belonged here. He had to remind himself these were experienced people. Surely they'd seen a black man with a white mother before. For all they knew, Frank had looked like Shaquille O'Neal.

"Lawan is moving in," Karen says. "There's no other option."

"I have to drive my route."

"That's no problem. I think Mom can swing a few hours alone."

Karen proceeds to list the things he should do before leaving. Food. Medicines. Bathroom. Phone. Glass of water.

Now is the time to bring up the Marines. He passed the test and it was only Gloria's fall that stopped his enlisting. Instead, he asks, "Long-term, though, what's the plan?"

They all shoot him a warning glance. Even Tricia looks uncomfortable.

"One day at a time," Karen says. "That's always what you say. Right, Mom?"

"That's right. Tomorrow might never come. Why waste today preparing for it?"

This had always been Gloria's mantra, and the older Lawan grew the dumber he thought it was. Every day kept coming at you, like a slap across the face. Better get your hand up.

At two o'clock he manages to slip away. "Gotta go get the kids."

Tricia sits beside him quietly for the first several minutes and he wonders what she thought of everyone, but doesn't want to ask. As they're pulling up to the first school, sliding in line behind a bus that picks up the regular kids, she says, "I take it you don't want to move in?"

For a second he thinks she means with her, then realizes she's talking about Gloria. "I don't know. I'm not sure she wants me to."

"Oh yeah, she does. She's just too proud to ask. Mothers don't like to be a burden."

Lawan would like to ask Tricia if Tyler is a burden, but he knows that's mean. If the answer is yes, she wouldn't want to say it out loud.

On days like this, blustery and cold, he takes a blanket inside and tucks it around the kids in their chairs. The first time he did it a kid got scared and he said, "It's okay. You're just going to be a hot dog, all wrapped up tight in your bun." The kid laughed and said, "Hot dog time," so that's what he calls it now and all the kids think it's hilarious.

From the start Lawan felt he understood them. As a child, he had a speech impediment, remembers sitting at the kitchen table with Gloria, watching her narrow lips, the color of raw salmon. *Your bottom teeth have to bite your lip,* she'd say, then she'd puff. *Fuh, fuh, fuh...* Something about it made him feel she was always on the verge of hurting him.

At each house, he pulls into the driveway, straps the chair to the ramp, then lowers the ramp to the ground. By then a mother or grandmother, rarely a dad, is already coming out. Some of them will take over at the curb, some need help getting the chair up the house ramp and through the door. If it's grandma, Lawan always waves her back inside. When he goes to leave, he whisks the blanket off like a magician revealing a rabbit and says, "I present to you, the Great Hotdogini!" The kids who can laugh always do.

Tyler is the last stop on the route. After Lawan helps Tricia get him inside, instead of going back to his apartment to pack a few things or returning to Gloria's, he goes to see Lawsandra.

It turned out to be easy enough to find her. Just ask around the right neighborhoods, spelling her name carefully so people don't confuse it with "LaSondra," of which there are several. But there is only one Lawsandra, and she is his mother. Lawan wasn't convinced of this until he asked, "So what's my birthday?"

She thought a second. "May twenty-second. You was born at ten fifteen at night, and I was up on my feet by eleven, sneaking a hit in the bathroom under the fan." She laughed. "They caught me and took my stash away and wouldn't let me see you till the next day. They afraid I was too high to hold you right."

Gloria and the rest know nothing about his finding Lawsandra. It's simple enough to keep a secret, Lawan the only overlap between the two worlds. Every month or two he hangs out with his mother and her boyfriend Booker, who works at a tire store. Lawsandra claims she's gotten clean, except for pot, which Lawan doesn't think counts anyway, and she works part-time at KFC. She hates it, is trying to find something better, so Lawan gave her a few lessons in Microsoft Word and Excel, but even though she's a fast learner, she doesn't have the patience—or maybe the interest—and he can't picture her in an office anyway, with her long gold nails and the way she oils her hair into the shape of a fan, like a chicken's tail across the back of her head.

Their duplex slouches on a mud-soft lot east of Collingwood, dirty white aluminum siding, spongy porch boards and the ghost outline of long-gone shutters. Lawsandra seems happy to see him.

"You want a beer? I got some chips and stuff. We having people over. You want to hang out?"

He tells her he can't for long, then ends up staying two hours, playing a game of blinding darts with Booker and the three guys who show up. You lie on your back, and throw the dart toward the ceiling, trying to land it in the old plaster, which is harder than drywall. If you fail, and they mostly do, you have to dodge the falling dart. One time a dart lands right on some guy's cheek, missing his eye by an inch. Everyone, including Lawan, laughs. When the moment passes, he puts on his coat and, without saying goodbye, heads back to Gloria's.

At first, he cleans. The house has been empty for over a month, except for the cats, whose crusted plastic bowls he tries soaking, but ends up pitching. Kevin was feeding them and apparently washing the bowls wasn't on his list. Lawan vacuums the cats' long, silky hairs from the furniture, washes all the towels and sheets and scrubs the bathroom, from whose dry drains wafts the faint odor of dead skin. Gloria insists it's unnecessary, but it is. Even before the fall she wasn't keeping the place very clean. Not that he blames her. She tires easily and some days relied on canes just to walk. That she had tried to go down the stairs carrying his laundry was ridiculous, except she'd been carrying her own laundry up and down those stairs, so who could blame him?

Lawan wants to leave the place better off than he found it so no one can say he didn't do his duty. He'd leave Gloria better off, and if she got worse later, after he enlisted, well then the others would have to deal with that because the Marines are not a part-time, come-and-go kind of thing.

On day four he finishes scrubbing, yet the smell remains, so Lawan empties the cupboards, convinced a mouse is decaying behind a stack of old Tupperware. Instead, he finds a bag of what, judging from the deli sticker, used to be roast beef. The fetid meat has decayed into a purple-brown gelatin whose enzymes have eaten through the plastic bag and started on the shelf's yellow paint.

"Why in the hell is there meat in the cupboard?" Lawan asks, suspending the bag for Gloria's inspection. It drips onto the plate in his other hand.

She looks upset at first, her bony, freckled face scowling from forehead to chin, then laughs. "I guess I wasn't thinking."

This isn't the first odd thing she's done. Gloria's been reading the Chinese farmer book for hours every day, but her bookmark looks to be in the same place, and the day before while he was mopping the back hallway, she told him the "roof" didn't need cleaning.

He asks, "Are you feeling okay? I mean, do you have a headache or something?"

Gloria admits to feeling "a little muddied," and Lawan thinks stroke or seizures. Either one would settle it. Assisted living, no question.

"Does Karen know about this?"

"She'd try to make me go somewhere and I don't want to. I want to stick it out here, until I can't, then..." Gloria pauses. "I was thinking of Dad."

Lawan's cheeks grow hot. They have never talked about what happened with Frank. Dennis and Karen were away at school, Kevin on a hiking trip, when Frank had a heart attack and his car ran off the road into a park, where a bike rack stopped it. The next day, Lawan and Gloria sat alone in the hospital cafeteria trying to make sense of what the doctors said about his chances. He was on a breathing tube and there was talk of organ damage, questions about how long he'd been gone before the EMS people revived him. Gloria looked at Lawan as if he would know. "What do you think Dad would want?"

Lawan wanted to say he wasn't his dad. They should wait for the real kids. He didn't, and by the time Kevin, Dennis, and Karen made it home,

Frank was at the undertakers' and Lawan felt like he'd killed him, though he couldn't even remember what he said to Gloria that day.

A new stab of guilt shoots through him. She'd clothed and tutored him and come to baseball games and student conferences. All the things a real mother would do.

"I want to die quickly," Gloria says. "I want to go with dignity. You know, not hold on for nature to do it."

Lawan takes a long moment to register her meaning, then pretends not to. He drops the leaking bag into the garbage. "Life's a crapshoot. What are you gonna do?"

Lawan always avoided calling Gloria and Frank "Mom" and "Dad" at home, where the terms took on an ingratiating phoniness. In public, though, he used to look for reasons to say it, and watch people's expressions, trying to guess their thoughts. He remembers this when he takes Gloria to IHOP and the hostess mistakes him for her driver. Would she have made that mistake if he were white? It might have been the van, parked outside the big picture window, but he didn't think so. And so what? Why blame the woman for a commonsense assumption?

Gloria corrects her in the vehement, offended tone she's always used at such moments. A tone that makes Lawan feel like a scruffy dog being reclaimed at the pound.

After breakfast he tries to keep himself busy around the house so he won't have to watch Gloria flog away at that Chinese farmer book or discuss her death anymore. She'd brought up the subject again at the restaurant, him trapped in the booth waiting for pancakes. He'd agreed, vaguely, to help her, knowing that if all went according to plan, by the time she's lying in the hospital hooked up to the machines they hooked Frank up to—the one that beeped every thirty seconds, and the one that sounded like an obscene phone caller's breathing—he'd be on some ship anchored in the Arabian Sea and someone else would have to do the dirty work.

Saturday night Karen invites everyone to dinner. Lawan carries Gloria up the four steps to the front porch, then down the three steps to the sunken dining room, feeling again what he felt that first day she came home from rehab, both proud and awkward with everybody watching. Alone it doesn't feel like this. Alone he is just Lawan, carrying Gloria.

Between dinner and dessert, Gloria wants to go outside for a smoke. Lawan lowers her into the wheelchair beside the back stoop. It's drizzling and cold and she waves him back in, popping open an extra-large umbrella Karen has provided.

"Give me ten minutes."

Kevin and Dennis have moved to the family room to watch a recorded *SNL* while Karen and Veronica, Dennis's wife, clean up. Karen's husband, who owns some kind of industrial parts business, is in China again. As far as Lawan can tell, he half-lives over there. Karen doesn't seem to mind. Lawan wonders if she'll mind after the baby is born.

Veronica pokes her head in the living room and scolds Dennis for not breaking up a fight between their boys, three and five, who can be heard in the foyer spitting at each other. Kevin gives Dennis a big grin to indicate how happy he is to be divorced, nobody to reprimand him, until Karen shouts, "And we could use some help cleaning up, Kevin!"

Lawan is exempted. He wonders if it's because he is supposed to be watching Gloria. He watches *SNL* instead, and then, having lost track of time, looks out the window, where Gloria sits, contentedly it seems, cigarette half-smoked. Or maybe it's her second.

Cleanup done and pie dished out, everyone resumes their places, Kevin in the recliner, Dennis on the couch, Veronica perched on the arm next to him, frowning at the show. Karen looks out the window, then taps on the glass. Gloria must indicate she's not ready to come in because Karen sits down next to Lawan.

"So how's it been going over there?"

This is the moment Lawan should tell them about the lunchmeat in the cupboard, the book that never ends. Instead he tells them he's been thinking of joining the Marines.

"What?" Karen says, aghast. "Why would you do that?"

Kevin thinks he's kidding. They all launch into a lecture about what an idiot he is.

"You want to go to the desert and get your legs blown off for some rich guy's oil contract?"

Lawan points out that the Marines are connected to the Navy. He doesn't think they go to the desert.

"If you like the idea of traveling, join the Foreign Service," Veronica says.

Lawan shrugs, unwilling to admit he has only the vaguest notion of what that is. Embassies or something. It sounds like paperwork.

"You need college for those positions," Karen says.

Gloria offered to pay for college and Lawan's not going has been a regular topic of discussion. Kevin used to argue college wasn't necessary if Lawan wanted to own a business. Karen and Dennis said what business? And where would the capital come from? Lawan didn't want to ask what capital was and when he found out later he thought, why don't they just call it money?

After Lawan turned down Kevin's offer to "apprentice" at the bike shop and took the job driving the kids, Kevin stopped defending him. But Lawan can't work at the bike shop. He hates people who take bikes seriously. Does not want to discuss why frame weight matters or how comfortable a seat is on their bony asses.

"You've never even mentioned the military." Karen's tone is exasperated. He wishes she'd just come out with it: what will they do with Gloria?

"I have a friend who joined." He details all the benefits, attributing to this fictitious friend what the recruiter told him.

"The few, the proud, the Marines," Kevin says.

Unsure if he's being mocked, Lawan replies, "That's me," hoping to sound ironic, worldly, while thinking yes, that's exactly what he'll be.

He slips on his windbreaker and puts the hood up. Through the window in the back door he can see Gloria staring at the yard the same way she had years ago, when as a kid he'd be flailing away with a jump rope or teetering across the patio on an old skateboard, shouting, "Look! Look!" and she'd nod, saying, "Yes, I see you, yes."

As he's closing the door, Dennis yells, "You do know the Marines are going to shave your head, right?"

The next weekend Lawan gets dressed to go to a Jay Z concert with Lawsandra, though he told Gloria and Dennis, who's coming by to stay with her, that he's going with a friend from work.

The tickets are his birthday gift. Beforehand they are going to one of those famous steak houses where they bring you a slab of meat two inches thick and you have to order everything else separately. For dessert he hopes they have carrot cake, and his piece will have a burning candle in it. After the concert they will go out for drinks, and she'll tell him what he wants to know that he hasn't had the nerve to ask yet, like who his father is, and if Lawsandra knows what happened to his sisters. He tried to find them, Googling their given names first, then trying versions the Millers might have substituted, like Kayla or Kay, Nita or Anita. He found several Millers with these white names and considered messaging them, but Lawkaya and Lawnita are only sixteen years old. If these other girls turn out not to be his sisters, trying to connect online could get him arrested.

At four o'clock, half an hour before Dennis is due to come over and stay with Gloria, he calls to cancel. Something about time zones and filing deadlines. He goes on, offering details as if Lawan knows what they mean. It feels like a way of putting him down, reminding Lawan he should have gone to college.

Lawan calls Kevin, who doesn't answer, then Karen, who says she woke up with a sore throat and doesn't want to risk getting Gloria sick.

While he waits for Kevin to call back, Lawsandra texts wanting to know where he is, and he tells her they might have to go late, skip dinner.

Finally, at six o'clock, Kevin arrives and Lawan borrows his CR-V. It's newer and more reliable than his own car, and it doesn't smell of cigarettes like Gloria's, which he knows Lawsandra hates. Dope is fine, but regular cigarettes nauseate her. The facts about her are piling up, and he is storing each one like the little slips of fortune from a Chinese restaurant.

At her house Lawan takes the musty stairs to the second floor. Booker answers, looking half-asleep.

"No, she gone to the concert."

"I was supposed to pick her up."

"She gone with her friend Cheryl. Left a while ago."

A few texts verify this. Lawsandra didn't want to risk being late, so she sold his ticket to Cheryl and they're already at the restaurant. No mention of his birthday.

Lawan hangs around, sharing a pizza with Booker, mostly to kill time. When he leaves it's still too early to go home, so he stops at the bar, where, without Booker and Lawsandra, the other customers make him nervous, hot girls in peek-a-boo skirts draped over guys who look like they'd take his eyes out for noticing. At ten he leaves and drives around, careful to snake through the city without backtracking. Doesn't want the same cop to see him twice. He'd get pulled over, a young black man driving in circles.

Monday, Lawan's actual birthday, he has just dropped off Danny, a sixteen-year-old whose problems started with a car accident, and is closing the back doors when he notices Tyler drooling. Lawan wipes his mouth with a tissue. "You okay, kid?"

Tyler can talk, but it takes a while for the words to make their way to his lips, so at first Lawan isn't worried. Then his hands begin to shake and Lawan realizes it's a seizure. He jumps in the driver's seat and shoots straight down Cherry to the big hospital, where his van and his uniform get the guard's attention and he hits the ER in five minutes flat, by which time Tyler is shivering and his eyes are just white marbles and the hospital staff don't need any paperwork or cards before they take him and Lawan stands, stunned, beginning to question if he did the right thing, or if he should have held the kid's tongue down. Wasn't that the risk? They could choke on it, or bite it or something.

When he calls Tricia he downplays the incident so she won't kill herself driving over. Once she's safely in the waiting room, he fleshes out the reality and they sit holding hands, until the doctor comes out and says Tyler seems okay, but Lawan can tell something's changed. There is a lot of medical talk which Tricia seems to understand. She begins to follow the doctor, then stops. "You coming?"

"No, you go ahead. Your time."

An understanding passes between them that he won't be there for her the way she'd hoped, and she accepts it gracefully, but he knows how she feels, and that drives him out to the van, which the guard has moved to a nearby lot.

The guy hands him his keys. "Kid okay?"

"Hope so." Lawan shrugs, safe inside the assumption that he is just the driver.

He'd planned to spend the evening at Tricia's. Birthday dinner, birthday sex. Lawan assumes that's off, but Gloria isn't expecting him home for hours, so he goes to Lawsandra's.

She answers the door without her wig, and it takes a few seconds for him to understand the rooster tail was fake. Her real hair looks like tufts of dryer lint.

"How was the concert?"

Lawsandra shrugs. "You didn't really miss anything. The seats were shitty."

She brought home KFC and gestures for him to make himself a plate. While they eat, she doesn't mention his birthday even though Lawan brings up Memorial Day and the change to his schedule in a couple of weeks after school ends for the summer. He can't think of any other way to get her to consider the date, so he asks if she knows what happened to his sisters.

"Huh?" She's looking for something in the fridge.

"The twins, Lawnita and Lawkaya. They went to a family named Miller."

Lawsandra looks at him as if he wasn't supposed to know this.

"I looked for 'em on Facebook, but that's a common name."

"Lawkaya and Lawnita?"

"Miller."

His phone rings and Karen leaves a message wanting to know if everything is okay. She's called Gloria several times at home and didn't get an answer.

Lawan's not worried. When he left for work, she was at the table with her Chinese farmer book, the newspaper, and a cup of tea. He'd prepped her dinner and she was going to microwave it whenever she got hungry. Still, he puts on his jacket. As he's moving toward the door Lawsandra says, "They're your half-sisters."

"What?"

"Half. Different father. Yours was named Ron and he died in a house fire. Police tried to say it was a crack thing, but it was electrical. The lights and stuff in that place were always weird, and some of the fixtures there, at the ceiling, they had these black marks, like scorches, around them."

Lawsandra points to the ceiling, at the hundreds of tiny holes their blinding game has left.

"You know where they are?"

"No. They was so little."

"What difference does that make?"

"They don't remember. It's all up here." She stabs at her temple. "You make your connections and then they stuck, right? Like you, you come back looking for me because you remember. They don't, and why confuse 'em now?"

On the way home Karen calls again, says Gloria is still not answering. After that, time gets thick. Lawan pushes through. At Gloria's he finds the bedroom door shut. She must have gotten herself up here on her bottom. There's no way she could do the stairs on her feet.

Lawan knocks. "I'm home. You okay?"

Nothing. He raps on the door with all four knuckles. "You all right?"

Silence.

He tries the knob and finds it locked.

"Mom?" The word sounds strange. He repeats it, louder. "Mom?"

Razor blades. Pills. Alcohol. The results flash across his mind in vivid pictures. He pounds on the door, "Mom! It's Lawan. You answer now!"

Then he hears the toilet flush, the faucet, her walker rattling. She opens the door, registers his expression and laughs. "What's the matter? Did you think I was dead?" Gloria is almost as tall as he is. She gives him a smacking kiss on the cheek.

"Why didn't you answer the phone? Karen and I were calling."

"I was trying to nap. My God, why is everyone so worked up? I can be alone for a few hours."

As Gloria starts to shuffle past him, Lawan blurts, "Why did you ask me?"

"What?"

"Ask me. Why did you ask me to help you, if you got worse?"

She takes a moment to register his meaning and it passes between them, the recognition that asking him to help her die is possible, but asking Karen, Dennis, or Kevin is not.

"That was stupid. I'm sorry." They are jammed face to face in the narrow hall. Gloria grips his wrist. "I love you, Lawan."

"It's okay," he says. "I get it. I know how it is."

She squeezes his arm. "I have your birthday present. It's downstairs."

"Come on," he says. "I'll carry you."

THE RIVER WARTA

Now that Caroline lived alone for the first time in her life, she began to be irritated by the cleanliness of her house. When she left something somewhere, it stayed there. If she didn't enter a room for days, it collected nothing but a thin, almost imperceptible layer of dust. Her daughters' bedrooms grew stiff and gray with disuse. In her own bed, Frederick's pillow remained plump and smooth, the case free of his coarse, white hair, and Caroline—though she knew it was ridiculous—took this as an affront. It unnerved her that nothing changed in the house unless she changed it.

So when the cat meowed, a ridiculous predatory supplicant outside her window in a golden twilight during Indian summer, Caroline did not broom it away as she would have a year ago. With the Depression on, she'd become used to homeless, hungry visitors. She stood at the window looking down at its twisting, black body, its chartreuse eyes, and whispered, "What's the matter? Are you lost? This isn't your house. Go on now, go," aware that her tone was more inviting than dismissing.

The next day, her youngest girl, Eva—who'd inherited too much of her mother even in her mother's opinion—came by. "There's a stray cat around the house. Where's the broom?"

"Leave it be," Caroline said. "It's doing no harm."

The night before, she'd watched the cat lap at the milk she'd slipped out on a tea saucer, marveling at the strange distance between herself and this woman who stood in front of the window. She who would not tolerate a cat's filthy tongue on her good tea service, especially now that she could no longer replace what might be broken. But this woman, who was using her dishes, her hands, her eyes, had carried the saucer out and watched with amusement and even pride as the animal satisfied itself.

"Where did it come from?" Eva asked.

"Nowhere," Caroline said. "I don't think she has a home."

Eva was Caroline's plainest daughter. She lacked Sophie's spunk—however annoying—and Addie's supple beauty. Sometimes, studying Eva, at once both diffident and haughty, Caroline felt embarrassed, as if she were looking too long in a mirror, and it made her love her youngest daughter with a humiliating ache.

"Everything comes from somewhere," Eva said. "What you mean is nobody wants it."

Caroline, then called Karolina, was born in 1880 in Poznań, Poland, a city on the Warta River. As a girl she liked to stand by the river when a thunderstorm was coming in, watching blue sky skitter to gray in the water's reflection, the mirrored clouds cut in half by waves. In summer the rain felt good on the insides of her wrists, where she rolled up the sleeves of her dress.

The river seemed a majestic, mysterious transport, always on the way to something else, and as she entered adolescence Caroline began to imagine what she might do if she were a boy. She'd escape for sure, maybe as far as America. At the very least she would have used her time down at the river for something useful, like fishing.

But the summer after she turned eighteen, her last summer in Poland, Caroline could no longer look at the river. It had become like her parents—a lonely, menacing thing with a dark, inscrutable surface. And it took a courage she would not have guessed she had, a will that even scared her a little—reminding her as it did of her parents' steely, stubborn resolve—to board a boat on that same river, a boat which would join a ship that would take her to America.

The cat did not leave, which, given how Caroline fed him, should have been no surprise. Since Black Tuesday not even an animal could afford to abandon a decent meal for the promise of something better down the block.

On Saturday her new son-in-law, Dobry, came to rake the leaves. After Frederick became too ill to work, he used to hire out such tasks to homeless men who walked the neighborhood looking for odd jobs. He'd send them off with a generous wage, Caroline's kielbasa sandwiches, and a dozen pickled eggs. Now that he was gone, though, Caroline didn't feel safe hiring strange men and making them meals. This left her with nothing to take care of—unless she counted the cat.

Dobry crouched, sliding his thumb against the tips of his fingers, and made kissing noises to the animal, who trotted up, stopping shy of his reach, and smelled the air appraisingly. Caroline stood at the back door, the screen breaking her face into a thousand tiny diamonds of shadow and light. "I don't know how to get rid of it. It's been urinating on my bushes."

"Looks well fed," Dobry said, scratching the hard spot between the cat's ears.

"Well, they are predators," Caroline said, seeing too late she'd forgotten to bring in the plate on which she'd left a smear of butter and ham rind that morning. It gave an odd satisfaction, having something wild, unreachable through logic or language of any kind, decide it needed you.

In Poznań Caroline's mother owned a white cat named Silk with blue eyes and an unusually long tail she used the way a ballerina does her arms. Silent and indifferent to verbal commands, the cat perfectly suited her mother, who had gone deaf at the age of four from scarlet fever and talked as if she had a marble on her tongue. She never used sign language because Caroline's grandmother thought it the recourse of the mentally deficient and had swatted her if she ever so much as gestured.

Caroline's father was a chemist. He'd been born with a deformed left arm, the hand a mere nub of tissue just below what should have been his elbow. He had a dog named Atlas—a black and brown shepherd with triangular ears that stayed upright even while napping—whom he'd trained to open doors. At the chemist shop and around town, if her father was carrying something in his good hand, Atlas would grip the doorknob with his mouth and twist, leaving teeth marks behind in the wooden knobs.

Caroline remembered her mother having all the knobs in their house changed to smooth, metal spheres on which Atlas couldn't gain any purchase. In retaliation her father had taken all the pens and pencils out of the house, forcing her mother to make herself understood with verboten gestures and futile attempts at proper pronunciation.

It was only after Caroline escaped to America and had to consider what she herself could expect from life—just another foreigner with a strange accent whose education and family lineage meant nothing—that she had begun to understand the seed of her parents' bitterness and resentment toward one another. And only now, in the time she'd had to think since Frederick died, had she finally found a single word for it: humiliation.

The next week the weather grew much colder and the cat began to cry at the back door. One night, when Caroline reached outside with the saucer, it darted inside. She couldn't find the thing until those glowing eyes gave it away, huddled beneath the dining room table. Caroline moved the chairs out and scolded, "You weren't invited in. What's the matter with you?" She clapped her hands and the cat ran.

It took several minutes to herd it toward the door and finally out into the dark.

The next day was colder again. Snow fell for an hour in the morning, then melted in the afternoon sun. The cat sat under the awning on the concrete slab of patio with its paws tucked tight against its body. At the kitchen window, Caroline shook her head. If she had allowed herself to indulge in the fantasy of cats having emotions, she might have said the cat seemed hurt by her treatment the day before. It refused to come onto the porch for its milk, and didn't meow when she poked her head out. It just looked at her a moment, then sat down, staring across the wet grass to the dark, dirty street beyond the fence.

The rest of the day Caroline tried to forget about the cat, and when she looked out around four o'clock, it was gone.

The last summer Caroline lived in Poland, after she'd finished school, her mother began a list of men—old men, young men, all rich men. She wrote them in her large, calligraphic script right across the printed text on pages torn from her father's books, then stuck the pages to the walls in Caroline's room with a paste made from flour and water. If the men were older, the rituals of questions and answers were private, passed among friends who knew friends who knew the man in question. If the men were Caroline's age, her mother would invite their mothers for tea.

In July, during the hottest part of the summer, her mother didn't allow anyone to open a window because of the flies, so when these women came, they sat in the formal parlor with the still air like a warm, moldy cloth across their faces.

The visits were an effort for Caroline's mother, requiring all her attention and focus. Her words were practiced, nearly identical from tea to tea, lady to lady, and they were few. While the other woman talked, Caroline's mother had to stare at her mouth to read her lips. Some people seemed to take offense at this, though they knew the reason. Hence there were long awkward silences in which the mothers would turn and smile at Caroline as if she were a picture on the mantel, and that was the face Caroline put on, the one she held for portraits, a mindless smile with fixed, wide eyes. Once in a while a boy's mother would deign to ask Caroline a question, but she was always careful to answer while looking at her own mother so her lips could be read. As she talked, she studied her mother's gray eyes, flecked with blackish-blue, the color of bruises before they turn, and tried to figure out if the narrowness was the study of pleasure or disgust.

During the meeting her mother would stroke Silk, who lay stomach down across her lap, paws dangling over her knees. At the end of the meeting, if things didn't go well—which mostly they did not—her mother would snatch the paper she'd written the man's name on off Caroline's wall, ball it up and slip it up her sleeve.

After her mother began the husband search, Caroline's father came into her room and stared at the papers. "My prospects," Caroline muttered. "Mother did it."

Her father nodded, then peeled one of the pages off the wall and licked its back. "That's the good flour," he said with disgust.

Caroline never heard her father talk to her mother about the papers on her wall, the flour, or anything else. He rarely spoke to her at all. Dare Caroline allude to this, he scowled and shook his head. "Why would I do that? How do I know what she thinks I'm saying?"

After the husband search began, her father began to move through the house as soundlessly as her mother, as if he didn't need to fidget with locks or open doors like the common man, as if his useless arm were like a fin to a fish, letting him slip through the world silently, effortlessly, on his way to somewhere else. And just as quietly, he would open every window in the house to let the flies in. For hours afterward her mother stalked the floor, swatting with a magazine or newspaper, Silk trailing behind, pawing at the black corpses. One time Caroline's mother broke her favorite vase. It was the only sound, that cracking china, all evening long.

After Caroline had children of her own and their noise filled the house, she realized she had often felt as though she didn't exist in her parents' bitter silence and that the invisibility had seduced her. She didn't want to contradict it. Sometimes her own girls would jump when she came into a room behind them. "Mother," they'd complain, "why can't you make noise like a normal person! It's like having a snake in the house."

By the end of the week the cat had forgiven her and come back up to the porch for its twice-a-day milk and scrap of food. Caroline's neighbor, Mildred Putramack, must have been watching her feed it all along. She came out on her porch. "Giving something to an animal, huh? Not enough food for us, even."

Caroline was not unaware of her good fortune—a generous pension from Frederick's company and a patent on a glassblowing technique he'd invented. The house was paid for and her needs had shrunk as she grew older. Shopping had become more a chore than a pastime. Recently she'd gone downtown to buy a new pair of hose and seen men on the courthouse lawn in pup tents, others sitting on stools selling handfuls of pencils, bushels of apples, and ears of corn.

Caroline stood up straighter. "There's been mice around. Seems like a sensible way to get rid of them."

Mildred huffed. "I've not seen any mice around my stoop."

All night Caroline worried about what Mildred would be saying to the neighbors. *She's giving meat to a cat when people are starving. Letting filthy animals in her house. Going a little batty living there all alone.* The thought of people talking about her made Caroline's skin feel tight, as if someone were pulling a million strings attached to her million pores.

The next morning, she began to clean the house. In the last several weeks she'd let her daily chores lapse. Now, the dirt and bits of leaves on the front walk and the sticky film on the kitchen floor inspired a mild panic. She scrubbed the tiles, shook rugs, dusted tables, swept the sidewalk. Then she remembered the windowsills. The first night she heard the cat, she'd pulled back the drape and noticed an accumulation of dead flies and spider webs. Now, as she tugged open each window, it occurred to her the cat may have been out there hours, even days, before she noticed him because she always kept the drapes shut to guard against sunlight fading her furniture. She thought of her daughter Addie, her favorite, who'd confided to Sophie, who later told Caroline, that she didn't like to bring friends home because Caroline made them nervous. Was she so formidable?

She left the drapes open. What did it matter if her couch faded a shade or two? And who could guarantee she would live long enough to notice?

Caroline was cleaning out the refrigerator—the new electric kind she bought just before Frederick fell ill—when Eva and Sophie arrived. They were arguing as they came in the door. Neither seemed at all surprised to see her cleaning, which relieved her sense of being the wrong person in the right body.

"Mother," Sophie said, "Mrs. Putramack waylaid us in the backyard. She said you've been feeding some cat, a stray."

"Is she talking about the cat I saw last time? The black one?" The note of displeasure in Eva's voice made Caroline angry. She also noted the surprise, remembering the plate and saucer Dobry must have seen.

"I don't know what that old woman wants me to do—firecracker it?" After Frederick died last summer, some kids put a stray cat in a cardboard box on the Fourth of July, then stuck lit firecrackers through holes in the box. Addie, who'd been helping Caroline sort paperwork, saw the boys do it. She chased them off, but too late, and came back in crying, saying she wished her father were here, he'd make those boys sorry. Caroline patted her back and looked out the window at the way orange shadows played against the house next door. For several days after that she'd felt frightened and out of place, as if she'd woken up in a world that looked like hers, but upon closer inspection was more like the props to a play, with hidden gears grinding behind paper-thin doors and windows without glass.

Before the girls left, Caroline said, "I thought Dobry was going to finish burning my leaves," a more imploring tone in her voice than she'd intended.

"He'll come by Saturday, Mother," Eva said. "I promise." Caroline never knew whether to take Eva's kindness as a sign of love or fear.

Later, Caroline was cleaning upstairs and opened Frederick's wardrobe. The smell of long-confined cedar filled the air. With the weather getting cold, she knew she ought to take his wool coats and suits to the Salvation Army. She was afraid, though, that one day she would pass a man wearing Frederick's brown and green checked overcoat and she would—for just a moment—think him still alive, then have to remember that, of course, he was not.

Caroline didn't want to marry any of the men her mother had chosen. She resented being discussed and measured like a piece of cloth. She wasn't something this man was going to wear around his skinny neck. But it felt impossible to avoid the marriage. Where would she go? How would she support herself?

One Saturday morning—another warm, wet day, the rag on her face—Caroline's father called her down to breakfast. He sat across from her mother at the dining room table in his undershirt, his short, shriveled appendage in full view. Caroline knew this annoyed her mother, who preferred he keep the embryonic limb out of sight.

Her father's arm made Caroline think of dried fruit, baked in the sun until all the moisture had leeched out. After she learned of gangrene, the way it begins at the spot of injury and, if unchecked by amputation, migrates toward the center of the body, it seemed impossible the desiccation would stop of its own accord. She began to study her father's shoulder and the right side of his neck for signs of wrinkling or flaking skin.

Caroline slid into her seat. The dining room table was set with the morning dishes, blue forget-me-nots on a yellow plate. Her teacup was full of orange juice because her mother disliked the way a juice glass interrupted the place setting, and her plate held toast and two eggs, poached, because that was the only way civilized people ate eggs. A cut-glass bowl in the center of the table held blackberry jam. Caroline didn't particularly like it, but she always ate it because her mother thought jam messy and her father considered it indulgent.

Caroline carefully ran her knife along the edge of the bowl, and spread the jam on her toast. It was in returning the nearly clean knife to the bowl that a black spot appeared on the table. Her mother's eyes didn't move. Her father's features remained still. The words, when they came, seemed to float in from behind Caroline, as if meant for someone else, someone in the neighboring house perhaps, and only through fault of the wind had they found her. *You've ruined the tablecloth.* She didn't even know who said them. The words were too distinct to be her mother's, the voice too high to be her father's. Caroline looked up and her parents were sipping their coffee. Then, in her marbled speech, Caroline's mother said to her father, "See, I told you she is making a bad impression. She's as clumsy as you with that stump."

Her father spoke slowly, looking directly at her mother, "Maybe they're afraid of you." He invoked an old folk saying. "The deaf cannot be trusted."

At the Salvation Army Caroline lay the coats and hats, the suits and shoes with laces tied together, on the desk. "I want someone to have these, someone who needs them."

The man at the desk, a face like a well-worn rock, nodded. "Sure."

Caroline watched him sort each item into different boxes, the suits folded against all good sense on top of work shirts and canvas pants.

At home the cat sat facing the door. "What are you doing? Hm? Get away from there, go." It was the end of October and Caroline thought of Halloween. She'd given out treats when Frederick was well—popcorn balls, cookies, and often, in her neighborhood, pieces of sweet bread or paczki—but after he became ill, she hadn't felt like it, causing her house to become the target of hooligans who tossed eggs at the front door, or left dog excrement in a bag of fire on the porch.

This year the expectation of harassment did not trouble Caroline as it had before. Nothing felt as it had when Frederick was dying, or right after he'd passed, the day Adelaide sat crying over the damn cat in the box. Now it seemed instead that the person turning the controls on her found the boys' petulant punishment amusing. They wanted their sweets, and this was her sentence for not providing them. Unlike the cat, who'd done nothing, she had refused them a treat. Fair enough. She would simply put gloves on, throw the paper bag away and scrub the egg off her windows. No harm done.

Dobry bicycled up the walk and around to the back gate about an hour before sunset, the evening cool setting in and Caroline closing the windows and making sure all evidence of feeding the cat had been cleaned up. The animal sat on the concrete walk behind the house where the sun came down hard at sunset, its face turned up to the warmth, the tip of its tail flicking like the tapping fingers of an impatient monarch.

Dobry raked the few newly fallen leaves into the burn pile while Caroline stood watching from the window. The cat watched too, unintimidated by the crackle of the piles or the twing of the metal rake as it sprung against twigs and tangled grass. Dobry was a good-looking, tall man with wide shoulders and curly dark hair. He was better looking than Frederick, and sometimes, in the secret part of her heart, she was surprised he had married Eva, a girl as plain as Caroline. Once or twice Dobry had said something that gave Caroline the impression he'd intuited her surprise and resented it.

Of course, he might also resent Caroline because she made no attempt to hide her opinion that Dobry was a disappointment for Eva. What she never explained is that it was his love—not his family's more recent immigration, or that they'd been farmers in the old country—that disappointed her. Dobry's feelings for Eva, nearly worshipful in their purity and degree, required no change or improvement, and so Eva would remain like Caroline forever because she'd found someone who would allow her to.

Caroline made coffee and went back to the door. The cat was gone and Dobry was burning the piled leaves on the far side of the yard, the hose at the ready in case any flames leapt free. A few minutes later, he knocked on the door. "You're all set." She noticed that none of her sons-in-law ever called her anything. She wondered if they would simply call her Busia when the children started to arrive.

"Why don't you come in and have some coffee?" Caroline said. "I want to ask you something."

Dobry wiped his feet and sat down at the kitchen table.

Caroline put his cup down with the bowl of sugar and a spoon. "I was thinking I might get the house painted next summer. Would you be willing to do that? Or know someone I could hire?"

"I'll do it. That's no problem. Save you some money."

"Oh no, I'll pay you."

"No." Dobry shook his head. "You hold on to your money. You never know when you might need it. Rainy day."

When Dobry stood to go, Caroline asked, "Do many children go to the houses in your block for Halloween?"

"I think there's more than there used to be. People feel bad for them. It's the only time of year they get a treat."

"Does Eva make paczki?"

"We didn't get too many children in the apartment. She gave them some coffee cake."

Dobry walked down the back stairs. It had grown nearly dark while he was inside. There were kids shouting a few yards over, on the other side of a chain-link fence. Boys, Caroline could tell, from their posture: jittery, absentminded, backs to the dark. As Dobry mounted his bike, Caroline caught sight of a box and the black body writhing in the boys' hands. She ran across the yard to the fence. The struggling creature cried out while the boys shut the box.

"Get out of there!" she yelled. "I see you! Go away! Leave it!"

"What's the matter?" Dobry jogged up.

"Chase those boys away," she said, pointing. Then hollered, "My son-in-law's coming down there and that cat had better be untouched! You hear me! I'll find you boys!"

The boys ran and Dobry loped over and retrieved the box, which had been taped shut. The firecrackers had fallen out, and lay around the box like a child's drawing of sunrays. Dobry opened the lid and the cat leapt for the bushes. Caroline told Dobry to wait there and went in the house, where she retrieved a can of tuna fish.

They lured the animal out and took him home, where he sprawled beneath the kitchen table, his bright eyes disappearing into the blackness of his vaselike face.

"I didn't think you much cared for cats," Dobry said.

"Well, I don't want to see anything murdered." Caroline wiped the counters with a sponge and ran it under steaming water.

As Dobry opened the back door to go, the cat scuttled into the darkness of the adjacent dining room. "You want me to chase him out?"

"Why not finish up this coffee with me?" Caroline said. "It'll go to waste otherwise. And I've got some cake."

Back at the table, she asked, "Do you know why I came to America?"

Dobry shook his head.

Caroline smiled. "Of course I never told anyone. I never even told Frederick. Can you believe that? Thirty years of marriage." She looked down at her cup, then into the dining room. The cat couldn't be seen in the darkness, but she knew he was there.

When she looked back up, Dobry's face waited like a blank piece of paper—neutral, open, empty.

Silk had disappeared. Her mother asked if she'd seen the cat.

"No, I haven't." Caroline looked under her bed, where the cat sometimes slept. Her mother waited a moment, then left.

Caroline could hear her walking through the house, whispering the cat's name in her slurred speech—"Sik, Sik."

When her mother was still whispering half an hour later, Caroline went to help. Silk hid when Atlas was home because he'd bitten her once, but when he was at the shop with her father, the cat normally sat with Caroline's mother. Sometimes, though, in hot weather she would sleep on the brick floor of the porch off the kitchen or under the parlor sofa. Her mother caught Caroline checking the latter on her hands and knees. "I've looked," she said.

"Perhaps she's in town," Caroline said, "getting mice." Silk liked to go to the docks and catch mice, which she'd leave in her food dish. She never ate them. She was too full from the chicken and fish Caroline's mother gave her.

Caroline suggested other possibilities too. None of them moved her mother to even respond. They sat until dark, skipping the dinner the maid had left in the icebox. Every few minutes her mother would get up and look out the back door. Normally Silk sat on the stoop when she was ready to come back inside.

Caroline's father arrived home later than usual, assembled his dinner and settled in without a word at the dining room table. Caroline could see him through the glass doors, his sharp frame wavy and dissected through the seeded panels and their wooden mullions, his arm almost whole in the shadows cast by the flickering oil lamps.

After dinner her father headed toward his study. He'd just passed the parlor, where Caroline still sat with her mother, when he stopped and she felt, rather than heard, him and Atlas come back toward them. "My dear," he said, his face close to a lamp to be sure her mother could read his lips. "I almost forgot. I think there's something wrong with your cat."

Caroline's mother almost didn't move. It was very close, but she did. Her eyes widened, just a moment, then back to normal. Her father went to his study. Her mother went out to the back porch and there Silk was, wet, limp, a potato sack next to her with a coarse rope fallen loose from her neck.

"Oh no," Caroline moaned.

Her mother whirled as if she'd heard her, but it must have been a motion caught from the corner of her eye. "Sh!" She picked up the dead cat and took her inside as if she were merely damp from the rain.

The next day and the next and the next was like any other in their house. Caroline's father and Atlas left for the shop at eight o'clock sharp. It opened at nine and he liked to be sure the money was in the register, the counters freshly dusted, the front window washed. At home Caroline's mother did needlework while she read in her room.

Sunday arrived, the maid's day off. In the morning they went to church, then her father went to his club. That Sunday, after he left, Caroline could hear her mother in the kitchen, pots being set down, a fire starting. Usually they ate leftovers on Sunday, so Caroline wondered what she was doing, but decided to stay in her room, pretending she couldn't hear.

When her father came home, her mother had already laid the table for dinner. Neither parent had said a word about her marriage all week. Though she hadn't liked any of the men her mother had chosen, and moreover disliked the very process of their choosing, it occurred to

Caroline the alternative to marriage would be staying here, with her parents.

Finished with dinner, her father pushed his chair out from the table.

Her mother tilted her head, drawing out her deaf-softened words. "Before you go..." Her father stopped. The same slight widening of the eyes. Caroline saw in retrospect that he'd already known, just that fast. "I wondered," her mother continued, "did you enjoy dinner?"

Her father looked at his plate, hardly anything of the meat left. Red meat. Unusual for her mother. Caroline looked at her own plate. Half-eaten. Her mother's gone completely. Then she knew too. Atlas never went with her father to the club. He wasn't allowed in.

Caroline ran out the back door, heaving, convulsing, choking on the red chunks of half-digested dog. In the distance, she could hear the slap-slap-slap of the water as the wind moved hard across the river.

WHEN WE'RE INNOCENT

O bi didn't want to go, but he believed there are some things you can't ask someone else to do for you. One of them is cleaning out the apartment your daughter killed herself in.

So he drove, the mood of a flight too cheerful, the planning too optimistic. The rules too absurd. He feared what he might do if a flight attendant instructed him to put his seatback in an upright position. Even the word "trip" angered Obi. He was going somewhere, but he wasn't taking a trip.

He climbed in his car on a Saturday morning and drove for four days at the speed limit, not below or above by even a single mile per hour. The navigation system's mellifluous, vaguely foreign voice, like a Swede who'd grown up with an American parent, kept him company only rarely. At five p.m. on Tuesday, Obi entered the outskirts of Phoenix, the sun a circle of heat on his right cheek until he took Highway 10 and it fell behind, chasing him down the walled expressway. Camelback Mountain, whose name he didn't know or care about, filled the windshield like a giant's boot in his path.

Obi and his wife Karen had been in Phoenix one other time, three years ago, when they drove from Toledo to Columbus, helped Jolly load the U-Haul, then made the slow journey west and south so she could start a new job. Jolly and Karen rode in Jolly's car. Obi drove the truck, a nerve-racking clatter-box with poor sight lines and a soft clutch that brought back the worst days of his life.

As they crossed the country, Obi's girls got off the freeway for fruit stands and flea markets, then caught up and sped past him, smirking kindly at his white-knuckled, right-lane progress. With every mile Obi prayed, and when he finally pulled into the Phoenix U-Haul, he resolved never to make such a grueling trip again. Staring now at the circle of sun in his rearview mirror, Obi realized that during this journey his habitual terror of driving had been entirely absent. His punishment had already been meted out, after all. No need to continue expecting it.

Still, the mountain unnerved him. No matter where he turned, it stood in his sight line as if it had something to say, but preferred to wait at a discreet distance until the time was right. Obi had lived his whole life in northern Ohio, where the sky remained above, as it should, and it took only twenty minutes driving any direction to see the earth's round profile shrink to a line of green, brown, or gold depending on the season. Here, the sky reached down and pulled the land up around the city like a knife raises a scar. That's what mountains were, Obi thought, a cicatrix on the planet. He glanced in each side mirror and saw more of them, thinking for the first time in many days about his own preferences. He preferred fewer reminders of the history of collisions and fractures.

"We need a psychologist sympathetic to rapists."

"I'm not a rapist."

"But that's what the prosecutor's going to be saying, and we need a psychologist who's able to present a more..." The lawyer Brian's father had hired paused, searching for the right word. Brian wished he wouldn't; he wanted to hear the man's disgust. "...a more nuanced portrayal of the situation. What we need is a person who can credibly explain to the jury the difference between..." The lawyer stopped again.

"Fetish and pathology?" Brian offered, clamping the phone between his jaw and his shoulder to lean down and pull out the cuffs of his jeans. They had become squashed inside the corner pocket of a fitted sheet during the dry cycle. Smoothed, the denim looked like rice paper, criss-crossed with fold lines.

"Yes," the lawyer agreed. "The danger in cases like this is that the jury will equate one type of behavior that is"—here he hesitated long enough for Brian to get out the word "aberrant"—"unfamiliar," the lawyer corrected. "We want them to make a clear distinction between two very different types of unfamiliar behavior."

Brian stood by his apartment's patio door. Outside, a metal balcony clung to the lumpy stucco wall. He'd secured a director's chair to the balcony's railing with tie wraps, though the desert wind seemed less inclined to take things away than the gusts in his native Chicago. The frigid blasts off Lake Michigan reminded truck drivers and ad execs that everything has its foe. The desert seemed less foe than abyss; it wouldn't come and get you, but you might fall into it.

"We'll talk more after I get a psych eval lined up." The lawyer cleared his throat and the scratch of a fine-point pen on paper traversed the phone line. Brian stepped to the right for a better view of Jocelyn's car in the parking lot. It hadn't moved. The front left tire remained at an odd angle, nearly ninety degrees to the wheel well.

The lawyer said, "We want to be careful because we don't want the evaluation done until we know what it's going to show."

From his father, also an attorney, Brian recognized this cornerstone of legal theory—only ask questions you already know the answer to. Increasingly, it struck him as a good policy for life in general.

"So I'll call you," the lawyer said. "And don't do anything between now and then, all right? I mean, don't go out drinking or ask anyone on a date. Just daily necessities. Nothing special, all right?"

"Yeah, okay." Brian hung up and went out on the balcony. Over the two years since he'd moved in, the director's chair had faded from navy to a dusty shade the color of old blueberries. He sat down.

Next door, Jocelyn's balcony looked the same as yesterday, and the day before and the one before that. The plants, a group of cacti in staggered-height pots, didn't divulge her absence. Even in containers and with temperatures over a hundred, cacti could go weeks without water. What worried Brian was her red bathing suit. It was Jocelyn's favorite, and it wasn't like her to leave it outside for days at a time, and yet it had been there ever since Brian returned from his last flight. Snagged on the spines of the tallest plant, its bright gold stars had tarnished to brass under the July sun.

Brian listened for movement or voices from her place. Hearing nothing, he leaned over the railing. Through the sheer drape he could make out her armless purple couch and yellow chair. The sun blinded him from the rest.

Brian had been off work for two weeks, having taken a leave of absence from his job as a commercial pilot. Before that he was doing overnights to New York and Detroit, and he couldn't say when he'd last seen Jocelyn, though he did know it was before his arrest.

They'd met at the complex's pool, where they both liked to do laps in the tolerable heat of twilight. Jocelyn swam every day, straight from taping the evening news, while Brian made it only when he wasn't flying. They swam in opposite directions. "This way it doesn't feel like we're racing," she said, squeezing her nose empty of water with her thumb and index finger in a cute, ladylike way. She never acted wary, as he expected her to, because she was on TV and he wasn't. It didn't seem to occur to her she might be the target of weirdos and stalkers. When he pointed this out, she laughed. "You aren't the type, and I'm pretty good at spotting things like that." It was the uniform—captain's hat and double-breasted navy jacket with four gold cuff stripes and six gold buttons. People had to see you in it only one time and they'd put their lives in your hands.

Last year Jocelyn broke her leg and Brian had carried her groceries and laundry and driven her to work while she was still on painkillers and couldn't drive herself. Still hobbling around in one of those black boots, her cast cut down to below the knee, she made him dinner as a thank you. While she cooked, he walked around her living room. She must have noticed his expression because she laughed, a little embarrassed. "I know. It's bright. Turkish monarch moves to Soho."

"I like it," Brian said. "It's a hell of a lot better than tan and turquoise."

On the balcony, mindful of being caught peeping, Brian sat back down. Jocelyn hadn't delivered the news since he'd been off work. If she was on vacation, why hadn't he seen her at the pool, or passed her coming and going? It was possible she'd taken a trip, but why would she leave her suit out? Maybe she'd heard about his trouble and was avoiding him. Maybe she was scared of him.

Under the Phoenix sun, Brian's jeans and long-sleeved shirt felt like a suit of armor sweat-welded to his skin, so he gave up and went inside, to the opposite problem—too-cold air conditioning, the annoying hum of the fan that never turned off. His apartment had come furnished, castoffs from another pilot who moved out to get married. Brown leather sofa with enormous saddlebag arms. A pine Adirondack chair with cushions in the ubiquitous, threatening Navajo pattern of expanding triangles. Scarred pine coffee table. Cut-pile, tan wall-to-wall carpeting and turquoise drapes. Besides toiletries and clothes, the only thing Brian brought with him was the faded director's chair. That ought to make prison a simpler affair.

Taking up a pad which bore the flight carrier's logo at the top and their slogan—*Travel made good again*—across the bottom, Brian sat down on the couch. After thinking a moment, he wrote, *As you might have heard, things haven't been going well for me. I promise, though, I won't bother you if you don't want to be my friend anymore. So I hope to see you around just to say "hi" and be relaxed where you live. Brian.*

And be relaxed where you live? He crossed out that part, reread the note, then copied the edited version onto a fresh sheet of paper, went outside, and walked the ten feet of squeaky metal planks that separated his door from Jocelyn's. As Brian leaned over, ready to work the note into the generous gap between the door and the frame—a gap he counted as another reason he hadn't bought a house here: what kind of craftsman could the desert produce who didn't need to guard against bitter cold, furious hurricanes, or sneaky earthquakes?—the lawyer's admonishment made him pause. *Just the daily necessities.*

Brian straightened up. Maybe Jocelyn had started seeing that guy again, or someone new, and was staying at his place. But wouldn't she have her car there? He raised his hand to knock, then stopped. Even if she wasn't avoiding him, she probably knew about the arrest. She was in the news business, after all, though his story had not garnered enough attention to appear on TV, thank God.

Brian reread the note, went back to his apartment for tape, then left it hanging on Jocelyn's door. If the note disappeared it meant she was safe and he'd let it go. If the note didn't move, he would call. Maybe screw up the courage to knock. If that yielded nothing, he'd have to ask around the complex. But Brian didn't know any other residents. They might not even recognize him. In the desert, where construction of gated communities never stopped, dozens of people transferred from these holding pens to their fake adobe two-cars on the last day of every month.

Brian walked back along the squeaky planks, wondering how long until his father called to find out what the lawyer had said.

Jolly for Jocelyn. The nickname originated in infancy or toddlerhood and stuck. Obi didn't remember why. As a child she wasn't particularly jolly, but she wasn't glum either.

After the medical examiner had cleared her body for burial, they flew Jolly home. "We'll bump you over and put her where you were going to go," Karen said, referring to Obi's burial plot as if it were a place setting. "That way Jolly can be between us." She nodded at this plan to protect their daughter in death as they hadn't in life.

Karen also made plans to clean out Jolly's apartment, booking them a hotel in Phoenix, but when Obi insisted on driving instead of flying, she refused to go. "I can't sit in a car for four days. I have to get this over with."

Karen preferred to chew her pain hard and swallow it quickly, while Obi let it dissolve on his tongue, the bitter flavor stored permanently, he feared, in every taste bud.

At the hotel, he signed the credit-card receipt, guessing Karen hadn't even looked at the room rate. Five hundred a night. He handed the signed charge slip to the clerk, fighting the urge to offer more, all the cash in his wallet, everything in their checking account. He might have handed over their 401(k)s if he'd known how. The woman, a brunette in a cheap red suit coat and navy blue pants, directed him with a polished finger down the hall. He carried his bag up four flights, suddenly repelled by the thought of elevators.

In the room, undyed hemp drapes framed the bright sky and the insistent mountain. Obi shut the drapes, dimmed the lights, took the coverlet—quilted squares of expanding triangles in rust and turquoise—off the bed, stuffed it in the closet, and turned on CNN, knowing it would sound the same in Phoenix as it did in Toledo. He felt dizzy because he hadn't drunk anything yet today, so he opened the warm bottle of water he'd bought in New Mexico, drank it in two long gulps, used the bathroom, washed up, and left for Jolly's place, unwilling to face going to sleep tonight without this part over.

The method: pills. The reason: no one knew. Not her GP, who, when Jolly shattered her leg falling down a flight of stairs, had prescribed the narcotics she overdosed on. Not the medical examiner, who'd looked for evidence of injuries on her body to suggest an abusive relationship or foul play. Not the police, who claimed to have interviewed all her friends and colleagues. Who had supposedly searched her apartment. They claimed there was no note. Obi didn't believe them. He would find something. They just didn't know how to look. During the long, quiet days on the highway, he had imagined a dozen types of code she could have used, from food arrangements in the cupboard to highlighted passages in the messy stacks of romance novels she always had around.

On the way from the hotel to her apartment, Obi's cell rang. Normally he didn't answer while driving, but he'd just stopped for a red light and the phone lay at hand on the passenger seat.

"How close are you?" Karen asked.

"I checked into the hotel. I'm on my way there right now."

"You're in the car?" Karen knew his rules. Obi's real name was Ken, but in college, where they met, she'd dubbed him Obi after Obi-Wan Kenobi. "You're just so damn good."

He'd tutored her in math, dug her car out of snowdrifts, driven her to class when it rained and, that first summer, turned down a chance to camp at Yellowstone in order to volunteer on Habitat houses. Nowadays, only strangers called him Ken.

He explained to Karen he was at a red light. "I can't talk long."

"Okay," she intoned, as if he'd reported disarming one bomb of several.

"I'll call you later."

"Yes," she agreed in that tone again.

He could see her sitting at the kitchen table with the phone in her hand, anxious for the all-clear. "It'll be a while."

"I know."

"He's looking for a psychologist sympathetic to rapists," Brian said. It was past six. He sat at the kitchen table, a two-person, glass-topped rattan outfit against the kitchen's end wall, his back to the apocalyptic

Indian upholstery, to the balcony and to the blank, burning sky. The days here stretched past the breaking point. No wonder these Indians never wove a circle. Everything had to imply not the sun, but its rays.

"I don't know anybody down there," his father said. "Do you? Any contacts in that world?"

"Not really."

"Well, that's what Chris is for." The lawyer. "How you doing on money?"

Brian thought he could hear his father's checkbook opening. It touched him. "No, Dad, I've got plenty. I save most of every paycheck."

"Good."

A pause allowed Brian time to think of the joke. "Except for what I spend on ads."

"You don't have an ad in now, do you?"

"I was joking."

"Yeah, okay, good."

"Dad, I'm sorry about this."

"Cool it on the ads, all right. We'll take care of it, just…" A brief pause, then his father said, "I have to go. I got a call coming in."

Brian admired his father's restraint. He'd never asked why Brian had to get his kicks by paying a girl to clean his apartment naked, though Brian felt sure his father's own sexual yearnings could be satisfied without money changing hands, unless you counted hundred-dollar-a-plate restaurants. In the twenty years since Brian's mother died, his father had dated several lovely women before marrying Carol, a divorced pediatrician whose two kids he helped get into Loyola. At Christmas her kids bought gifts for Brian's father at the local mall which were more creative and apt than what Brian picked up on his flights to Paris and London.

He wondered what his father had told his other family about the arrest. That's how Brian thought of Carol and her son and daughter, even though they had a good relationship with Carol's ex and had lived with his own father for only a few years of high school.

It was possible, even likely, Brian's father hadn't told them anything. In front of Brian, he'd treated the arrest for rape—technically vaginal penetration with a digit, in this case his finger—with a lawyer's professional indifference. The details—that Brian's ad had specified if the girl came to the job interview without a bra, he'd give her thirty dollars; without panties, fifty dollars—he'd taken in dispassionately, explaining that what mattered most was contact—Brian touching the girl's genitalia—vs. penetration—his finger entering, however briefly or shallowly, her vagina.

"So when you're talking to Chris, this is what you keep in mind. Contact gets you a year. Penetration, you're looking at five to fourteen." Guilt or innocence never came up. Maybe his father took one or the other for granted. Brian couldn't tell.

It was nearly time for the news, so Brian turned on the TV. If Jocelyn was at the desk, he would assume she wanted nothing to do with him and go take the note off her door, saving himself another irrevocable humiliation.

Jolly's apartment complex wrapped a large asphalt lot. The three buildings had no red-tiled roof or rounded eave; their Spanish style relied entirely on the stucco, painted a dirty yellow and punctuated by metal balconies whose railings reflected the sun in blinding shards like knife blades.

Who kills themselves in the summer? Someone who lives in Phoenix, Obi realized. If she'd lived at home his daughter would be alive. No one kills themselves during July in Toledo, Ohio. There's January, February, March, and most of April for that. In July there is sun, and such a shame to waste it. But in the desert, no matter how many Targets and Costcos you build, how many fluorocarbons the air conditioners pump into the atmosphere, the biggest star remains a malevolence.

Star. Jolly had seemed like one, smart and beautiful, blond hair from somewhere in the family they couldn't identify. Blue eyes from grandparents who hadn't managed to give them to either him or Karen. Jolly majored in journalism at Ohio State, took a job in Columbus, then the promotion to Sun City. Being a newscaster wasn't the same as acting, though Obi had feared it, too, would deliver an unnatural life, your face known by thousands whose names you never heard. So that was something else he had to do: find out whether things were going well at Jolly's station.

The other cause Obi planned to investigate was the boyfriend they'd never met, a first-generation Lebanese guy Jolly had been on and off with for a year. Obi and Karen considered Middle Eastern men sexist and authoritarian. They worried Jolly would get taken advantage of. Obi had been able to give only the guy's first name—Sam—to the police, and realized as he did that even that was most likely just a nickname, some truncated, Americanized version of the truth. They tracked him down anyway, through a coworker at Jolly's station. Sam claimed he hadn't seen Jolly for over two months. A hundred witnesses and a paper trail put him in Sonoma at a wedding the day she died.

In the parking lot, Obi took a stack of flat boxes out of the trunk along with garbage bags and a roll of packing tape. Karen had instructed him to send Jolly's clothes and furniture to charity but to bring home anything personal, like letters, diaries, financials, jewelry, and trip mementos. To make sure he didn't make a mistake, she'd written a list. He could throw out Jolly's toothpaste and toothbrush, but he should bring back her makeup, her hairbrushes, and her perfume. He didn't ask why. These were the things that had littered the bathroom counter for years, that her mother always complained she didn't clean up.

Struggling with the boxes—too awkward to carry horizontally, yet slipping against one another when he tried to grip them in a vertical stack—Obi made his way across the lot and up the three flights of stairs to Jolly's apartment. The day he moved her in, after the fifth climb up, he'd said, "I'm too old for this schlep. Next time you can hire movers like the rest of us grown-ups."

Jolly kissed him on the cheek and handed him a lemonade. "You're doing fine for a chubby schoolteacher."

At her door Obi propped the boxes against the walkway's railing and from his pocket fished out the keys the police had mailed. They still bore the tag with the evidence number. Sliding them into the lock, he looked up to see a note taped to the door. Her name on the outside was written in a masculine hand—large and messy, with alternately blocky and jagged lettering. Whoever put it here did so after the police had come and gone or they would have taken it. Obi stared a long moment. Would there be fingerprints? What if he smudged them? *No crime,* Obi reminded himself. *No crime had been committed.*

He looked at the boxes, then at the door handle and the dangling keys, trying to fight the feeling coming up from his knees. It entered his stomach, then his chest. As it invaded his throat, Obi sunk to a kneel, hands pressed against the apartment door. Grief took his breath away, then returned it in gulping sobs. Obi let his forehead fall with a clunk against the metal door, its heat a blank brand, and beat his palms against the beige indifference, cries turning to shrieks like a baby seal.

"Excuse me?" a deep voice said.

Obi looked up. A man stood there, not swarthy, but dark enough to be Lebanese. He'd come out of the neighboring apartment. "You!" Obi said, pushing himself to a stand. He tore the note from the door. "Is this yours?"

"Yes," the man said.

Obi started forward. The man flinched, features puckered as if ready to take a hit. Obi stopped. "What's your name?"

The man opened his eyes. "Brian."

Obi unfolded the note and read it. "Why wouldn't she be your friend?" he snapped.

"What?"

Obi flapped the note at him violently. "What did you do to her?"

"Nothing," Brian said. "I never did anything."

Obi took Brian in. He wore socks, jeans, and a long-sleeved shirt. "Why are you dressed like that? It's hot. You aren't supposed to be dressed like that." Though Obi himself was dressed like that.

"Air conditioning," Brian said. He looked suspicious. "Who are you? How do you know Jocelyn?"

The yelp broke from Obi again and he shook the note in the air. "Did you kill her!" he shouted. "Did you kill my Jolly?"

The man's expression was enough to exonerate him. "Kill her?"

Obi leaned on the wall, pressing hard against the jagged stucco.

Brian whispered, "Somebody...killed her?"

Obi bleated, "I loved her. I loved her," and covered his face with his hand.

There was a long pause before Brian said, "You must be her father."

Obi nodded.

"Come into my place. Come in here for just a minute."

The man's apartment hummed with cool. Obi felt as if his execution had been stayed.

"Will you sit down?"

Obi looked at the furniture. "Here," Brian said, fetching one of the rope-backed rattan chairs from the kitchen. Obi sat facing the living room, like part of an audience, and thought of the days when Jolly put on shows for them. Dances, skits, sometimes readings of stories about princesses and rocket ships.

Brian sat on the edge of the coffee table, his folded hands clamped between his big knees. Despite his size, he looked incapable of hurting someone, which disappointed Obi.

"I don't understand." He shook his head. "I just watched her newscast and they didn't say anything."

Obi ground his fists into his eye sockets. "I'm supposed to clean out the apartment. Her mother is waiting."

"In the car?"

"Ohio."

Several seconds passed. Obi was looking at the floor. "I was supposed to find out why. Did they say anything about why?"

"The news?"

"Yes, it was her station, wasn't it?" Obi looked up with a glazed, desperate hope in his eyes.

"They didn't say anything, sir."

"There's got to be a reason, you idiot!"

"Right, right," Brian agreed. "Do they know who did it?"

Obi looked at him with disgust. "Jolly did it."

"Jolly?"

"The police are telling us Jolly killed herself," Obi said, his voice accusing.

Brian shook his head. "She wouldn't do that."

Obi nodded, his tone now beseeching. "That's what I said. She had no reason to do that. There has to be a reason." The sun had sunk near the horizon. It shone straight across the room, a hot spot on the far wall above the kitchen table. Its careless light made the tears at the edge of Brian's lashes glisten.

"So you knew her?" Obi asked.

Brian shrugged. "I moved down from Chicago for my job. We both liked to swim at night, and when she hurt her leg, I helped her get around a little."

"Are you Lebanese?"

"No, sir. Italian and German, a little Greek. Maybe some Russian. Nobody remembers exactly."

Obi looked around the place. "Did the police talk to you?"

"The police?"

Obi explained about the investigation, the lack of a note. "They said they talked to everyone who knew her." His voice had grown suspicious again.

"They probably did look for me. I'm a pilot, though, and I've been out of town." Brian spoke like a job applicant, striving to explain himself without giving the impression he thought his personal views or circumstances worthy of discussion.

"They should have left you a note, or a phone message. Idiots!" Obi shook his head. "I knew they had missed something."

"I'm sorry. I wish I could help. I don't know why..." Brian raised his hands in a helpless gesture. "Can I do something? You're hot. How about a drink?"

Obi shook his head. "I'm supposed to pack up her things and bring them home."

"Do you want some help?"

Next to Brian on the coffee table were the TV remote, the pad and pen he'd used to write the note, and the first draft. Obi narrowed his eyes. Brian picked up the note and casually crumpled it, as if he were just keeping his hands busy.

"Give me that."

Brian reluctantly extended the paper. "It's stupid."

Obi read the note. "Why wouldn't she be relaxed here?"

"I got in some trouble recently. It was reported in the papers. I thought maybe that's why I hadn't seen her around since I've been off work. I thought she heard about my trouble and was staying away from me. I didn't want her to feel like she had to avoid me. I wanted her to know I wasn't going to bother her."

"Drugs?"

"No, sir."

"Stealing?"

"No, sir."

Obi examined him a moment. "Rape?"

Brian looked down and squeezed his folded hands together until it hurt. "Yes, sir."

"Well, aren't you going to tell me you aren't guilty?" Obi's tone implied this would be futile.

"I don't know for sure."

"You don't know?" Obi sneered.

Brian shook his head. "I really don't."

"We always know when we're guilty. Were you drunk?"

"No, sir."

"Were you in the room with the woman? I assume it's a woman?"

"Yes, sir."

A long moment of silence passed before Obi asked, "Why did you scratch out that part about being relaxed?"

"I thought she might think it was dumb, or that I was sort of, like, threatening her. Like when you say the opposite of what you mean to make someone uncomfortable. I wanted to be plain. Not misunderstood."

"Did the girl, that other girl, misunderstand?"

"Maybe. Maybe I misunderstood."

"You better tell me exactly what happened." Obi sounded like the police.

"I put an ad on Craigslist." Brian never planned to do anything the woman didn't want. "If I did, why would I place an ad? Or meet her here, where I live?"

Obi leaned forward and nodded. "Okay, yes. But what did you want from this girl?"

No one had asked Brian this question, and until this moment he would have said he didn't want anyone to, but now that someone had, he wanted to answer.

Brian described that afternoon. It had been a little like using an escort service, except because the girl wasn't a professional, that had made it better and more difficult at the same time.

Obi nodded. "Yes."

When she sat with her legs apart to show Brian she hadn't worn any panties, he'd reached up slowly and she'd had plenty of time to close her legs or tell him to stop. He couldn't say for sure what he'd touched. "It just made me so happy that she trusted me."

Obi turned toward the patio door.

"Sir?" Brian asked. "Sir? Do you believe me?"

Obi was sixteen, barely three months into his license, when he ran a red light, T-boning Gerald Sorens, a paunchy father of four with a bumper sticker across his rear window. *Everything we see is a shadow cast by what we don't see.* Forty years later he still couldn't account for it. He hadn't been speeding or drunk or fiddling with the radio or talking on a cell phone. There were no cell phones back then. It was broad daylight, but the sun was at his back. Despite all this, Gerald Sorens died on a gurney in the middle of the intersection, five police cars directing traffic around him while Obi knelt in the plastic shards of shattered headlights, praying.

"Sir?" Brian asked again. "Did you hear me?"

Obi looked down at the note. "It's when we're innocent that we're confused." Then he smoothed the rough draft and the edited version he'd pulled off Jolly's door over his knee, one on top of the other, folded them together into a perfect square and put them in his pocket. He and Brian sat in silence, staring at the sand-colored carpet. Neither man wore a watch and there were no visible clocks, no audible ticking, nothing at all to mark time, not even the sun, which shone fixedly on the opposite wall like a bare bulb. Time made no difference now. If you cannot understand or be understood, if you cannot make amends, what good are the hours and the days and the weeks?

But Karen was waiting. Obi made himself speak up. "I think they missed something. Jolly must have left a note. She had to have left something."

"Did they look at her computer? Emails and stuff?"

Obi brightened. "They said they did, but maybe not. Or they didn't understand."

Brian went next door and brought back Jolly's laptop. In a few seconds he had it booted up and he'd opened her emails. Sitting at the table, they analyzed each message, memo, and PowerPoint presentation for hidden meaning. Finding nothing by way of explanation, Obi slumped in his chair. "I thought for sure there'd be something."

"I'm sorry," Brian said.

"If not a note, then a clue. Something."

"Maybe it's in code. Something the police wouldn't notice."

Obi looked at him strangely.

"That's dumb. Sorry. I watch too much TV."

"No, that's what I thought. That she might have left a code."

They sat for several more seconds considering this until Brian said, "What if I taped her place? You know, before you touch anything, I'll video it exactly as she left it. Then you can study it all you want."

"You have a camera?"

Karen kept saying she wished they'd bought a camera so they would have video of Jolly, but Obi was secretly glad they didn't. He felt pretty sure he wouldn't make it if he had to watch her or hear her voice.

Brian retrieved the camera from a black bag under the TV.

"Don't touch anything," Obi said. "Just tape."

"Yes, sir. I got it."

Brian unlocked Jolly's door and went in, leaving it wide open. From where Obi stood, in the doorway of Brian's apartment, he could see a trapezoid of beige wall that could have belonged to anybody.

Brian was gone several minutes. Occasionally he would call out what he was doing. "I'm in the kitchen, looking in the dishwasher." When he was done, he and Obi sat side by side on the edge of the coffee table and watched the playback over the TV. Repeatedly, they freeze-framed the video to discuss the arrangement of objects—how book titles might be combined to spell out a message, if seemingly innocuous bills and shopping lists could have hidden meaning. They discussed what significance there could be to Jolly having no medicine of any sort in the house except the Percocet she'd overdosed on. No Tylenol or Advil, no NyQuil or Sudafed or Pepto-Bismol. While they dissected and discussed, writing notes and rewinding the tape a hundred times, the sun finally gave up for the day. At some point one of them turned on a light.

"Sir, I don't think there's anything here," Brian said. They were seated across from each other on the floor, the notepad from the airline disassembled, its pages scattered on the coffee table and covered with anagrams of the words Jolly left behind via cereal boxes and shopping lists.

The feeling made its way from Obi's knees to his chest again and he began to sob. "What am I going to tell her mother?" he bleated, bowing his head and pinching the bridge of his nose until his knuckles went white. "She had to have a reason."

"Tell her it was my fault," Brian said. "Tell her Jolly lived next door to a depraved soul unworthy of her, and if he'd only been a better man, Jolly would still be here."

Obi looked up, sobs still shaking his shoulders.

"Tell her it was me, that I'm the one to blame," Brian repeated.

Obi sucked in his breath several times. When his shoulders finally went still, he whispered, "Can you do me one more favor?"

"Of course."

"Can you bring me Jolly's things?"

Brian nodded. Obi gave him the list and one by one he carried Jolly's things to her father. Her hairbrush. The tarnished silver spoon ring Karen's brother had made. Her college diploma. Her key ring with the Siamese cat that looked like the cat she had in grade school. A box of warranty cards, receipts, and instructions he'd already videotaped and dissected for secret meaning. Perfume bottles and a tray filled with lipsticks and blushes. Old yearbooks and greeting cards. A swimming trophy from high school. A camera, a boom box, and an iPod. A stuffed frog she'd carried everywhere until she was seven.

When Obi satisfied himself that everything on Karen's bring-home list had been collected, he sent Brian back to pack the remaining things for charity. At three a.m. Brian touched his shoulder. Obi had fallen asleep on the floor in front of the balcony door, which looked like the black mouth of a deep cave.

"Sir? Sir? You want to lie on the couch?"

"Is it all done?"

"Yes, sir, it's done."

Obi struggled to a stand, stiff from lying on the thin carpet. Outside the heat sat waiting, even without its sun. Brian stayed in his own place while Obi went over to Jolly's.

A neat line of boxes along one wall. Across the room a purple couch and yellow chair, a silver coffee table, sheer drapes layered below velvet side panels, an enormous mirror framed with black glass. Somehow, in his zeal to find the smallest clue, Obi had not noticed the furniture itself on the videotape. It wasn't what Jolly had brought from Columbus. That had been a profusion of flowered slipcovers and tables in need of a fresh coat of paint, a rickety coatrack made of old canes lashed together with twine and picture frames whose original life had been as racket presses. Obi opened the empty cupboards one by one, then the medicine cabinet and the closets. He made himself glance at the bed, but it was stripped bare, a mattress on a metal frame that could have belonged to anyone, to a complete stranger.

Movement on the balcony caught his eye and Obi rushed over to the dark glass, flipped the lock and pushed open the door, for a crazy moment thinking Jolly had been out there all along. Brian was leaning over the railing of his balcony, the hook of an old-fashioned umbrella employed midair to snatch a red bikini from the spines of a potted cactus. Looking up at Obi, Brian lost his balance and for a moment dipped forward like a gymnast on the uneven bars. Obi lunged to catch him as the umbrella dropped three floors, its metal a sharp crack on the stone garden below. Brian righted himself. He and Obi looked at the suit, still snagged on the cactus.

"Sorry," Brian said. "I didn't want to leave it there."

Obi picked up the bikini's top and examined it in the light from the living room. Dangling cords connected two small red triangles decorated with gold stars. It didn't seem like clothing at all. Jolly swam in a one-piece blue Speedo with wide shoulder straps. Obi tossed the bikini across the gap to Brian. "This is nothing like Jolly. I don't think it belongs to her."

Brian folded the suit carefully into a single neat triangle like a flag. "Yes, sir. I'll take care of it."

Obi turned away. Now he could go home. Jolly didn't live here anymore.

HALF-LIFE

Sarah didn't apply for the job with a plan. She just wanted in.

Melanie Cuppernell was returning to work as a third-grade teacher and needed a nanny for ten-month-old Grayson and almost five-year-old Beatrice, who'd missed the kindergarten cutoff. "You'll have to keep her entertained." Melanie laughed. "And let me tell you, that's no easy task."

During the interview in a bright room with yellow sofas and paintings thick with color, Melanie asked questions Sarah could answer truthfully. Where was she from? Here. Age? Twenty-two. How long had she nannied for Melanie's friend Rachel? Two years. How long had she worked at the daycare before that? Two years. Melanie didn't ask about her family, so there'd been no need for lies, though Sarah had a string prepared because Nancy, the social worker assigned to her when she aged out, had warned against telling employers Sarah grew up in foster care. "Some people see it as a negative."

If asked, Sarah claimed her father died when she was two and her mother, a retired secretary, lived in Florida. This narrative had satisfied Rachel and it would satisfy Melanie. Sarah had refined it to such simplicity, it was impossible to forget. To such banality, no one ever wanted more. If she ever married, Sarah's husband might want more, but husbands, like other family, were bestowed by the universe, and so far the universe had not been all that forthcoming.

At the end of the interview, Sarah affected a lighthearted voice and asked, "So, are you related to Judge Cuppernell?"

"He's my dad," Melanie said. "Do you know him?"

Sarah shook her head. "Just the name." Judges' names appeared in the newspaper and on yard signs every few years. Sarah wasn't worried about her own name being recognized. Melanie would have no reason to know it and the Judge, if he remembered, which seemed unlikely, would probably dismiss it as coincidence. Before scheduling the interview, Sarah had gone to the library and checked. There were nine Sarah Andersons in Toledo's white pages and so many on Facebook the computer crashed trying to load them all.

As Melanie backs out of the driveway that first morning, the first time Sarah is alone with the children, Beatrice looks at her with trusting eyes. "What do you want to do?" Her voice rides high with anticipation.

"Nothing," Sarah says, trying out cruelty.

"Well, we have to do something. That's what Mommy hired you for."

Melanie had not lied when she called the girl precocious.

Weekdays Sarah arrives at seven thirty, by which time Melanie has left for school and her husband Aaron stands by the front door, tapping at his phone. Every day he says, "Bea's in the kitchen and the baby's up, I think," until one morning Sarah says it before he can and after that Aaron smiles and salutes her as they pass in the foyer. "It's all yours, Captain."

She imposes a schedule similar to the daycare. "It will get you ready for kindergarten."

Beatrice balks. "I do what I want."

"Not anymore."

Grayson waits, half awake, in his crib. Diaper change, face wash, breakfast, tooth brushing, clothes, then a walk, though Sarah allows a little variation here. Bea can take her bike or scooter. Snack time, reading time, playtime, lunchtime, nap time (Grayson) and craft time (Bea), TV time, another walk, song time, snack time (kids) and cooking time (Sarah). At Rachel's cooking was both harder—her twin infants liked to be held a lot—and easier—unlike Bea, the babies never questioned why there were two dirty pans but only one loaf of banana bread.

Sarah makes spaghetti because no one counts pasta strands. She makes casseroles because women like Rachel and Melanie don't have plans for the leftover ham or the vulnerable half of last night's green pepper. When Sarah tells Melanie, "Just warm it up, it's all baked," Melanie, like Rachel, doesn't notice the ragged edge of the casserole, which attests to its having been cut and the larger portion transferred from the 9x12 to the 9x9 bakeware.

"You're such a good cook!" Melanie exclaims instead. "I can't believe what you make out of stuff I throw away."

"My mom taught me." It's one of the few true things she's ever revealed about her mother, who made delicious meals out of things Sarah couldn't name, like a blade-shaped lettuce she put in a pan with black water. One time Sarah tried describing the black water's taste to a stocker at the grocery store, but the woman looked at her like she was nuts. Embarrassed, Sarah switched stores, afraid to run into her again. Months later, at Rachel's, she sniffed the contents of a brown bottle on the counter. Balsamic vinegar. A taste confirmed: this is what her mother cooked the lettuce in.

Week four, Thursday afternoon. While Grayson is napping and Beatrice is in the basement making Play-Doh cupcakes, Sarah sneaks out, locking the door to make it appear as though she's still in the house, then stands behind the garage knee-deep in yard clippings and mounds of white-veined dirt dislodged from last year's pots. Disturbed by Sarah's footsteps, bees emerge from beneath one of the mounds and draw their turbulent pattern in the air. Sarah takes several steps away and regards the lurch of her watch's second hand. One minute. Two.

It takes only three and a half minutes. Three and a half lousy minutes!

Beatrice's muted voice hollers Sarah's name, the "ah" long and echoing, while the bees slowly retract into their nest. As the minutes grind on, Sarah strains to detect any change in the child's tone, but fear is not discernible in so muffled a version. Beatrice doesn't come out, or even open the back door, and Sarah remembers how it is to be a child, the unspoken boundary between your life and out there. Your apartment. Your mom. Your kitchen table. You do not cross that boundary alone, and no one has to tell you that. Sarah's mother never told her. She just knew: you wait.

Twenty minutes and the shouting has stopped. The feeling in Sarah's stomach is both familiar and strange. A memory she had not remembered until now.

She slips from behind the garage, forces herself to sidle past the climbing rose she will later learn Melanie's mother planted forty years ago. The Judge's wife comes by several times a year to fertilize and trim the plant, worrying over its blooms because Melanie lacks a green thumb.

Sarah opens the door and hears Grayson crying, finds the two of them in his room. Beatrice has somehow gotten her brother out of the crib and sits with him on the floor, paging through his favorite book, her high-pitched voice wavering through tears, trying to interest him in what the zebra is going to do about his stripes.

When Sarah appears, instead of rushing to her, Bea levels a knowing, angry look. "I thought you left."

"I just went outside a minute." Sarah sits down cross-legged and takes the baby, rocking him against her chest, his feet anchored in the flesh of her folded thighs. "You should have come out."

"Gray was crying."

Sarah scowls. "Did you wake him up?"

Beatrice shakes her head. "He was crying and you weren't here. I had to get him out of his crib."

"Did you drop him?"

"He was crying because you left."

Ah, Sarah thinks. Smart girl. Knows how to turn things around. But so does Sarah. "He was crying because you panicked. I'm gone a few minutes and you panic."

"I didn't panic." Beatrice looks both defiant and ashamed.

"I was just in the backyard. Did you even look out the window?"

Pause. "Yes. You weren't there."

She's lying, yet it's Bea's truth now. The narrative she will continue to tell herself. And her mother probably. Sarah's chest tightens again. By four p.m. today she needs a more compelling narrative for Bea to pass along.

The narrative she provides is pain and pleasure.

Grayson sits in his highchair, swirling fingers in the crushed, seedy remains of raspberries, which he eats by the carton, as if they weren't a dollar an ounce. It seems unlikely, but Sarah remembers picking raspberries with her mother. Unlikely because they had no car, so they must have gone with a friend. Sarah remembers only a few first names. Barb. Joan. Mindy. Without last names, there is no way to claw back the years.

With Bea back at her Play-Doh bakery, Sarah takes the baby outside and sets him near the bees' nest, glancing around to be sure she's unobserved before prodding it with a stick. When several bees emerge, she traps two in a glass jar laced with sugar water, then slides the lid of the jar away and presses its mouth against Grayson's bare back, tapping hard on the bottom to startle the bees. To her surprise it works and one of the bees stings the baby. He lets out a wail that tumbles into gulping sobs.

Sarah pulls out the stinger, then rubs the wound, pressing hard enough to distract the nerves. "Oh, I'm sorry. I'm sorry," she tells the baby. "I had to do it. I had to."

Inside she shows Beatrice. "Stay away from the back of the garage. There's a bees' nest in the ground. One of them stung your brother." The red circle with its center puncture has already bloomed to two inches. While Grayson wails and Beatrice sits beside him singing, "It'll be okay, it'll be okay, my baby," Sarah makes an ice pack and applies it to the baby's back.

Slowly, his crying diminishes and Sarah turns to Beatrice. "Do you want to make some real cupcakes?"

"It took no time at all to spot him," Melanie tells Sarah.

They're in the kitchen, Sarah washing frosting fingerprints from the cupboards while Melanie pretends to make headway on the counters. Long smears mixed with sprinkles and Red Hots—which Beatrice inexplicably adores—Pollock the white marble, but Melanie is only pinching individual candies, making no real progress, in an attempt to protect her silk blouse.

Bea greeted her mother nearly quivering with excitement—"Grayson almost died!"—and Sarah quickly intervened.

"A bee stung him. You have a big nest in the backyard. I iced the spot and watched him carefully. He had no trouble breathing, and the swelling was very slight. I gave him a dose of Tylenol for the pain."

Melanie is pleased at her handling of the crisis. "I knew you were the one for us."

Now Grayson is playing with some pots and plastic spatulas, Bea has taken herself off and Sarah knows she's gotten away with it. There will be no mention of her disappearance. She applies another squirt of soap to the sponge and waves Melanie off.

From the safety of a counter stool, Melanie continues her story about a student. "He's one of my Ethans." There are three in her class, the name's popularity having surged at the turn of the millennium. Melanie considered it herself, she tells Sarah, but aware of name contamination—

every teacher develops strong associations with previous students that ruin otherwise good names—she chose Grayson instead. "Because it's my dad's name, I knew I'd always love it."

Ethan K. is new at school and Melanie declares, "He's going to be my problem kid."

She ticks off the "flags" she found in his file. #1: He lives in an apartment on Moss Road. #2: No father listed. #3: Only one emergency contact listed, a man's name, and under "Relationship" it says "friend."

"Today I kept him in because he's behind in language, so I have him there trying to squeeze out a paragraph about his summer, and I find out he's alone all the time. His mother 'works.'" Melanie does air quotes. "Okay, so has she ever heard of a babysitter? Or summer camp? I asked what he did all day and he says he plays his Nintendo DS. Lovely, right? No wonder he can barely eke out an English sentence. And he eats peanut butter sandwiches every day for lunch."

"They're filling, and cheap."

"Right." Melanie rolls her eyes.

As she details the many angry outbursts Ethan K. has had in the weeks since school started, Sarah realizes it could have been her fourth-grade teacher, Mrs. Schuppe, who reported her mother. She'd always assumed it was the neighbor, Mrs. Zabik, because she left the door to her apartment open, would have seen Sarah's mother coming and going, and her mother had often warned Sarah not to give Mrs. Zabik any information. "Anything you say can and will be held against you."

But what about Mrs. Schuppe and the teachers before her? They knew of all those days missed, heard her mother's excuses. A rash. A doctor's appointment. A family reunion. Or maybe Sarah herself told Mrs. Schuppe something incriminating. Listening to Melanie, she learns again what she already knew: everywhere, by everyone, things can and will be held against you. Things you never even thought to hide, like the street you live on or the emergency contact on your school form. It could have been something as simple as that which brought Sarah to the attention of Judge Grayson Cuppernell.

Four bedrooms. Eight closets. Three bathrooms. A basement storage room full of boxes.

Sarah makes her way through it all during TV time, when the kids are too captivated by Disney to notice her whereabouts. In the hollowed-out pages of a book about the Lewis and Clark expedition she finds a pair of diamond earrings and a couple of old-looking pieces of jewelry—a pin and an engagement ring—all of which she leaves untouched. In the master closet in a shoebox under other shoeboxes she finds a blue rubber dildo. She knows instinctively what it's for, but not what it means. Does Aaron know it's here? Is it normal to have such a thing? Sarah washes her hands.

Their medicine cabinet conceals the usual supplies—tampons, toothpaste, fungus cream, Benadryl, Advil—plus something called Zovirax, which Sarah looks up on Wikipedia using Melanie's computer. Usually Wikipedia sends her mind dodging and weaving in too many directions, one article pushing her forward to a web of a hundred more, until she quits not because she understands, but because she never will.

In this case, though, it's only two links to the answer: a picture of the familiar cluster of blisters on the edge of a lip. They bloom on Sarah's every three or four months.

That evening Sarah rides her bike to the drugstore, looks on the shelves, then goes up to the pharmacy counter.

"You need a script," the pharmacist says.

Sarah assumes she can get one at the free clinic. "How much is it? I don't have insurance."

The pharmacist taps at the computer. "A hundred and fifty."

"Dollars?"

"I know. It's expensive. Have you tried the new exchanges?" The pharmacist explains Obamacare.

It sounds like an innocent enough trade: information for medicine. But the government took her mother and gave her nothing. She is reluctant to exchange with them again.

The next day Sarah puts the Zovirax from Melanie's medicine cabinet in her pocket. It is a very small piece, she figures, of what this family owes her.

Wednesday, two p.m., she announces she's going to the neighbor's for an egg.

"You can't," Bea says. "Grayson is sleeping."

"You'll stay here and watch him."

"I can't do that." Bea flashes a big grin. She thinks Sarah is kidding.

"Sure you can. Just sit here and wait. If he cries, go upstairs and talk to him. He won't, though. I'll be back in a bit."

"What's a bit?"

"Ten minutes," Sarah says.

Bea looks at the big grandfather clock she can't read. "I want to go with you."

"You'll be fine here. You have to stop panicking about being alone. It's no big deal. I was alone all the time at your age."

"You were?"

"Yeah, sometimes overnight." Sarah stops herself from saying more, in case Bea repeats this to Melanie.

"Okay." Bea sits down on the couch and crosses her legs, her tiny hands cupping her tiny knee.

Outside Sarah stands in the bushes next to a window sneaking looks into the living room, where Bea sits rigidly, glancing repeatedly at the clock. After two minutes, she looks at the TV remote lying on the end table. House rules: no more than two hours a day, and that's reserved for an hour after nap time and an hour after dinner, for Melanie and Aaron to grab some quiet time.

At Bea's age, Sarah watched a lot of TV because TV hours are different. Faster. Fuller. They make it easy to pretend your mother is in her room napping and they count the day for you. When the shows about evil twins and men saving women from kidnappers come on, it's lunchtime. The news: dinnertime. Shows with men on a stage telling jokes: bedtime.

Very slowly, as if Bea is afraid the remote will bite her, she picks it up and turns on the set. It springs to life with a happy brown-haired woman talking about how to grow a vegetable garden. Bea taps at the remote until *Tom and Jerry* appears, then scoots back on the couch and relaxes.

Good girl, Sarah thinks. These are the things you have to learn.

She thought she would know him. Only now does she realize she's been picturing his robes, his desk, the great seal of the state of Ohio behind him, but not the man himself.

He's short, 5'7" or 8", her eye level. His right cheek is mottled light and dark in large, irregularly shaped patches and she knows instinctively this is a disease or defect of some kind. It will get worse. Do they hurt? No, she decides. Maybe unsightly, even embarrassing, but they do not cause physical pain.

"Hi, I'm Melanie's dad. Did she tell you I was coming by?"

Sarah eyes the Judge, then looks behind her toward the kitchen, where Beatrice and Gray are eating lunch, to reinforce her role: she is the one in charge.

They hear his voice and Beatrice comes running down the hall. "Grandpa!"

He hauls in a dirty canvas bag filled with tools. "Mel say's you've got no water pressure in the kitchen. I'm going to take a look."

He removes a small screen from the spout's end and cleans out a buildup that looks like hardened baking soda. "Mineral deposits," he explains. "Mostly calcium." Getting rid of it doesn't help the pressure, though, so he heads down to the basement to shut off the water. "I'll have to replace the valves."

Sarah empties the sink cabinet, stacking the cleaners and plant food out of Grayson's reach. The Judge lies on his back, reaching into the cabinet over his head. The knees of his jeans are white with wear and a triangle of hairy flesh shows where his old button-down pulls free of his belt.

"Can you hand me the wrench with the red handle?"

She looks in the bag for anything with a red handle.

"These are pliers." He hands them back. "The wrench is the one with the round head."

They work like that for an hour, the Judge asking for various tools and a cookie sheet to protect the back of the cupboard. "I'm going to use the blowtorch to solder this in, so keep the kids away."

Bea asks what a blowtorch is and when her grandfather explains, she says, "I already got burned today."

Sarah stiffens.

The Judge slides out of the cabinet and sits up. "You were? What happened?"

Bea presents her leg. "I was cooking."

That morning Bea and Sarah made cookies, another food of uncountable raw ingredients and indeterminate portions which makes it easy to squirrel a few away in her tote. Sarah had explained the oven's heat, showed Bea how to use a potholder, but Bea leaned on the door while taking the cookies out. To her credit, she didn't even cry. Good girl, Sarah told her. Brave girl. You'll know better next time. You'll be more careful. Pain is an efficient teacher. Fortunately Bea doesn't repeat these words to her grandfather.

The Judge kisses the red line on her knee. "Ovens are hot. Nothing for little girls to mess with." Then he winks at Sarah, assuming Bea being near the oven was an accident.

•

"So what was it like," Sarah asks Melanie, "having your father be a judge?"

Melanie shrugs. "There were a few interesting moments."

"Like what?"

"This one time, I was maybe seven or eight, and these people were upset about a ruling Dad made on an abortion clinic. They were protesting in front of our house, this house, actually."

This is Melanie's family house. Her parents gave it to Melanie and Aaron two years ago.

"My mom had the twins in the bath, so my brother Tim and I were watching this out front and trying to figure out what was going on. The people had signs with fetuses on them and stuff like 'Cuppernell kills babies.' Finally Tim, who was just starting to read, goes into the bathroom and asks my mother, 'Does Daddy murder babies?'

"My mom loves to retell that story," Melanie says. "She always says Tim was waiting until he'd been told what to think of this act Daddy supposedly performed, ready to side with him in case it turns out killing babies is something Daddy is supposed to do."

"So what happened?"

"Mom locked us in the house and marched outside and told the people she had four children in there and they were scared and could read those signs and could those people please go."

"Did they?"

"Yeah. They actually apologized. My mom always said it was because they never thought of Dad as someone with four little kids of his own. I guess they thought that meant he was a good guy." Melanie shrugs again. "I never did figure it out. I mean, if it was so easy to give up, why had they come?"

The next day Sarah Googles Aaron, Melanie, the Judge and his wife. Wife: zero hits. Melanie and Aaron: two each. Judge Grayson Cuppernell:

five thousand eight hundred and twenty-four.

As the leaves redden and fall, Sarah works her way through. Most are official documents and news articles of little significance, but she feels increasingly powerful with the gathering of his facts. Where he went to law school and college. What year he graduated. Newsworthy cases. One day she finds an article about a gavel he gives to kids finalizing adoptions. The other judges who do adoptions—it's called "Probate Court" Sarah learns—give them too. The article shows Judge Cuppernell handing the gavel to a pretty white girl being adopted by her uncle. Sarah stews on this. Gavels are a symbol of power. Instead of pretty white girls with nice uncles they need to give them to children being put in foster care, something to slam and say, "No! Order, order in this house!" Or they could give them to kids aging out. You are your own parent now. Call your life to order.

The lessons continue. Sarah teaches Bea how to slice the neck of a banana laterally so the top won't bruise. She teaches her how to mix Grayson's formula and change his diaper, how to crack an egg and how to set the heat level on the stove. "Five is usually good. If you aren't sure, choose five." It's too soon for spaghetti, pouring out the boiling water too dangerous, but she teaches her how to make rice, which Sarah used to put in her mother's shopping cart by the five-pound bag.

"Really?" her mother would ask, lightly knuckling the top of her head. "Five pounds? That's a lot of rice."

On the days her mother slipped away Sarah would eat it for lunch and dinner with big pads of butter and lots of salt. When they ran out of butter she'd put on ketchup or mayonnaise, and when her mother returned after a night or two, sometimes three, fuzzy-eyed and penitent, Sarah would make twice as much, then her mother would take a bath and Sarah would sit on the toilet and tell funny stories, or ask lots of questions, vainly trying to keep her awake. When she drifted off, Sarah drained the water and covered her with towels.

Sarah teaches Bea how to work the cordless phone and about 911. "It's only for emergencies, if there's a fire or Grayson chokes."

The notion of confronting the world alone unsettles Bea. "You can call."

"What if I'm not here?"

"Then Mommy or Daddy will call."

"What if Mommy and Daddy aren't home?"

"Then I'll be with Grandma, or Aunt Lydi."

"Someday you'll be alone."

"I will?"

"Everybody is. You have to keep your wits about you."

"What are wits?"

Sarah puts the girl on her lap. "Your smarts, your thinking. You can take care of yourself, Bea. You just have to learn some stuff."

"I don't want to learn stuff. I want you to do it."

"And what if something happens to me?"

"What is going to happen?" Bea starts to cry, little hiccuping bursts that tighten Sarah's throat.

"You need to toughen up." She lifts Bea off her lap and gives her a light swat on the butt. "There's nothing even wrong right now. What are you crying about?"

Sarah lives in an efficiency apartment in a complex off Bancroft Street. The Saturday after Thanksgiving she is watching reruns on TBS while the microwave blasts away at leftover spaghetti when a thunderstorm comes up, rain beating the single-paned windows. Sarah has always liked storms, so she takes her dinner and stands watching the lightning, feeling the thunder through her slippered feet. Then, a cracking noise reaches through and before she knows what is happening out there in the dark, Sarah drops her plate, covers her head, and her knees skid across the carpet, the cold air and rain on her. When the cracking noises have stopped, she looks up to see an oak tree suspended above her bed.

"My God, that's terrible," Melanie says. "Where did you go?"

"I checked into a motel."

"A motel? Really? Don't you have a friend or somebody to stay with?"

Sarah shrugs, embarrassed. She attended seven schools after she was taken from her mother. Kids' names surface. Amber. Tanya. Ricky. Pat. Julie. She doesn't know where any of them are now. That was Sarah's life. One day she was sharing a toothbrush holder with you, the next she never saw you again.

"Do you have renter's insurance?" Melanie persists. "Maybe it covers motel."

"No, actually my mom said I shouldn't bother. My stuff, it was so cheap. Not worth the premium." It was actually Nancy who said this. In her delicate way, with a tilt of her head and a sad smile, the way Nancy said everything.

"What about your lease? Do you have to honor it?"

"I don't know."

Before she can stop her, Melanie gets the Judge on the phone. "Dad, yeah, I have a legal question."

Sarah has nothing to worry about. The Judge says she will definitely be able to break her lease.

Melanie insists she stay with them until she finds a new place to rent, but the fourth bedroom is crowded with a huge desk and two bookcases, so she'll have to sleep with Bea.

"Do you want the top or the bottom?" Bea asks.

Bunk beds make Sarah feel as if she's in a coffin, so she takes the mattress off and sleeps on the floor, tells Bea it's like a magic carpet. Of course Bea wants her mattress on the floor too, and they sleep like that, side by side, flying all night.

Evil. That is the word Sarah finds in the blog about Judge Cuppernell taking away Reginald Diglio's grandchildren. It appears entry after entry. One hundred thirty-eight times. Sarah counts. She finds a news article from five years ago profiling Diglio, who at the time was circling the courthouse in his pickup truck from eight a.m. to five p.m., Monday through Friday, protesting the placement of his grandchildren in foster care. He had a sign mounted in the truck's bed. "Cuppernell took my kids." The picture of the sign shows a poster board with slanting, furry-edged letters that had bled, from some sort of homemade stencil she guesses, and Sarah feels an upwelling in her throat. The tears surprise her. *Yes, yes,* she thinks. *He took away your kids.*

But the article itself is like reading a blank wall. Simple facts. Only one is useful: Reginald Diglio lives on Mester Road, a two-lane stretching from the western edge of the city into the country, where houses give way to cornfields and scrapyards.

It takes more than an hour to bike there. Sarah's legs are used to it though, and it's a warm day for early December in Ohio. Sunny, high forties. She's feeling strong and optimistic when she enters the last stretch and the signs change over, white with fat black numbers: County Route 24. Half a mile later three giant children's faces come into view.

Sarah stops across the road. The sign is enormous, wider and taller than either of the rusted trucks sinking into the yard. Superimposed on the kids' smiles are foot-high letters: "judge cuppernell took my grandchildren." The rest of the yard is cut into rows by dozens of white paint buckets with metal pipe cemented inside and a piece of plywood lashed to the top displaying a name. Headstones for pets, perhaps. Rudy. Polly. Iris. Tim. Between the rows are other metal, plastic and wooden things intended, she assumes, as sculpture. Behind them stands a dilapidated two-story wooden house. One side disappears into a thicket under which Sarah glimpses what appear to be a mattress and couch slowly rotting.

For five or six minutes she takes in each sculpture, their menacing shapes, like bodies mid-attack, until the front door flies open. Someone shouts, words lost to her as she gets her feet on the pedals, fumbles, turns her tire onto the grass, slides, regains her grip and pedals off, heart like a crack of thunder against her ribs.

"The other kids sense something's off. It's because he's angry all the time. Abused kids are always angry." Sarah overhears Melanie saying this to someone on the phone.

She has come home mid-conversation, Bluetooth earpiece in place, waved to the kids and Sarah in the sunroom and slid into the kitchen. Sarah strains to hear the rest of the conversation while helping Beatrice finish a Lego princess castle.

"So he walked home today, and I watched out the window. He's always alone, always, then today these other kids ran up to him and for a second I thought he'd made friends, you know? Then suddenly he slaps one of them across the face. They all stopped, but Ethan never even paused. Just kept walking. There's something wrong there, don't you think?"

Melanie's voice is hard. "I'm sure it's his mother. I talked to her. She doesn't care. Too busy with her boyfriend, or her bongs, or something.

"Believe me, I know," she says, in a tone that makes it sound as though whomever she's talking to may be questioning how she can be so sure. "She's skinny, too skinny."

Melanie considers being too skinny the same thing as being too fat: suspect. "Drugs," she says. "Maybe alcohol, but I bet drugs."

A few days before Christmas, Melanie asks about Sarah's plans. "I take it you aren't going to Florida? Is your mother coming here?"

Sarah claims her mother is in town staying with an old friend. "I'll go over there Christmas Day."

"Okay, then I'm going to give you your present now."

It's a gift certificate to Williams-Sonoma.

"You're such a great cook. I'm sure you can find something you'll love there."

Christmas morning Bea shakes Sarah, who pretends to be groggy, though in fact she's been lying awake for an hour.

"Come on, Santa came! Santa came!" Bea pulls at her arm, but Sarah sends her off.

"I'll be down. I have to go to the bathroom."

She listens to the baby's cry, Bea's cheerful shouts and Melanie and Aaron's muttered permissions. The scent of pancakes and bacon, the only two things Aaron can cook, reach her.

At eight Sarah dresses quietly and slips out of the house. First the bus to the Catholic church on Cornish, two warm Masses, then two rides around town, switching every twenty minutes so the driver doesn't get suspicious, and an early dinner at the Chinese restaurant on Passe Road, the only place open on Christmas Day. From there it's a two-mile walk back to the Cuppernell's.

The house is dark, as Sarah expected, Aaron, Melanie and the kids having gone to her parents' for dinner.

Sarah gets out the pan she bought at Williams-Sonoma, the important one. Her mother owned its twin, the words "All-Clad" engraved on the handle. She had the small saucepan and a stockpot too, but these were indulgences. "The only pan that really has to be top quality is the large sauté," her mother explained, "so your meat and fish sear evenly and you can scrape the fond off with a metal spatula. Never use non-stick for this. No good. You can't get the fond." Her mother showed her how to polish the pans with a white powder and hang them on a rack above the sink in their mint-green kitchen.

Sarah isn't hungry, but defrosts a chicken breast anyway and while it sizzles, wonders where the pans ended up. She never thought to ask for them. Then again, she was ten when her mother died and a month passed before her foster parents said anything. By that time, the pans were probably long gone.

The chicken is perfect, browned without burning, juicy in the middle. Sarah wraps it up, then polishes her pan with the powder the saleswoman recommended. She hadn't recalled its name or what the label looked like. She knows this is the right stuff, though, because the pan shines, brand-new again.

The Saturday after New Year's Sarah has an appointment to see an apartment and Melanie insists on driving her. She's long since discovered Sarah has no car.

Stained tan carpeting, white walls. It's another holding cell, like the bedrooms she slept in as a foster child, but it's partially furnished with a leather couch, bedframe, table and chairs, and the rent is the same as her old place.

"Furnished?" Melanie sneers, turning to Sarah. "Did you want furnished?"

The landlord, a skinny guy wearing yellow pants, loses interest. No sale here.

On the drive home Melanie pulls into another place with a "Units Available" sign out front. Much newer, the complex is set back from the road behind a rolling lawn. The cars line up, protected from the light snow by a long peaked roof. White numbers reserve each spot.

They look at a one-bedroom. It has floors Sarah thinks are wood, but Melanie informs her it's "just laminate. Looks nice for an apartment, though."

The pan could hang here. And she'd keep her laundry quarters in a bag in this drawer. Except it costs three times her old place.

Sarah says she'll think about it. Feeling the need to justify her delay, she claims to be saving for a car.

On the way home Melanie asks if she knows anything about cars.

"No," Sarah admits.

Melanie smiles. "I've got just the man for you, then."

Within a week Judge Cuppernell has found a used Civic thirty miles away and he's coming to get Melanie and Sarah to look at it. They ride south on a blustery Sunday in the Judge's Suburban. Melanie is laughing because Aaron has never been alone for this long with both kids. "Can you believe it? He's just going to die."

Her father seems to find this just as funny. "That poor guy. Fathers really have it tough these days."

Melanie slaps him playfully on the arm. "Oh right, tough. Really tough. How about grandfathers? Have you ever even changed a diaper?"

The Judge laughs. "Avoiding that is one of my main goals in life."

The Judge looks under the hood and examines the tires, asks questions of the owner, a Hispanic man with a goatee, then has Sarah start up the car and gun the engine. "No blue smoke," he says, taking her place in the driver's seat. "Let's take it for a spin." As they drive the Judge explains what he's testing for—alignment, noisy brakes, stopping distance—then pulls over and tells Sarah to take the wheel. "Let's get on the expressway. See if you feel comfortable with the acceleration."

As they pull back into the seller's driveway, the Judge says, "It seems pretty solid to me, and these have good safety crash ratings, for their age anyway. I want you to take it in, though, and make sure the airbags check out." He gives her the name of a mechanic he trusts.

Sarah swallows hard as she writes the check. Five thousand dollars. Nearly her entire life's savings. She's close to tears, but that's not why.

She doesn't go back to the furnished place Melanie sneered at or the complex with the rolling lawn. She finds a place with carpet not as stained and nothing by way of furnishings except a smelly chair in the bedroom. Sarah moves in early February, taking delivery of a brand-new mattress which she puts on a metal frame scored at Goodwill, where she also bought sheets, a blanket, dishes, and silverware. She's started from scratch before, knows the priorities.

Melanie gives her the yellow couches from the sunroom.

"They were my mom's. I've been looking for an excuse to get rid of them so her feelings won't be hurt. If you take them, she'll be happy and I can get something I like. I mean, don't feel you have to keep them. As soon as you find something better, just toss them."

Sarah spends the last of her savings paying two guys from her old apartment complex to haul the couches up and heave the stranger's chair in the dumpster. Watching it go over the edge—gone, forget it, she doesn't need it—is exhilarating.

Now that Sarah has a car, Melanie begins leaving her money to buy groceries. She tries new vegetables and spices every week, makes casseroles from recipes rather than remainders. One day she goes to a store that sells nothing but fish because she's going to try making seafood paella, a recipe she found in one of Mrs. Cuppernell's old cookbooks. At the counter she explains to Bea why the fish are on beds of ice and what "deveined shrimp" means.

On the way home they pass Melanie's school. It's lunchtime and the students are out playing, so Sarah texts Melanie, who brings them in to see her classroom. While Bea looks around and Grayson dozes in the stroller, Melanie and Sarah stand at the window.

"Is that him?"

Ethan stands alone against the building, his thick, uncombed hair snagged on its bricks, trying to feign preoccupation with a stick, though it's painfully obvious he's just standing, excluded from four-square, basketball, the climbing wall, the monkey bars.

"The way he acts, nobody likes him," Melanie says. "It's heartbreaking." She goes over to help Bea feed the fish.

Ethan twirls the stick like a baton, scraping his fingers on its rough bark. He examines his hand, rubs the pain away, then begins rolling the stick against the building, trying to sand it smooth, until one of the playground monitors, a surly woman in a bright yellow jacket, tells him to quit. Sarah can't hear every word, but it's clear she's telling him he'll damage the building and Ethan is pleading his case: it's just a stick against brick. The monitor shakes her grumpy face and points to the ground. Ethan throws the stick down and walks several feet away, to stand behind the trunk of a massive oak. The woman yells something else and he sulks back toward her, forced to take up a position in full view of the other kids.

Childhood, Sarah thinks: a prison made up of lack. A lack of words, of knowing better, of being believed. You are at everyone's mercy.

Back at Melanie's house she looks through the toys and comes across a Rubik's Cube, its edges pockmarked by Gray's teething, its colors hopelessly jumbled. On the way home, she buys a new cube and the next day prints off tips on how to master it. That evening, she gives them to Melanie.

"He'll have something to do on the playground at least."

A week later Melanie reports that Ethan takes the cube out every day and that some other boys have started gathering to watch him.

"It's really improved things for him. It was a brilliant idea. You should be a teacher. Have you ever considered that? Going to college?"

Sarah dodges the question with a vague plan about saving money. The truth is she has no idea how to go about getting into college, let alone paying for it. Melanie suggests federal loans, scholarships. "Didn't the school counselor help you with any of this?" Sarah has no recollection of such a person at any of her high schools. A few weeks later, while watching a show about Albert Einstein, she wonders if that's what went wrong. Maybe you couldn't switch schools, houses or families too often or too quickly. It frayed the net of space and time. You had to stay put, let the moments link themselves like runners passing the baton. If you don't, your life slips through, like her mother's pots and pans.

Rubik's Cube as anodyne has a short half-life. Within a month, Melanie reports that Ethan is being made fun of because he is too attached to the cube.

"He's amazing at it, actually, very, very smart, and at first the other boys were impressed, but they can't do it as well, so now they're mad, and he just won't put it down. I finally had to take it away. I mean, I give it to him during recess, that's it. Otherwise he'll never listen or do anything else."

Melanie says watching him align the squares, his face no longer a simulacrum of absorption, but truly captivated, makes her cry. "I mean the thought that a colored block of plastic is all he has."

"He has his mother," Sarah says.

Another eye roll. "He comes to school in the same clothes all week and when we have food, you know, for holidays or birthdays, he eats like he hasn't had a meal in days." Melanie shakes her head. "I wish I could get some evidence on her, something to report to child services."

"Don't do that." Sarah hears the sharpness of her tone too late, but Melanie is oblivious.

Unloading a stack of papers covered in large, loopy handwriting, the lines of text sloping up and down, she says, "I'm keeping my eye on things. I don't like that woman."

Sarah finds Ethan's last name in Melanie's grade book, looks up his address and drives by several times thinking vaguely of warning them:

be careful, they're watching you. Their building is a yellow brick fourplex on a street that backs up to a grocery store and gas station. The windows are the same type of silver ones she has in the new apartment and she wonders if they ice up the same way.

One Sunday Ethan is sitting on the front stoop in a jacket and no hat, hands clasped between his knees. Sarah circles the block, then pulls over and gets out. "You okay? Are you locked out?"

Ethan looks at her a long moment as if he doesn't speak English. "No."

"Well, what're you doing sitting out here? It's awfully cold, and you don't have a hat or gloves."

"I'm okay."

"That's a light jacket. Do you have a coat? A winter coat?"

Ethan stares at her sullenly. "Who are you?"

"I'm a friend of your mom's."

"She's inside." Ethan scoots over for her to pass.

"Aren't you coming in?"

"I have to stay out here."

"Have to? Why?"

Again he gives her that look that lets her know she has no business here.

"Is your mom making you stay out here?"

The door opens. Sarah looks up, startled.

Ethan's mother is very skinny. She has a pale face pockmarked lightly around the mouth and thin hair dyed the color of a brand-new penny. A dark line cleaves its two halves.

"Your friend is here," Ethan says. His voice is high, almost broken.

"I don't want anything. And I don't appreciate you talking to my kid."

"I'm not selling anything," Sarah mumbles.

Ethan looks between his mother and Sarah.

His mother steps outside. "Are you looking for somebody?" Her voice is hard and annoyed.

"Sorry, I just stopped because I thought maybe he was locked out."

"You just drive around talking to strange kids?"

"Well, it's pretty cold."

"What?"

"It's cold, so I was worried." Sarah has to use the bathroom. She contracts her muscles and the urge recedes.

Ethan speaks up. "She said you were friends."

The mother looks at Ethan, registering his claim, then back at Sarah, alerted that something is wrong. "Is that your car?"

Sarah looks behind her. The license plate is fully visible. "I'm from Children's Services," she blurts.

Immediately, the woman's attitude changes. She becomes both stiffer and more friendly, a smile stretched across her face as if it's being pulled by a string.

Sarah introduces herself as "Ms. Adams." "May I come in?"

The woman stands back, swinging open the cracked storm door. "Of course, of course, we got nothing to hide."

An unfamiliar feeling of power washes through Sarah, loosening her stomach and slowing her heart. "Ethan is coming in too, yes?" she asks, glancing behind her as she steps into the building's common hall, a wide space dimly lit by a single bulb recessed behind a soiled plastic cover.

Inside the apartment the living and dining space is one long room. The table is covered in stacks of mail and various other misplaced things. She spies a screwdriver and several bottles of nail polish. Unopened boxes stand in the corner, and the drapes, little blue and yellow flowers, must be left over from previous occupants. They were not chosen by the same person who owns the overstuffed brown couch and red chairs.

"Would you like a drink? A pop or coffee?" Ethan's mother asks.

"No, thank you."

"Please sit down. What's this about? Did someone call you or something?"

"Maybe we should talk privately." Sarah mimics the cadence of

Nancy's voice and the kinds of things she used to say.

Ethan's mother tells him to go to his room, then motions for Sarah to sit and both women perch on the edge, Sarah on the couch, Ethan's mother on the nearer of the two chairs.

"I'm just here to find out a little information. So I see Ethan was outside. He said he had to stay out there. Why was that?"

"I just wanted him to go play a little while. He doesn't do anything but those video games. I thought he needed the exercise."

"It's pretty cold. Does he have a heavier coat? Some gloves and a hat?"

"Oh yeah, yeah." She goes into the hall, opens a narrow closet where coats half-conceal an old vacuum cleaner and yanks out a blue ski jacket. "See, he's got a good coat, and I told him to wear it, but he likes that team jacket. He's a Broncos fan."

"Well, he shouldn't be out in this cold dressed like that."

Ethan's mother nods. "Right, sure. Absolutely."

Sarah wonders if this is how the Judge feels behind the bench: everyone must listen.

"So Ethan's father? Does he live nearby?"

"He's out in Texas. Maybe Arizona. The moron moves a lot." Ethan's mother rolls her eyes just like Melanie.

Sarah asks about friends, if Ethan has other boys over to play, and his mother shrugs. "We're pretty busy."

"How are his grades? Does he do well in school? Does he like his teacher?"

At the mention of Melanie, his mother's expression changes. "Is that who called you? That woman?"

Sarah fumbles, then grabs hold of the obvious: it's confidential.

"His teacher's had it out for me and Ethan since day one because Ethan, he's got the ADD, and he's a handful, but that's not my problem. It's her job to deal with it."

Sarah asks a few more questions, random ones she's not even sure seem reasonable or professional, but she doubts his mother has the experience to know the difference.

"Okay, I think it's all good. I appreciate your time today."

Sarah's bladder hurts and at the last moment, when the blast of cold air hits her, she decides she can't make it.

Ethan's mother takes her back inside, points down the hall to a peach-and-black-tiled bath. The peach toilet seat has yellow spots. Sarah stands, holding the towel rack. The tub has a charcoal rim of filth, and a tangle of dark and red hair completely covers the drain. The place could definitely use a scrubbing.

She flushes and after washing her hands leaves the water on to muffle the sound of the rusty medicine cabinet hinges. Nothing remarkable except one bottle of OxyContin. It has a script label, though. Luanne Holman. Probably a maiden name.

Ethan's mother is waiting for her in the hall, by the entrance to the kitchen. Behind her Sarah glimpses a mess of pots and pans, plates and cups.

"Maybe you should do a little cleaning, I mean, just in case. It would look better, you know."

"Right." The woman glances behind her. "Right, I will. I've been really busy. I will, though."

On the front step Sarah puts out her hand. "Sorry to bother you."

"No problem, no problem. I'm an open book."

Sarah steps down to the walk, then turns. "I'm sorry. To be honest, I missed your last name. Was it the same as Ethan's?"

"Oh, yeah, yeah, Kiebach. Sorry." She offers to shake hands. "Kim Kiebach. People call me KK."

Sarah considers every scenario. Obtained under a false name? Left by a friend? Borrowed for a bad toothache or migraine? There are several plausible, innocent explanations for the pills.

Over the next few weeks she avoids the topic of Ethan, then one Friday Melanie comes home and slaps her leather tote on the counter.

"We had Ethan K.'s mother in today. He was in a fight on the playground again, so we call her in and she says they're moving. It's almost April for crying out loud. She's going to move the kid two months before school is out? Like he doesn't have enough problems fitting in."

"Maybe it's a job change or something."

Melanie snorts. "Right, a corporate relo."

Sarah escapes quickly and drives home thinking about what she's done. They're moving because of her. Which might be good. Or disastrous. There's no way to know.

She spends the summer staying home with Grayson so Melanie can take Bea to the pool and clean her classroom or go out with friends. One week Melanie and Aaron go to Nashville and Sarah stays with the kids and sleeps in their bed, remembering the big blue dick in the shoebox. Does it mean Melanie isn't happy with Aaron? Maybe it means he has a small penis.

In August, when Aaron and Melanie take the kids to her parents' cottage on Lake Michigan, Sarah spends her vacation in bed watching TV. The hours are different now, still faster, but not fuller. At the end of the two weeks they've accumulated to nothing. She doesn't remember a single show.

School starts, Bea goes to morning kindergarten and returns to report being the only one in her class who knows how to cook, what 911 is and her own address and phone number. "Some kids didn't even know the name of the street they live on!"

In September, Bea turns six and the family throws a huge party. Aunts, uncles, cousins. Aaron's parents are divorced and remarried, so there are six grandparents. Sarah is invited because, as Melanie says, "You're like family. Bea would be devastated if you don't come."

Saturday morning Sarah considers calling to say she's sick. Bea needs to learn: devastation is just a state of mind.

But she goes. She goes, and there is the backyard strewn with balloons bobbing on fish line strung from tree to tree. Several folding chairs and tables are set up, including a table with the cake she made. Sarah baked and decorated it yesterday afternoon, Bea in awe of her ability to transform five regular square cakes into Dorothy's slipper. Covered in Red Hots, of course, which the guests will have to pick off because only Bea could stand to eat so many.

Everyone knows Sarah even though she doesn't know them. She is the famous nanny, who taught Bea to cook, who made the cake, who, Melanie has joked, stole Grayson's first word. Instead of "Dada" or "Mama" it was "Saha."

Sarah eats a burger and flirts with Melanie's cousin Michael, a guy just good-looking enough to make her tingle, but with crooked teeth that give her confidence. Michael is finishing a master's in engineering at the local university. They talk for twenty minutes before he's yanked off to provide piggyback rides. Sarah has little experience with men or their signals, but she thinks he looks reluctant to go and for a while she watches him play, hoping he'll break away, until he doesn't and she becomes self-conscious and moves off toward the food tables.

It's eighty-five degrees out, one of the last hot days, no doubt. Melanie offers Sarah a beer.

"No, thanks."

"We have wine coolers and a couple bottles of Pinot for the grownups if you want that instead."

"I don't drink."

"Never?"

Sarah makes up an excuse about allergies.

The party is winding down. Fallen balloons float at ground level among the remaining guests. One of them drifts into the climbing rose on the garage and the crack makes Sarah jump. She glances around, but no one else looks startled. Michael is nowhere in sight.

She wanders around trying not to look as though she's looking for him, then returns to the tables, where she tidies up the pile of presents, stacking dolls and Lego sets, more Play-Doh and bubble wands, gathering up the wrapping paper before she realizes the garbage is overflowing. She'll have to take it inside, bring out another bag. Hands full, she moves to the back door and, catching a glimpse of people through the screen, is about to raise her voice and ask for someone to open it when she hears Aaron say, "Well, yeah, next year we'll probably do preschool for Gray instead of a nanny. It'd be a lot cheaper and get him more socialization, more academic prep. Bea's smart as a whip, you know, and I think in a way it's held her back, being home. Next year she'll be in first grade, so Grayson can go to Montessori. He'll be three. He can handle all-day."

Sarah's cheeks go hot, shame washing over her as if she's been caught holding that blue dick. Yes. Of course. This too will end.

"Need some help?" The Judge is there, opening the door, and Sarah has no choice but to step up into the kitchen. Aaron and the two people he's been talking to smile, seeming unconcerned about what Sarah may have heard. Aaron plucks a garbage bag from the box on the counter and holds it wide for her to stuff in the paper, then the three go back out while Sarah ties the bag, prolonging the process to calm herself. The Judge sits at the table, mopping his sweaty, blotched forehead with a handkerchief. He wears tan shorts and a golf shirt.

"Honey," he says, "can you get me a glass of ice water? I think I overdid it running around out there with the kids. It's damn hot today."

Sarah runs him some water without waiting for the tap to cool or adding ice.

"I saw you talking to Michael," he says. "He's my nephew, known him his whole life." The Judge takes a drink of water and wipes at the sweat still beading his hairline, which is now the midpoint of his skull.

"He likes pretty girls."

"I'm good. I can take care of myself," Sarah says.

The Judge looks unconvinced. "Melanie tells me you helped her with a kid she had this year, somebody with problems."

"I just gave him something to do on the playground. You need something to do when you're alone."

The Judge drinks his water. "So you grew up around here. What high school did you go to?"

"Several," Sarah says. "I was in foster care."

The Judge's expression changes. Alert is the only word for it. "Foster care? Here? In Lucas County?"

Sarah nods.

"For how long?"

"Nine years."

"You aged out?"

Sarah nods. "My mother died."

"She died?" The Judge seems to relax a little. "Is that why you went into foster care?"

"No. They took me away first. My mom wanted me back. She was fighting, but then she drowned."

The Judge pauses. "I'm sorry. That must have been terrible."

"In the bathtub. She fell asleep and slipped under. There was no one there to drain the water."

This settles on the Judge like déjà vu. She can see it in his wrinkled brow, the intensity of his stare.

"What is your last name?"

"Anderson. Sarah Elizabeth Anderson."

For what seems a very long moment they stare at one another, each knowing what this means, and yet not. The back door slams. Bea is shouting, "It has my name! Sarah, it has my *name*!"

At Goodwill Sarah found an old doctor's kit, complete with white lab coat, and sewed Bea's name on the pocket. Bea starts with her grandfather. As she bangs away at his knee and shines a light in his ear, Sarah imagines becoming a doctor, but quickly decides the stakes are too high. Maybe she could be a teacher. So much to explain. Buy one good pan and scrape the fond. Stay put if you can and remember last names. Weave tight the net of space and time.

Bea has finished with the Judge and moves over to Sarah.

"I have to listen to your heart." She rests the stethoscope on Sarah's stomach.

"I don't hear anything."

Sarah moves it to the right place. "Try this."

"It's loud." Bea's expression grows serious and her lips begin to move, counting the rapid beats.

"Well, what do you think?"

Bea nods. "You're healthy."

"Thank you," Sarah says. "That's a relief."

These stories, sometimes in slightly different form, first appeared in the following publications:

"All the Sons of Cain": *The Kenyon Review*, May 2015

"Half-Life": *Alaska Quarterly Review*, Spring & Summer 2015

"Prisoners Do": *Printers Row Journal, Chicago Tribune*, Issue 159

"AKA Juan": *Cimarron Review*, Issue 190, Winter 2015

"Coyote": *Ascent*, March 2014

"Unattended": *PRISM international*, Vol. 50.2, 2012

"You Should Pity Us Instead": *The Massachusetts Review*, 2012

"When We're Innocent": *Confrontation*, Issue 107, 2010

"Goldene Medene": *Ballyhoo Stories*, June 2006.

"The River Warta": *Natural Bridge*, Issue 16, 2006

"An Uncontaminated Soul": *Black Warrior Review*, October 2005

ACKNOWLEDGMENTS

Support came in many forms from many people. First thanks go to my good friend and fellow writer Paul Many for hours of craft talk, encouragement, and reading more drafts than anyone should have to.

To my other longtime friends and fellow toilers Barb Goodman, Ann Epstein, Danielle LaVaque-Manty, Lori Eaton, Eleanor Shelton, Julie Babcock, and Jeanne Sirotkin for their thoughtful, generous feedback on the many pieces to which I've subjected them over the years. Particular credit and gratitude go to Keith Hood, around whom so much has pivoted.

I thank those who offered up pieces of themselves that inspired or enhanced these stories.

Special thanks to Caitlin Horrocks for going out on a limb and to Sarah Gorham, Kristen Radtke, Kirby Gann, and the whole Sarabande staff for their enthusiasm, advice, and hard work on my behalf.

Final and greatest thanks to Patrick, with all my love, for making it possible.

ABOUT THE AUTHOR

Amy Gustine's short fiction has appeared in several magazines, including *The Kenyon Review, North American Review, Black Warrior Review, PRISM international, Confrontation, Natural Bridge,* and *The Massachusetts Review.* Her story "Goldene Medene" received Special Mention in *Pushcart Prize XXXII.* She lives in Ohio.

Sarabande Books is a nonprofit literary press located in Louisville, KY, and Brooklyn, NY. Founded in 1994 to champion poetry, short fiction, and essay, we are committed to creating lasting editions that honor exceptional writing. For more information, please visit sarabandebooks.org.